Notes from a Cannibalist

ULTAN BANAN

Also by Ultan Banan

Meat

A Whore's Song

Copyright Ultan Banan © 2021

All rights reserved

No part of this publication may be reproduced, stored in a retrieval system or transmitted in any form or by any means, electronic, mechanical, photocopying, recording or otherwise, without prior permission of the author.

Cover art courtesy of Dave Migman © 2021
Editing by Paul @ Seminal Edits

blacktarnpublishing.com

ISBN: 978-1-914147-05-0

'They mustn't die,' he thought.
Then, as though awakening from sleep, he called the gardener and ordered him to cut all the roses.

Notes from a Cannibalist

September, 1848

I

We think a man is dead. No one's sure. Seems the captain kept it quiet for a day, but the man's wife is now running about the ship upsetting everyone. We're in the middle of the ocean. No one needs this. A mad passenger on a ship is no good thing, and I'm no seaman, but it seems some things don't agree with being on the water. Screaming women's one. People that's missing, another. How many's on the ship? Close to three hundred, now every one of them nervous and edgy, and we got near six weeks of travel ahead of us too. Still, she'll be off at Rio. They say her and the husband were travelling there. I hope to Christ they were, cause we can't have her on the ship all the way to London. She'll jinx the lot of us. Some kinda sea hex. No, get her off, best thing for everyone. He'll be dead anyway, nowhere he can be but overboard. Ship's been searched high and low, galley to decks, and not a sign of him anywhere. They say he was some politician, too. They took the wife below an hour ago, filled her fulla laudanum. But we know she's there, drugged, just waiting to rise up and kick off again. It's not just me, either. We all feel the same. Isn't there some kinda sea law about that, too? Self-protection first and all. We're all waiting for Rio. Can't come quick enough.

Meanwhile, your other one's up there on deck, doesn't seem to have a care for anything. Veil down, head in the books. Still haven't had a good look at her. Nestled away in her corner, reading her tomes.

I told her in the morning a man was missing, she shrugged. 'Keep me informed of the news,' she said. Went back to reading, no cares at all. Queer woman. Still, there may be a job in it for me at the end of it all. So I'll just go along with it. Eighteen months in Buenos Aires, never managed to land a job I could stay in. Did a bit of farm work, bit o'rustling, bit o'this that and the other, but never found anything I could stick with. Now we're going back over the ocean, and to London of all places. Stinking city, but all the same, she paid handsomely for the trip just to have a porter to see her over, and like I say, she may keep me on. Seems she has money too by the get-up of her. Fine dresses and all those fancy trunks. Yeah, she's well off. I'll stick around, see if an opportunity arises.

I go up on deck for a touch of air. Nice out today. Middle of summer, of course, all the way down here. Fine summers, too, with cool air and warm nights and cool mornings. Yeah, I have to admit, it's no bad land this, and it'd be a paradise if they weren't cutting the heads off folk night after night. Gone savage they have, that bastard at the top, a tyrant if ever there was one. But they got a country all right, they got a fine one – not like Ireland, that's for sure. Or England. *And now you're going back, you clown. And for what? Hopes of a job that may never happen? That said, you've a little silver in your pocket now, which is the best you've had in a long while.*

I roll myself a smoke. Got the good tobacco here, they do. Something else to miss. I puff and look out at the ocean. That's the Atlantic, out there. She's a fearful old bitch. *She'll carry ya all the way back to Antrim, if you're not careful. That's the way you're headed. Keep an eye on the winds, son, make sure she's sailing in the right direction.*

Saw a humpback whale yesterday. Great monster of a thing, broke the surface of the water all *end-of-the-world* like, scared the Christ outta all us, but a finer thing I never saw in my life. Been out here looking for another but they've gone under. Heading south I heard one fella say, and him a fisherman. I'm sure he knows the score. Still, I'd love to see more before we get north. The da said he saw them, up west of Scotland, came home with stories of schools of them feeding off the Hebrides, great tales of fish and monsters, and then one day he never came home again. Always said the ocean would kill him, or maybe he shacked up with a little Scottish mermaid, we never knew, nor did the ma care all that much. There was no bliss at home when he was there, and quiet enough when he was gone. I'd like to go home with a tale or two myself, not that the last two years have been shy of a few. Tales, and a bit o'tail too, there certainly was. And I get to thinking about the young farm girls as I sit there looking over the Atlantic, waiting for a whale, smoking that sweet tobacco and feeling the salt on my face.

It's not long waiting before someone disturbs the peace.

'Facking Paddy,' he says, the big bull coming up behind me. 'Got any baccy?'

'Georgie,' I say. 'Captain light on the rations, is he? You with a job and bumming smokes from myself.' I hand him the pouch.

'Fack you doing?' he says.

'Whale watchin,' I tell him.

'Yeah? Where is they?'

'Hidin.'

'Forget the bloody whales. Captain's ordered everyone below so's we can search the ship again.'

I flick my butt into the wind. 'No point. Guy was overboard a day ago.'

'Could be, my son, could be. Still, procedure is procedure. Gots to get everyone below.'

'Aye. I'll head down in a bit.'

'Good man, Paddy,' he says. He claps me on the back and wanders down port side.

Damn English. The plague of us Irish wherever we go. Not a corner of the world they won't follow us to – even to the jungles of the Americas. Steal the food from your mouth then scab a cigarette from ya.

I wander down aft of the boat, eyes on the horizon. Nah, the whales aren't coming up for air today. You know who's not coming up for

3

air, either? She isn't. I go round the corner where I got a view of her table, nestled away back there like she don't want no bother from the rest of us. Doesn't wanna be troubled, like, just left alone to her books and her solitude. I can't argue with that, who doesn't wanna be by their lonesome now and again, but it's not often you see it in a woman, not one of good breeding like her. I lean against the guard rail and watch. There's something about her. Self-contained, doesn't need no one. A devil of a mystery what she's about. A gentleman comes by, tries to engage her in conversation. Now, I can't see nothing behind that veil, but something comes off her: the tilt of the head, the slow deliberateness of it... some kinda fury. I mean, I can feel it here, the death stare, and I'm thirty feet away. The fellow flees. I mean, he's outta there like shite off a shovel... legs it he does. Never saw a man put to flight like that in my life. Something about her, there is for sure. There was a woman back in Camlough, never saw her myself but tales of her were far and wide – Maggie Lung, they say she could send the devil into men without so much as touching them, just a look or a glance was enough to put the fear o'God in them, and she'd a voice on her like an angel too, hence the name, like a siren they say she was, and so fine her song it'd put fishermen on the rocks. Maybe my own father gave himself up to her, who knows. I know Gabriel Leary cut his own throat over her, cause the da himself was by his side after. Lived through it, the old bastard. Told my da the story of Maggie, how she could make gold appear from her petticoats just by singing, saw it himself, gold coins spill from between her legs like confetti, a proper witch, and when you tried to spend them they turned to copper, swore it true the poor bastard. He was bewitched, of course, gone mental at a bit o'skirt. The town put her out in the end and she went wandering. Nobody heard of her after, none from Camlough anyway. Maybe the old da took her to Glasgow in the end. He was always a man for the stories. Any old hen coulda whispered in his ear and took him off on a dance. Too soft a man by far. Maggie Lung. The thought of her back on me now, fifteen years later and a million miles across the ocean, somewhere between Buenos Aires and Rio. Some memories just come at ya from nowhere. Still no whales, though. Her siren song hasn't called them back up, but we got six weeks for another sighting of them yet. About a mile off starboard, another ship passes heading south, heading for the city no doubt. It's the only city down there. Maybe come from Rio, or down from New York itself, or Germany. Lots of Germans heading down there – us and the Germans, God knows why.

A man passes me. 'Everyone's to go below,' he says.

'Mate's already told me,' I say.

I take out the tobacco, roll myself another. Maybe I should go tell her she's to go below. What'll she have to say to me? Doesn't look like she takes kindly to being disturbed, but I am in her employ, after all. There's cause for it, too. I light up and ponder my dilemma. I'll finish the cigarette then I'll go tell her. No sense rushing headlong into it. Give her a minute. Give me a minute. Then I hear it: —*Ryan*. Clear as fucken day, I hear it in my head. *Ryan*. It's her. I glance over my shoulder but she's not looking in my direction. But by Christ, I heard her. I fucken heard her. That's too much. I take another look at her then turn and walk up fore of the boat. I'm spooked now, I admit it, but I know what I heard. That was her voice in my head, in my head like Maggie Lung. *Naw*. I pull on the cigarette til it's burning my fingers and flick it into the ocean. What do I do? I gotta talk to her, don't I? She's paying me, for chrissake. So I wander back down the ship, the deck mostly clear of folk now, all gone below at Captain's orders. I go round the corner to where she's sitting, all quiet and intense like, and I mosey up beside her.

'Ma'am?'

'Hmm?' She looks up from the book.

'Did you want somethin, Ma'am?'

'No.' She shakes her head. 'Oh, you know what – could you ask Constancia to bring me some tea?'

'Sure, ma'am. There's somethin else...'

'Yes?'

'Captain's ordered everyone below. A man's missing. They want to search the boat.'

'The captain has no problem with me sitting here, Ryan. Don't trouble yourself.'

Can't argue with her. 'Sure, ma'am.'

I turn to go. *Fetching tea for her now, am I?*

'Ryan?' she says.

I stop. 'Yes?'

'Were you watching me before?' She looks up from her book.

Is she smirking below that veil? 'No, ma'am.'

She goes back to her book, leaving me standing there like a fool. So I turn tail and go, go to get the young mistress to fetch up some tea. I take a last look at her before I step inside, still with her head in that great tome, and she lifts a leaf between her fingers, fingers in elegant green gloves, and turns the page.

August, 1847

2

I walked across the land, eating my brother as I went. I had him cooked and parcelled up into edible pieces, and I calculated what I had left of him would carry me across the country.

I'd said goodbye to his remains and those of the ma and left their graveside for a new life. The meat of his left arm took me into Letterkenny. It was two days walking. From Letterkenny, I walked to Strabane on the eating of his right calf, and from Strabane to Omagh on his thigh. Two days from Omagh took me into Armagh, on which I was sustained by meat from his shoulders, small and inconsequential as they were. Then I walked from Armagh to Belfast, three days on the hoof, on the eating of the brother's buttocks, which, it must be said, was probably the tastiest part of him.

Some hundred and forty mile I walked through shite and stream, passing only ghosts as I went, the living dead, who lay by the sides of roads and in holes in the ground, much like the one I'd been in just a week before. They watched me pass, and in their dead eyes I saw a flicker of wonder at how there was a man among them who was marching across the country with the strength of the living towards a new life, a future. They wondered and I marched on, for there was no life there only death, and one can't remain long in a place of dying. I left it behind me and soldiered over the land.

I got to Belfast, me, a poor fowl who'd lived all his life in a field, and had my first view of the city. I walked into Belfast on my shit-stinking feet, and exhausted from a week's walking, sought somewhere to sleep. I found shelter under the awning of a butcher's shop, wrapped myself in my great sodden coat and ate the flesh of the brother's neck, now rotten. There'd be food on the boat and I had only to hold out til then. I shivered through the night, poor eating in my belly, and got up with the first light of day, ragged and sore.

It was coming on September. I had to get out, and quick.

I went down to the docks to ask after a boat to the new world. America – that's where I'd be headed. And when I got down to the docks, such a mass of shattered humanity I saw, all tired and wasted and hungry, with cardboard cases and filthy children, wrapped in shawls and ancient coats, and even some of them with boots on their feet. Faces blackened with soot and the filth of the field, eyes like pissholes in the snow, desperation on their faces, fear too, for they had tickets in their hands but not a penny in their pockets, and no idea what they'd be finding on the other side. I'd heard tell that some were even dying on the journey, wracked by dysentery or worse, without even the strength to take them across the water. That wouldn't be me. I'd make it, for I had fortitude and a will to live, and now I had a week's worth of meat in my belly and that'd be enough. I had meat and so I'd cling to life. My hand went into my pocket where it clasped the last pieces of my dead brother in my pocket, rotten flesh but all I had.

I found one young fella and asked him the date.

'Wednesday, twenty-third,' he told me.

I stood in line for an hour at the ticket office. No availability for another two weeks, I was told. I'd have to wait. And tickets were seven pounds.

'I've five,' I told him.

'Seven,' he said.

So I sat down by a wall and took out the last parcel o'meat, a piece of the brother's flank, and I looked at the rotten meat and considered throwing it into the lough. *No*, I thought – *No. For I'd killed him, and it was my brotherly duty to eat him and not cast him into the sea for the fish.*

Yes, I'd eat him so he came with me. I'd carry him to America.

So I ate the rest of his rotten flesh, the brother, the stonemason from Gortahork, whose only memory would live on in the dry stone walls of the west of Ireland, those useless walls dividing nothing from nothing, or perhaps only the holes where forgotten souls lay buried, a great web of stone across the land segregating the dead from the dead. That would be his legacy, that and the remains of him I'd carry to the New World in my belly. I swallowed the rest of it and kept it down with great difficulty.

That was it, the last traces of the brother, buried for eternity. Dust to dust and what have ya.

I wrapped my coat round me and wandered about the city. Some fine people I saw there, and they looked right through me they did, but I suppose I was a ghost to them. Part of me died back there, it's true. But now I'd another chance, a chance at life again, and all I had to do was get on the boat. I walked round the city til evening, my stomach doing strange and wonderful things, cramps and stabbing pains clawing at me, but it was nothing to what I'd gone through back home and it wouldn't stop me now. I waited til dark and I sought out that old butcher's shop in Castle Place and lay down under its awning and drew my coat up round my shoulders. I closed my eyes, for night was on us.

The next day I went back down the docks. We were all there, the great mass of lost souls crashing wavelike onto the shore, begging to be carried out to sea. I was one of them. I was carried along on the great wave, with nothing but five pounds in my pocket and a desire to live again. I wandered through the harbour looking for a man who might take a backhander and let me sneak on the boat. I kept at it til I was kicked back down the quay by a foreman who threatened me with the law. I left, dejected, but I knew my chance would come, and it wasn't long before it did.

A ways down the road, I saw a sorry-looking family stumble, dragging their belongings behind them in sacks. For the boat too, no doubt, and as they drew close, I saw they were sick. The father had trouble moving and his wife was half-gone with it too, and as they passed me the man collapsed on the road. I watched, the wife trying to raise him off the ground, carriages passing and nobody stopping, all the good people looking away. The woman's young'uns stood with their hands in their mouths as she tried to drag their father to the pavement. She clawed at his coat and looked round desperately, and she caught my eye. I stood up and hurried over.

'Help you, miss?' I said.

She fell to the ground and started weeping.

I looked at the man, his face blue and waxy. He was choleric, and if he wasn't dead already he would be soon. My two sisters had died of it and I hadn't caught it then, so I lifted the fella for her and dragged him off the road and laid him against a wall. I sat down from the effort. The woman sat next to her husband, took an old rag from her shawl and wiped his face.

'How long's he been ill?' I asked her.

'A week or so,' she said.

'You come far?'

'From Ballycastle.'

'Where you headed?'

She wiped the tears from her face, long streaks of filth smearing her cheeks. 'We're supposed to go out on the boat th'morrow.' She looked at the husband.

'He's not gonna make it,' I told her.

She didn't reply. He was dead even then, even if he still had a breath in him. There was nothing to do, so I sat with her and waited for him to die.

I went down the port and came back with a health official, and a cart was brought and the man loaded in and carried away.

The boy, maybe five years old, watched it happen. 'Where's Daddy goin?'

The mother had nothing to tell him.

'Your Daddy's goin to the hospital,' I told him.

'Is he not comin with us?' the girl said.

'He'll come after,' I told her.

The two children watched the corpse of their father disappear down the street while the woman drew up her knees and rocked gently. I took off my coat and put it round her, and sat down next to her.

'Where were you headed?'

'New York,' she said. Her eyes were hard and blank.

'You've tickets?'

She nodded.

'Look,' I said, and I pulled five pounds from my pocket. 'I'll take the ticket off ya. I'll take it and I'll ride with ya.'

She looked at the note in my hand. 'Tickets are seven pounds, mister,' she said.

I shook my head, sorry-like. 'This is all I have.'

I saw her wavering so I pushed. 'You gotta get on that boat. You can't go back to Ballycastle now. What's there for ya?' And I could see that there was nothing, maybe just a few shallow holes in the ground, like the ones my ma and brother lay in.

'You have to get on that boat. I'll go with yis, and I'll help ya with the wee'uns and make sure you're safe and ya get to the other side.' I pushed the coins into her palm and closed her hand. 'Five pounds'll go a long way to getting ya started over there,' I said.

She'd no fight left in her. I knew before she said it she'd agree.

Evening, we huddled in a corner and had tea together. I filched a pot of hot water from the Harbour Office and she pulled a lump of bacon out of her bag, and we ate bacon and drank tea and fell asleep the four of us in a heap by the wall.

In the morning, she produced a ticket with the name 'Robert Moffatt' on it. She handed me his papers and that was it. From then on, I was her husband.

'What's your name?' I asked her.

'Eliza,' she said. And the young'uns were Molly and Jake, her nine and him five.

So we headed down the port, me, Robert Moffatt, with my wife

Eliza and two children. It was around six in the morning, cold and with a thin rain falling. We got wet, everything got wet, and little was I to know we wouldn't get dry again for another six weeks. We pushed our way through the great nothing mass of men and women, produced our tickets at the gates and were ushered onto the pier, where we got the first look at the Constitution.

Five hundred and fifty-eight of us queued to get on her. One hundred and eighteen would be dead and consigned to the ocean by the time we reached New York. My wife included. But the signs of the cholera were already on her as we lined up for passage. It was probably her that took it on the boat, but there must have been others. We took a teabag and ruddied up her cheeks; it didn't give her any appearance of health, just made her look dirty, but it covered her up. A nurse took a glance at the four of us and waved us on the boat. Young Jake took my hand as we climbed aboard the Constitution. I was his new father, the old one already dumped in some hole in the ground and sprinkled with lye.

We found our way to the hold and our berths. Eliza laid down with the kids in one, a damp mattress six by six and stuffed with straw. I laid down on a half of one next to them. They all filed on, Ireland's ruined: hunched, decrepit, filthy and desperate. I knew even then many of them wouldn't make it. They'd already given up, even if they held out some hope for a life across the ocean.

A family of three made their camp in the bunk above me: a man, his wife and a boy about seven.

'How're ya?' I said.

The man tipped his cap. 'Is she seaworthy, d'ya think?'

'I hope for our sakes she is,' I said.

'The brother left six months ago, haven't heard hide nor hair of him since. He'll be living a fine life in New York. Clean forgot about us, no doubt.'

I could tell by the way he said it he was sure the brother was dead.

'No doubt,' I told him.

He held out his hand. 'Thomas.'

'Robert,' I said, and we shook hands.

I glanced at Eliza. First time she'd heard me introduce myself as her husband.

'This your good family, is it?'

'Aye,' I told him, and I introduced the family.

'This is the wife, May, and the young fella, John,' Thomas said.

Awkward hellos and handshakes. Bags were unpacked and bedding unrolled, and the spaces were claimed for the weeks ahead.

'Bit of a squeeze up there, is it?'

Up above they'd barely two feet of space above their heads.

'Christ, it is,' Thomas said.

'Tom!' cried his wife.

'Jaysus, forgive me,' he said. 'The wife takes offence at the name of the good Lord.'

'And so she should,' I said.

And then, up walked the ship's mate, next to him a priest in full getup. The mate took off his cap. 'Good day to yis. We've had a bit of a mix-up above, folks. The good Father here had a cabin, but so has a fine couple gone and booked the same one. Thing is—'

The priest took over, turning to me. 'I think it's better if only one is put out instead of two, don't you think? And by the looks of things, you wouldn't fit two there anyway.' He looked at the space next to me.

'So if yis don't mind,' the mate said, 'the good Father would be wanting to sail next to ye. If ye agree.'

And what could I say? Surrounded by good and praying people, and a wife and two wee'uns next to me, what could I say?

'Aye,' I said. 'The good Father can go here.'

'Bless you,' the priest said.

'So we're all alright, then?' The mate thanked me, put on his cap, and hurried away.

The priest held out his hand. 'James Carmichael,' he said.

And thus I met the man I would soon become.

3

Father James Carmichael took his hat off and laid it on the bed next to me. I'd never seen one like it before and I wondered what kinda priests they were breeding here in the city. I watched him while he unpacked his small case. Delicate hands, thin wrists, sober gait – not a working man. Certainly never was in a field. Never swung a hoe or an axe, never shovelled shite, never hauled rock from the earth. A gentle, soft man. Studied, no doubt. He gave me an embarrassed smile.

'That's a quare hat you've on ya, Father.'

'I'm a Jesuit,' said Father Carmichael.

'A what now?'

'A Jesuit.'

'That some kinda Protestant, is it?'

I heard a gasp from May. She blessed herself. Eliza turned a hard gaze on me. I realised suddenly that with a name like Moffatt, I was probably a Protestant myself.

'What way is that to talk to the good Father?' Eliza said.

'Apologies, Father.'

'No need,' Father Carmichael said.

Then he explained what a Jesuit was all about. 'We're sons of the holy church in Rome. We're engaged in bringing the word of God to the uncivilised corners of the world, spreading God's message and ministering to the poor and unblessed.'

'The poor and unblessed, eh?' *Sure wasn't there enough of us here in this bloody country?*

Father James laid out his bedding and sat down, and took out some books and set them on the floor.

'Plan to get some readin done, Father?'

'The mind is a muscle. I try to exercise it daily.'

'True, 'tis,' I said.

'Been on a ship before?'

'Not one like this, Father.'

'She's a beauty, alright.'

'Let's hope she's fit for it. We'll be needin our sea legs, you can take it from me,' I told him.

'The good Lord'll watch over us.'

'Here's hopin,' I said.

It wasn't long before 558 people had crammed on board, and we all went up to the deck to see off the old country. A black cloud sat over the city with the hum of industry coming off the port, and in the distance we saw thin trails of smoke seep from the chimneys of the linen mills. Above us the ship's horn blew, a great horrific noise betokening terror, uncertainty, hope, giddiness and the unknown. I didn't know where I was going, but I knew what I was leaving – Ireland. Ragged shrew, abused Jezebel, wretched fury... *We're off now. Be seein ya*. Wives blew reckless kisses into the air in the direction of the quay, kisses caught by no one; husbands stood looking at the Black Mountain wistfully, a tear in the eye and torn poetry in their hearts for a blighted isle, home no more. Me, I was looking at the faces, wondering why they were weeping for a land that put nothing in their mouths but the taste of ash and unanswered prayers.

The horn blew three short paps and then we were moving over the waters, the cold face of Ireland at our backs and open sea ahead.

August 25th, 1847.

I looked round to see Eliza at my side with the two wee'uns next to her. There was sorrow on her face, and why wouldn't there be? She'd one dead husband behind her, and a new one, just as poor and sick as the last, standing next to her.

'Will we have a tea?' she said.

'Aye. I'll fetch us some water.' I pinched the cheek of the wee'uns as I passed.

I went and collected the pot below and joined the queue for water. This is how it'd be now: waiting for water, waiting for bread. Waiting to piss, waiting to shit. Five hundred people on board, all waiting.

I filled the pot and went back up on deck. We gathered round the fire on the fore deck and waited for a space to open up so we could boil the pot. All humanity's itinerant, waiting.

Eliza sliced some bacon and we sat on the deck and we ate and drank. There was a jovial atmosphere alright: families sat around in the cold air, drinking tea and eating whatever scraps they were holding on to, a bit of bacon or cabbage or bread, and I thought of the brother in my belly and how he was coming with me across the ocean.

Then I remembered there was half of him lying in a hole in the ground next to a wall in Donegal, and I got to wondering what the essence of a man was... was it in his head? In his hands and feet, or in his bones? Or in his meat and gristle, his flesh? Regardless, I was taking some part of the brother away from it all, and for that, I think, he'd be grateful.

Young Molly looked up at me. 'So are you our daddy now?'

A few heads around us turned.

Her mother leaned in, all hush like. 'You'll call him Daddy 'til we get to New York.'

'I want my daddy,' Jake said.

'He's comin after,' I told him. Eliza was too exhausted to come up with a better yarn.

'My daddy's a fisherman,' Jake said.

'Is he now? What's the biggest fish he ever caught?'

And the kid threw his arms out wide as he could.

'Oh, that's a monster. Can you fish?'

'Yes.'

'Then we'll get you a rod and you can catch us a big fish to eat,' I said.

He nodded, chomping on the last of his bacon.

'What can you do?' I asked Molly.

She could think of nothing, so Eliza said, 'You can make tea and boil eggs, can't you?'

And the child nodded.

'You have any eggs?' I asked her.

'No.'

'Well that's alright, cause I lay two eggs every day and four on Sunday,' I told her.

'No, you don't!'

'Yes I do,' I said.

And the kids laughed and yelled, and I shouted, *I do!* and I started making noises like a chicken, and they both howled and even Eliza had a laugh, and just for a moment, we were all alright.

Night set in early and we were soon off the coast of Donegal, and I saw it pass, the black land, before all became dark. Night fallen, we retreated to the hold, the shivering dregs of Éire, and we closed up the portholes and we got ready to sleep. The priest was reading by the light of a gas lamp which hung next to the bed.

Eliza strung up a couple of blankets so her and the kids could get dressed. I sat on the bed next to Father James.

'What you readin there, Father?'

'An account of the Jesuit missionaries.'

'That what you be headin out for, is it?'

'I've accepted a missionary post in the Argentine Republic.'

'Where's that?'

'In the south of the Americas,' he told me.

'You'll be livin down there, will ya?'

'Yes.'

'That's some adventure.'

'I think we're all on the cusp of a great adventure, no?' he said.

'Well, you're right at that.'

'It's a rough trip to be makin with young children though, isn't it?'

For a moment I forgot myself. I forgot that I was Robert Moffatt and I'd no idea what he was on about. He indicated past me to where Eliza lay with the children.

'Oh. Oh it is,' I said.

'Brave man.' Father James Carmichael closed the book. 'Perhaps I'll get some sleep.'

'Right you are.'

He turned off the lamp. I looked over at Eliza with the wee'uns behind her. I tried to see them through Robert Moffatt's eyes, the wife, the kids, lying there all peaceful like, and me, the good husband, protector, provider, trying my best to give them a new life. Some men were cut out for it, I guess. Some, like me and the priest here, had a different calling. *To each his own.*

I was awake at five. Five hundred people round you, you wake early. There were two main holds split in the middle by a dividing wall. That was 279 per quarter, so sixty berths running either side of the long room, stacked double. Two to a berth, except with families, where you had a mother on a bed with two, maybe three, children. With everyone in strange surroundings, many were already stirring. I decided to get my toilet outta the way before the whole ship was up.

I headed to the corner. The toilet was a bucket behind a curtain. You shat in the bucket and when it was full the mate came along and tipped it over the side. The bucket was already half-full and stinking. I squatted over it and did my best to squeeze something out. I gave my arse a bit of a rub with my hand and washed in a bucket of salt water, then got my jacket and headed up on deck.

We were out on the ocean now, no land in any direction. There was a ship off port side, maybe a mile away. Another passenger ship by the looks of it. Astern, folks were already making tea. The air was freezing but clean and I took great gulps of it. Never had been this far out before. Never was out so far out I couldn't see land, but it was thrilling. *A terror too, she is, the ocean. No mistakin it. Would swallow you up and not a trace left of ya.* My hands tightened on the guard rail. I gripped it, feeling the salt coated on its coarse surface. I spat into the churning waters, then headed downstairs to see what the family was at.

I found them awake on the bed, Molly crying into her mother's bosom.

'What's the matter?'

'She doesn't want to go in the bucket,' Eliza said.

'You know chickens poo in buckets, too?' I told the child. I was thinking I'd get a giggle out of her, but she wasn't having it.

'Maybe she can just go on the floor, then you can take it outside and fling it into the sea.'

'Jaysus,' Eliza said.

So we held a blanket up round her and Eliza put down her handkerchief and the child went on it. Eliza picked it up, wrapped it, and took it up to the deck.

'Feel better?' I said.

The child sniffled.

Father James came back from the direction of the washroom. He was pale, obviously just introduced to the bucket himself.

'You alright there, Father?'

He nodded. 'Fair rough conditions we're living in, isn't it?'

He went straight for his Bible. *Comfort where you can find it, I suppose.* I suspected the pages of his books'd be finding a different purpose before we were off the ship. The Father knelt and blessed himself and set about praying for patience, or strength or grace, or whatever he needed to get him through.

Eliza came back and we joined the line for our daily bread. A pound per adult and a half for the children. The bread had already seen better days and we were only on the boat since the day before. I'd a good idea what it'd look like in a week's time, and who knew, maybe we'd be on the boat for five. There'd be a riot if the mate wasn't careful.

We took our bread and got a pot o' clean water, and headed above to make our morning tea.

4

Before a week had passed, Eliza was confined to the bed. The boat tore a line across the foul Atlantic and my 'wife' grew sicker. I played the part of concerned husband. I sat by the bed while our daughter wiped her mother's face with a rag, and young Jake sat at the end of the bed with his thumb in his mouth, growing more and more distant. Eliza had to suffer the indignity of me, a stranger, lifting her so she could shit in a bucket and not all over herself and the bed. She shat and she vomited, and with the depletion of her bodily fluids she lost all shape and became cold and limp and rag-like. Father James upped his prayer regimen. The others became nervous, and soon the entire hold was on edge. Sickness had set in and many knew what that foreboded. I did my best to shield Eliza from the contempt that was growing around us, but she was beyond noticing at that point. She wasn't making it to the other side and she knew it.

I made sure the two children got fed. It was only seven days into the trip and already the bread was unfit for eating. So every morning I collected our rations and we went up on the deck and I boiled a pot of water for tea. I made tea for the three of us and we sat in the cold spray of the ocean and dipped rock-hard bread into piping hot tea, then forced the foul mess down our throats to our wanting stomachs. I made a game of it with them, and we would race to see who'd be the first to swallow a fistful of stale bread. Then, if the weather allowed, we'd sit and look out at the ocean and banter and jibe as best we were able. Their mother was below dying and Molly knew it, young as she was. Jake clammed up. Mornings, up on deck with the cold air blowing down our necks and salt on our faces, I tried to pull him out of himself. He was five years old, lost his da only a week before and was now watching his ma wither away before him. I'd lost my whole family too, but I was thirty. Jake was little more than a baby.

We went back downstairs to check on Eliza. We found Father James by her side, holding her hand. They were praying. He'd more of a backbone than I gave him credit for, did the priest. Strong enough for God's work after all. I still wasn't sure what a Jesuit was, but we coulda done with a couple more of them, there on the Constitution.

Worse was coming.

First two weeks of the trip, we had sunshine. It was cold up on deck, no doubt, but the sun was a fine thing. Day eleven, we carried Eliza up to the deck for an hour. The air below was becoming rancid; portholes were open for an hour or two in the morning but it wasn't enough to chase the festering smells. Sweat, muck and the rank odour of bodily fluids filled the air. And now, with sickness on the boat, new smells were rising up – smells of decay, putrefaction and the hum of the dying. We all knew it; we'd all watched someone die from hunger or cholera and we knew the smell of their impending hour. Death had an odour; it crept into the room and announced itself, and you knew the next time the one lying in front of you closed their eyes it'd be the last.

We took her up on deck, sat her in the sun and wrapped a blanket round her shoulders. Molly sat with her head in her mother's lap and Jake stood next to her. She was wan, skin like wax and eyes sunk. Her hair was plastered to her face, so I took her comb and tried to bring some kind of order to it. I did the same for my own mother before her hair all fell out, then there was nothing left to brush. Molly wasn't having it, said I wasn't doing it right, and took the comb off me and set about it doing it herself.

'Some girl you've raised,' I said to Eliza.

She smiled weakly.

'The wee man's grown awful quiet,' I said.

Eliza stroked her son's head. He sat sucking on his thumb. John, the child from the berth above us, wandered up on deck. 'Can Molly come and play, Mrs Moffatt?'

Him and the girl had become good friends.

'Take Jake with you,' Eliza said. She took the comb from Molly. 'Go and play,' she told them.

Molly took her brother by the hand and the three of them skipped away up fore of the boat. We sat alone, me and Eliza. We looked out over the Atlantic, the boat lurching side to side, with the horizon disappearing and reappearing behind the boat's trim.

Eliza spoke. 'Are you a good man?'

I looked at her. I wasn't sure what to answer. 'What do you mean?'

'Just that – are you a good man?'

There's a question. Never was asked such a thing. What did a man who only ever dug potatoes from the ground or help put up a few stone walls have to be doing with good and evil?

'I dunno, Eliza,' I said. 'I never hurt no one, if that's what you mean.'

She looked at me, then back at the sea. 'I'm not gonna make it.'

'Oh, now—'

'I'm no fool. I'm not gonna last another week,' she said.

'Look, Eliza—'

'I'm as good as dead. I'm not gonna make it to the end of the week and don't try and tell me otherwise. But I've two children…'

We could hear Molly shouting on the other side of the boat.

'… and I want to know they'll make it someplace safe.'

'Eliza,' I said, 'I'll do whatever I can for em when we get to New York.'

'Do you promise me?' She caught my eye and didn't waver.

'I promise.'

'Thank you.' She nodded. 'You better take me back down.'

I lifted her up, all that was left of her.

'Maybe you'll tell me your real name, so,' she said.

I told her. 'But you can call me Robert.'

She smiled weakly. It was a poor jest.

She died three days later. After a pretty serious bout of convulsions which had the children distraught, she slipped into a coma. She passed away in the night, a shadow of the woman she'd been only ten days before. Such was her sickness. Molly hugged her mother tightly and wept, and the young boy sat off at a distance, watching and sucking his thumb. The mate was summoned, a hearty fella called Tadhg, and we stood with him over the body as Father James administered the last rites. We blessed ourselves, even me, as a blanket was pulled up over her head.

'What do we do?' I asked.

'She goes overboard,' Tadhg told us.

'Is that the only way?'

'It's the only way.'

I nodded.

A cold silence fell over the hold as we lifted her body from the bed. She was laid in an old sail and sewn up, and the children got the last look at their mother as the needle closed the shroud. I caught Molly's eye as Eliza disappeared, and I understood the passing of her parents was not her first acquaintance with death, for she'd clearly lost folk already and her only nine years old.

It was eight in the morning when we took Eliza upstairs. The sun had seen fit to abandon us that day. The sky was black, heavy; we all felt a dark new fate had befallen us.

We had a brief service, rites were said. I said a few words over the body of my dead wife. Then we cast her into the sea. People filed away to collect their rotten bread.

Later that day, it was announced that due to corruption of several of our barrels, our rations of drinking water would be halved. Tempers flared. There were a few who wanted to have a go at the mate but there was nothing that could be said to the man. He was merely the bearer of bad news. Some sagely asked whether the first-class cabins would be seeing a reduction in rations, or was it just us in the hold. Tadhg assured us the rations applied to all. Whether there was any truth to it, I don't know, since there were five hundred of us and only fifty of them. My hunch was there was an unequal distribution. I noticed, too, since he was my bunkmate, that the priest disappeared above for a time every day, and I suspected he was receiving first-class benefits, which was fair, I suppose, since he'd been the holder of a first-class ticket.

Molly and Jake, having witnessed the death of their second parent, turned to me in the following days and I, their surrogate father, had no choice but to take them under my wing. Since it would've been cruel to let them lie in their mother's deathbed – it was seeping with more than the memory of her passing – they came in with us, me and Father James, and now the poor man who'd gotten on the boat with the expectation of a lovely big bed all to himself was sharing with three others: one big human and two small ones. He remained courteous, however, and my admiration for him grew.

The next morning, May came down with a bout of vomiting. There was a hateful fear among the people.

I went on deck with Father James to make tea. The children had run off in search of distraction.

'It's started,' I told him.

He nodded.

'You think much about death?'

'It's part of my job,' he replied.

'And what about all this? All this needless dyin? What's the point of it all?'

He was gaunt-looking. He knew what was coming. 'I don't know.'

And I coulda kissed him. He didn't give me any bull about God testing us, or grace through suffering, or any of the other shite that priests like to throw around. He admitted he didn't know. There was a man among them after all, the priests, and here he was, with his thin wrists and delicate hands, and his books and his eyeglasses. Father

James Carmichael, a Jesuit.

So I told him the truth about me and Eliza, how she wasn't my wife and how I'd watched her husband carried away on a cart with the cholera and me giving her five pounds for the ticket and getting on the boat as Robert Moffatt.

'So you knew she was sick?' he said.

I lied. 'No. She was fine gettin on the boat.'

'We'll be lucky to get off alive.'

'We can't blame the poor woman, her with two children and a husband just dead, and tryin to make a new life for herself.'

He shook his head. 'I suppose we can't. We're all entitled to that, a chance at a better life.'

'Why are you leavin?' I asked him.

'I consider it my duty to bring the word of God to the world.'

'There are plenty in Ireland who could be doin with a man like you,' I told him.

He shook his head sadly. 'I, too, want a better life.'

'You're the only honest priest I've ever met.'

'I hope that's not true.'

'It is. And that's why Ireland is fucked.'

We woke up in the night with water falling down round us. The whole family above us sick, watery diarrhea was running from them, through the mattress and down on top of us. The children were in distress, but what could we do? There was nowhere for them to go, so in the middle of the night we carried the family down from their berth, switched out the mattresses, and moved up to the top bunk. When we got up in the morning, the floor round us was swimming with vomit and bowel water; not shit, but water, that ran out of them in a ceaseless flow. We watched the whole family turn waxen with the disease, all three. Then three became six, and six became fourteen, and soon there was a couple of dozen ill with it. Father James continued to help and I did my bit too, but much of my time was taken with keeping the children distracted, keeping their minds off their dead mother and their current situation.

We took to fishing. I scraped together some old line from the mate and a few hooks too, and we soaked some of the rotten bread and cast our lines into the ocean, and didn't we pull them out with big fat mackerel on the hooks. We all hooped and giggled deliriously, even the young fella, who hadn't said a word since his mother died. Molly got into it too, and soon we were passing out fish to the other passengers. We fished in the morning, getting wet if needed be, for now the weather had turned and we often got lashed by a squall or soaked by the spray whipped up by hard winds, and in the evenings we cooked our mackerel on the fire and ate a bit of proper food for the first time since getting on the boat. We felt good. Others took it up too after seeing our success, and the smell of grilled fish became common at teatime. The abundance of fish gave everyone a boost, and for a day or two things seemed like they might be alright. Then Molly fell ill.

5

Just nine years old. I had a few questions for the priest, but now wasn't the time for asking. Besides, with a sick child sleeping next to us, it was only a matter of time before we fell ill ourselves and we knew it. But Christ, I was gonna do what I could to get that child off the boat alive.

The vomiting started two days after the passing of her mother. Then came the diarrhea, so I took her from the bed and made up a small cot for her at the foot of the berth. There were four people round us struck with the sickness: Thomas, May and John were all dying right before our eyes. May, she'd taken something else, cause now she was swelling up; her feet and hands were puffed up to an unnatural size and her head was all outta shape. Another six in the near berths were showing signs, if not already bedridden.

The floor of the hold was a river of shit and vomit, and as the boat listed to this side or that, so the river ran. The two second mates came down twice a day and scrubbed out the floor, but it was useless. Those who were ill were, one way or another, losing their fluids and there weren't sufficient buckets to contain it all. Those who were bad could only shit themselves, and if they could muster the energy they would shit over the edge of the bed right onto the floor. The place stank. We opened the portholes but it did nothing. The mates came down with shirts wrapped round their faces but the terror in their eyes was clear. They knew they were walking into a cesspool, and it was only with a miracle that they'd walk out of it healthy again.

I entreated the captain for some medicine for the girl, and when that came to naught I had the priest go beg the captain for me. That also came to nothing. The captain insisted they didn't have medicine on board. I was sure he had his own stash in his cabin, but I couldn't go robbing his berth for they'd put me in chains and I'd be no good to anyone, certainly not the girl.

When she ceased vomiting, I took her up on deck for a bit of fresh air. We were well into September now and it was proper cold, but any respite from the hell below was welcome. The fishing had stopped for the sea was too rough, and we were back on rations of stale bread and tea. I tried to make her eat but she couldn't keep her food down.

'Are they gonna throw me over the side of the boat like mammy?' she asked.

Christ, I wept.

'You're gonna make it to New York,' I told her.

And I spun her some auld shite about the New World, any auld shite, just to keep her mind off it. 'You know, in New York they have women with beards and men with two heads, and you can pay a penny and go and see them, and when you're tired of women with beards you can go see a little midget fella with a belly made of glass with fish swimming around inside, and if you give him a penny he'll let you feed the fish. You'll see him swallow a worm—'

'*Eww!*'

'...and the worm will slide down his gullet and appear in his fish-tank belly and you'll see the fish eat the worm, and if that's not interesting enough for ya, you can go see a woman with an alligator for a baby – an alligator is a big scaly lizard thing with razor sharp teeth that can bite off your leg – and it's true, she went to the hospital one day to have her baby and out popped this big lizard... and next to the woman with the alligator baby is a fat man who pees confetti—'

'*Eww!*'

'...it's true, the fat man pees confetti and he has a big tall fella for a pal who has a lamppost for a leg, and at the bottom of the leg is a gas lamp, and just by slapping his knee he can turn the lamp on and off. And not only that, in New York they have people of all colours, they have red men and black women and yellow people and even green and blue, you may not believe me but it's true...'

And on and on I went all day.

That child was a warrior. She listened to all my shite and even believed some of it. But still she got worse.

There was no one on the boat who wasn't terrified. Some had taken blankets up on the deck and were sleeping there, and were waking up in the morning wet and frozen and with a good coating of salt on them. I suppose they thought it was a good idea, but if the cholera didn't kill them the chill certainly would. I'll admit that dying of pneumonia seemed like the preferable way to go.

It became clear cholera wasn't the only thing killing us. Some of the sick were plagued with great black sores, others yellow ones filled with pus; some of them were covered head to foot in a torturous rash, and they clawed at themselves from morning to night til their flesh bled, yet others were shitting and vomiting blood, and more of them began to swell up all unnatural like. The priest said it was some combination of cholera, typhus and dysentery, perhaps all three, and possibly other afflictions we weren't aware of. We saw the first-class passengers come stare in at us, and they looked on in horror at the hell within before crossing themselves and running back to their first-class cabins. I wanted to spit in their faces. I wanted to infect them, drag them below into the shit and the vomit and the poisonous airs in which we lived, have them touch the pus-filled sores and the cracked, bloody skin, and inhale the stench of the dying.

You wanted to see. Here – see.

We weren't animals, but suffering human beings. But those faces that appeared in the portholes saw only curiosities and horrors.

Pay a penny and see the freaks.

I won't deny it scared the living Christ outta one to look upon us. May... *Jesus.* May was unrecognisable. All swollen up, her head about twice its natural size, sores bursting all over her. She must have been in agony. I sat with her and Thomas and the little fella in the evening when Molly was sleeping. Father James whispered hollow and meaningless comforts:

'Another few days and we'll be in port in New York. Hang in there.'

'Sure the doctors in America are great.'

'You've only an auld virus. It'll pass if you just hold on.'

'You gotta be strong for the young fella.'

She was beyond weeping. Her eyes were red and sore and she said little, but when she looked at her husband her eyes communicated a very simple message: *Kill me*.

I swear she wanted to die.

We woke the next morning and she was dead. Thomas was stoic. He'd wept through the night, but he was sitting next to his dead wife, her with a blanket over her, the young fella still asleep. He stared vacantly out past her corpse, hand on her belly. I thought there was something else in his eyes, some shame or guilt. Perhaps he'd killed her, maybe with the pillow over the face, suffocated her like. The priest got this impression too, cause he went over to the man, put his thin arms round his shoulder, and said, 'It was the only thing.'

That's what he said. *It was the only thing.*

'No one should have to suffer like that,' I said to Thomas.

Somehow I felt me and the priest had our condolences mixed up, him with the hard words and me with the compassionate ones. Perhaps that's what happens when people lie next to each other for long enough – their thoughts get mixed up. I'd absorbed some of the priest, him some of me. We were melding.

May was the second funeral.

Dust to dust. Water to water.

My own family had been returned to the earth, these people were being returned to the sea. Which was more natural? We're all born swimming after all, aren't we?

May was wrapped in some old sail, sewn up, and cast into the ocean.

We had to carry Thomas up on deck to see his wife off and his son to say farewell to his mother.

They were dead themselves two days after, father and son. They too were consigned to eternal rest.

Five more days, fourteen more. They just kept dying.

But Molly hung on. I don't know what kinda fighting spirit she was gifted with, but she clung to life. She made sure we looked after her little brother too. For some reason the young fella was fine, not a lick of any kind of contagion on him. He wasn't right in the head, though; he didn't speak at all now, and his thumb only came outta his mouth to put down a bit of bread, and that only at the fiercest insistence. We hadn't fished in days, the weather didn't allow it, and besides, with all the dying it was hardly proper to be sitting up on deck with a rod, even if it did mean the difference between eating and dying.

Me and the priest took the two young'uns up on deck one afternoon to get them outta that shit-filled hole below. We watched out for the sharks that had taken to following us since discovering the abundance of flesh that followed in our wake. There was plenty of them, popping up every few minutes, waiting on the corpse that would appear sooner or later. Molly didn't make the connection, thankfully, between the sharks and the dead, herself not far from dying. We talked about home.

'What do you miss about Ballycastle?'

'Yellow man,' she said.

'What's yellow man?' said the priest.

'The Father doesn't know what yellow man is,' I said. 'That's a strange fella doesn't know what yellow man is.'

She looked at him like, *How can you not know what yellow man is?*

'Yellow man, Father,' I explained, 'is a little yellow man that comes outta his hole in the rocks once a year, and you give him a coin to have a lick at his tiny head, and his head tastes like blackberries, only the best blackberries you've ever tasted.'

Molly giggled, in a way she hadn't giggled since I saw them chase each other round the boat when we first caught a mackerel.

'A little yellow man?' he said.

More giggling.

'Aye, Father, and if you give him an extra penny he'll let you chew on his leg which tastes like honeycomb.'

We all had a laugh.

It was rough out, but dry. And the air, the sea air, was *oh-so-sweet*. We were high on it. We were a long way from yellow man and dulse and the fair, but we still had the sea. The ocean. And with a little luck, she wouldn't eat us all before we reached the other side.

We nursed the child as long as we could, but it was inevitable she would go. She died in her sleep one night with six others, all of them under the age of thirty. Young Jack woke up in the morning with an arm round his dead sister. He didn't start or weep; he watched noiselessly as we lifted her limp, waxen body from the berth. We laid her out and tidied her up best we could. I tried to fix her hair up like her mother did. We left her dressed but took off her boots, and they were added to the pile of stuff the dead were leaving behind. It'd be auctioned off later.

We were outta sail by then, so we were reduced to wrapping her in old meal sacks. We took two: one over the head and one over the feet, but I told them she wasn't to be sewn up yet.

Six bodies were consigned to the ocean that afternoon, one after the other. Less and less folk were appearing on deck for the funerals. Most were too sick anyway, without the strength to crawl from their beds. Lives ended, their stories finished here on the foul Atlantic, folk cast into the deep waters with barely a witness. Nobody cared to see anymore. We'd had enough death already, and that was only a third of them that would be dead before making port. In the two and a half weeks that followed, another seventy or eighty would meet their end there in the frigid, unremembering sea.

We didn't bury Molly in the morning. I made them wait. I went to the first mate and asked for some tackle. He wasn't ready to part with it but I got pushy. In the end, he gave me three old blocks and a couple of cast iron cleats. The weight was for the child. I'd weigh down her down so she'd race to the bottom and the sharks wouldn't have her as she sank. I was no fool – I knew something else would have her at the bottom, just as long as it wasn't the sharks.

We put the weights in round her feet, sewed up the sack and carried her up on deck after nightfall. No one else came with us. The boy was asleep so we left him be.

The night was dry, the water black. I waited for the priest to say a few words.

He said, 'Let not your hearts be troubled. Believe in God, and believe also in me. In my Father's house are many rooms. If it were not so, would I have told you that I go to prepare a place for you? And if I go and prepare a place for you, I will come again and take you myself, that where I am you may be also.'

And I wondered about the rooms of his house, in particular the one where we were sending the young'un, nine years old, headed to the big black room below, to be companion to the cuttlefish and the octopus and the spider crabs. I'd a good idea what was below. Did God? Would he be waiting there for her, to welcome her to his black abode?

Eternal rest in the deepest hole of earth awaited her.

'Bless you, child,' I whispered.

We cast her over the side into the black water.

6

Four weeks in we were all praying for the end. Expecting sight of land any minute, it never came. We waited, hour by hour, for a glimpse, or maybe a waft on the air of God's green earth, but we waited in vain. I was lying next to the priest who was now suffering in a pool of his own shit and vomit. Of those round us, only me and the young fella were unscathed, everyone else in some bitter agony, rife with sores and dysentery and whatever else, and I wondered: Why me? Hadn't I killed my own brother and mother, and hadn't I eaten the flesh of my own kin in order to escape that island? So why was I now graced with good health? I didn't have the answer. I thought maybe Father James did. I sat with him in his sickness, now no longer afraid of those cruel maladies. I changed his bucket and wiped him down, and brought him water and black, stale bread. He couldn't eat it. So I talked to him instead. I told him he was gonna make it and that he'd be well, and to hang on for another week and we'd be in America, and we'd share a cup of tea on the streets of New York.

'You can drop the schpiel,' he said.

I guess I could n'all. 'Are you prayin?' I said.

'I don't have the strength for it.'

'Can I ask you something?'

'Go on.'

'You're dyin...' I said.

'I am.'

'Is there anything waitin for ya? I mean, is he doin somethin for ya, the God above? Is he there for ya?'

Father James waited for a dose of retching to pass. 'When we enter the church, we do so because we believe there's a higher power greater than ourselves. We join the church to submit to that power, and to accept that we trust God to make those decisions for us. We can only bow our heads and surrender.'

'And what about all this, then? What kinda higher power can allow this to happen?' I gestured round us at the sallow and haunted people writhing in their own dirt.

He was silent for a long time. 'It's a terrible thing,' he said eventually.

'It's an evil thing,' I said.

'We can't call God's work evil, no matter how tragic it is.'

'You know what's evil, Father? The smell of a boatload o'people shittin themselves to death for want of clean water. That smell does things to ya. Cause I'll tell ya, and this is the truth – will you hear a confession from me now, Father?'

He nodded, and there was something ridiculous about it all, me nursing him in his final hours and him taking my confession.

'Is it evil, Father, that I want to kill these people? Want to get up in the night and take a wet pillow to their faces til the life's out of em?'

'I would have to ask why,' he said. 'For what reason?'

And I know what I should've said, what the answer of a reasonable man would be, the answer of a human, but the human wasn't in me and I couldn't lie to the priest on his deathbed so I told him like it was.

'Because I've had enough of it, the stink of it. Death. I've been suffocating with the stench of it for over a year now. I've choked on the rot of my own family – the father, the sisters, the brother and the mother, and each time I inhaled the rot somethin in me died too; I felt myself decay, and I felt the man squeezed outta me and something else make its nest there in the absence of me, something dead and cold. I'd choke the life outta all these people, Father, not so's to ease their pain, but to put an end to the inhuman stench.'

The priest said nothing. So I went on.

'And there's a question for ya, Father – say's I got up in the night and choked the life outta eight people, eight people with barely a day to live between them and not a hope of clean air or water in sight, people only destined for the sharks, what'd it matter if I killed em for themselves or killed them for my own comfort? What'd it matter?'

'Your soul. It'd mean your soul.'

'I told you already, Father, my soul choked to death on the stench of my own rotting family.'

'It's not dead. Your soul may have been tested, but it's certainly not dead. It's still there. All you have to do is give it time to flourish again.'

'If you wanna try and find it, Father, you're more than welcome. I haven't been acquainted with the fella in a brave long time.'

Father James smiled, but I could see the life slipping outta him. He wasn't swollen or covered in sores like some of them, he was just shrivelling up, skin taut against his bones, his face sallow. I dabbed his face with a cloth. His skin felt like mackerel. I remember those final hours cause I remember the talk, and night was coming on when we stopped chatting. His last words to me were: 'Don't let me sleep.' That's what he said, took me by the arm, squeezed it and whispered the words to me. He knew it was coming. I squeezed his hand and nodded, but who's the man can fight it when he knows it's coming on him? He drifted into a tortured sleep, and I did too, and I woke around three in the morning with Father James gripping my arm like a vise, and I turned to look into his face, his eyes wide, white in the darkness, and he passed with a holy silent scream. I thought of his words, then, as I saw the life go outta him: *In my Father's house are many rooms*, and I thought, *Well, be glad you're gone from this room, for in this room we know only one thing, and it's not life... and Christ do I hope your soul is intact and it's taken to a fine place, for you're a good sort, Father, you're a good sort. Farewell.*

We buried him at night, a moonless night as with the child, but without all the weight to sink him. He was cast into the ocean, only his own insubstantial frame wrapped in sack and his own prayers still on the wind. I prayed, in my own strange way, for him to reach the rooms he so believed in. Father James Carmichael. Believer. Deceased. And I decided at that moment, as his body disappeared into the cold waters of the Atlantic, that I would, also in my own strange way, carry on the man's memory. I would honour him by carrying on his mission – it would be me that carried it on to America, whatever hardships or obstacles be put in my way, I would bear the good name of Father James Carmichael. I would carry his torch. I would see with his eyes and touch with his hands, and it would be with his good feet I walked the earth when I ventured out across the world. I decided at that moment to become a priest.

There were sharks in the hold, too, that had to be fought off. They came for his things, they did, like they came for everyone's. I fought them. The captain sent the mate for the priest's books, and I stood over them and told the mate he'd be clawing them from my dead hands. They came for his boots, his good leather boots, and I told them they'd be kicked black and blue before they ever wore them. They came for his trousers and his spectacles and even his hat, his big strange hat, and I fought them all. Nothing of the priest's would be auctioned off, and the only reason they relented was I threatened to bring the curses of God down upon their heads, I who had no knowledge or acquaintance whatsoever of that same God. I swore and blew and kicked and eventually they relented, and the priest's affairs were left in my care. They were mine now.

So I got acquainted with his books. I had some reading, though I'd little use for it since I was at school, but it came back to me now as I explored the priest's letters. I found his invitation from the Order in New York, asking him to come and spread the good Word to the lands of the south. He had a Bible, of course, which I'd need to become familiar with. He'd a book on the Americas, by a Mr Dickens. So I got my head down. It was just me and young Jack now, his parents and sister dead, the priest dead, the family above us dead, just the two of us and he needed little looking after. So I read. I read as the rest of them kept dying round me, and when I was needed I would help ready bodies for burial, and help carry them up on deck and over the side, for it was only me and the boy and a few others were still any way healthy. So I did what I had to do, and when I wasn't doing it, I read. And then it came. We all heard the shout.

'Land!'

Four more died from the moment land was sighted til we got into port, and that took the number to 118; 118 souls who dreamt of a life in the New World but found only eternity in the deepest, coldest parts of earth. Eternal sleep with the fishes is what they got, and God bless. I wept a tear for them as the boat pulled into the quay, for Eliza and the priest and for Thomas and May, and for all of the dead women and children alike, but mostly for Molly, who was an angel put on this earth for too little time, and of whose smile and laughter we would be deprived ever after. I held Jack's hand as we landed in New York. The boy, thumb in mouth, watched silently. Despite the stench on our boat of death and shit and vomit, which reached even the decks, I could smell the New World, which smelled of oil and smoke and apples. It made my heart jump, and my belly too, for I was six weeks eating stale bread and, Jesus forgive me, but I'd kill a man and eat him for a taste of an apple.

'What would you do right now for an apple, son?' I asked Jack, but there was no reply outta him.

Half the boat was carried off, or simply dragged. Those that were sick and clinging to life by their dirty fingernails were hauled off by the sanitation department and away towards some unknown fate in the care of the city of New York. I was sure it was better than what they were getting back in Ireland; in Ireland they'd only a hole in the ground waiting and not even a stone for remembrance.

Then I collected the priest's things in his nice leather case and took the boy in hand and got off the boat. I found a nice, plump woman from the sanitation department and explained the boy had lost both parents, dead of cholera or dysentery or typhus, and that he was traumatised and hadn't said a word in three weeks. The kind woman took the child by the hand and led him away, and with a single look over his shoulder he was gone, thumb still in his mouth, him away too into the great unknown. I wished the best for the child, but he was beyond my care.

I was stopped on the way outta the port by another plump lady from the sanitation department, who looked down her nose at me, til I explained I was a priest and I would now need to change into my cassock, if that was alright with her. She said it was. So I went behind a curtain and changed into my robes, and stepped out. She was the first, that plump nurse, to see me in my priest's cassock.

'Oh, Father,' she said, and that was all she said, and then she put a thermometer in my mouth and scratched something in a nice little paper book with my name, Father James Carmichael, and said I was alright to enter America.

'Bless you,' I said.

She pointed to my old clothes as I left, my wretch's rags, and I told her burn them.

He was gone now, the wretch who crawled from a hole in the West of Ireland, who ate his brother and buried his ma and the rest of his family and crawled across Ireland and got on a boat where a hundred died, even some of the best he'd ever met, and him not with a breath of sickness on him the whole way, but who was born again as he stepped off the boat onto the new land, the New World, New York, and was a new man with a whole continent laying open before him.

So I stepped outside, out into the sunlight and a new life. And wasn't there a man waiting there, dressed just like I was, in a black cassock and a strange hat and with his arms crossed on his waist.

'Brother James Carmichael?' he said.

'Yes,' I said, and smiled.

October, 1847

7

'Brother Michael Flynn,' he said. He held out his hand and I shook it.

'Irish?'

He nodded and smiled. 'They thought it fitting that you were welcomed by one of your own countrymen. We've been waiting for you for five days.'

'You've been here every day?' I said.

He smiled, and took me by the arm and lead me out to the street and towards a horse and cart.

'What date is it?'

'October ninth. It's impossible to say when the ships come in. We had a German come in last month from Bremen... our brother was nine days waiting for him here at the port. The ship hit weather mid-voyage and had to travel around a storm front. Six hundred extra miles on the journey and an extra week and a half on travel time. The crossing can be three and a half weeks, or it can be six. I consider myself fortunate.'

He explained all this as he climbed up on the cart.

Meanwhile, I was lost in the great hustle of the place, Belfast the only other city I'd seen my whole short life. With the great rattle of capstans and the hollow, throaty horns of the port behind us, I climbed up in the cart next to Brother Michael Flynn, and he gave the reins a crack and the horse trotted off down the street, down the filthy and glorious New York street, past all the people – the people! Such a conflagration of folk I never saw, with the Chinamen and the Hindoos and the Blacks and the Cossacks, and Turks and Italians and Dutch, and beggars and street wretches and ragged children, and I marvelled, for I'd never seen a Turk or a Black or a Chinaman, and the whole scene was like some picture book come alive, and swarming among them all, the Irish, sure as shit stinks, the Irish, ragged and drunk and swearing and kicking, but alive... insane and broke, but alive. Here they were, my countrymen, in the New World, with the Hindoo and the Black and the hoors and the Cossack, a part of it all, mad life in all its wonder, and I wept for my people and my country, but for once, for once, they were tears of joy.

Brother Michael Flynn glanced at me, saw me wipe an eye as the cart careened down the street, sending pigs and Irish and lost children scooting in all directions.

'It's a shock,' he said. 'It's a wonderful, frightening shock.'

I nodded but didn't speak, for I was overcome with emotion and the words had left me.

'I'd say you'll be glad of a square meal. Most of our brothers come off the boat with a great hunger. What've you been eating this past month?'

So I told him, rotten bread and water, not for sympathy but because it was the God's honest truth and there was no sense hiding it.

'You'll be pleased to see a bit of bacon then,' he said.

Christ, I would, I thought, and I told Brother Michael it'd been over a month since I saw a bit of bacon, and I recalled the brother, the eating of him, and sent a little thought his way for his sacrifice.

This is my body...

It was his flesh that'd carried me here. *Here we are, brother, this is it, the New World – see them all, how they swarm and kick and swear and blaspheme – isn't it fine? And I'm glad you're here to see it with me—*

'Fucken papists!'

The scream came from the side of the road, and a foul head of cabbage was flung our way, striking me on the shoulder.

I watched the man give me two middle fingers as we flew past.

'What was that?'

'Sorry you had to see that. There's a lot of anti-Catholic sentiment in the city. All of America, actually. And if I'm honest with you, you're going to see more of it. May the Lord give us strength.'

'People throwin things at you in the street?'

'They do. And spitting. And even physical violence. Some of the brothers have been attacked. You'll have to be careful out and about but don't let it worry you too much. Aren't you leaving in a few days?'

'Aye.'

And I'd be out soon enough. But I wanted a week to see the city, to taste it, to smell it; already I was inhaling great lungfuls of its stink and loving every minute of it.

'Is there a ticket south?' I said.

'I don't believe so, since we'd little idea when you'd be in. But you'll have to talk to Brother Larkin about it. He's been left in charge of your arrangements.'

'Brother Larkin?'

'Yes. Brother Larkin's in charge of our mission here in the city. A great man, a great man altogether. He's done amazing things here.'

'Is that so?'

'Oh, yes. He came down from Fordham a year ago with five cents in his pocket, not a penny more, and within six months had raised the funds to buy a church here on Elizabeth Street. Isn't it remarkable?' I saw Brother Michael beam. 'Yes, our quarters are next to the church – that's where you'll be staying until you depart south. It's a great place, it is. We've a school in the basement with seventeen children taking lessons there from our own brothers. We're doing wonderful things, even if we see some aggravation from the locals.'

'What do you mean?'

'It was a Protestant church before we took over – they just didn't have the numbers. And even if our congregation is growing day by day, there are a few in the area who resent our presence. We do our best. It's getting easier.'

I listened to Brother Michael. I saw hatred in the eyes of men in the street, and women too and even children, minds poisoned by their elders, but it didn't matter, for filling my head and lungs with the air of New York it was all golden to me. I smiled. I beamed. I was alive, alive in the smoky murderous clamour of the world's greatest city; I felt it all round me, in the sooty streets and the heavy air, even in the cold intent of eyes that despised me, despised the church and Ireland and the Irish – I was alive and living and no one was taking it from me, not the King nor the President nor the Pope himself.

'This is Elizabeth Street,' he said. We'd turned onto a long wide thoroughfare and I marvelled at the great sprawling streets of the city. 'Now do you see it?'

I saw it, a church in front of us of wooden build, as nice as anything we had in our own country, and Brother Michael beamed as if he'd built it with his own hands. We pulled up out front.

'Now, if you'll just come with me,' he said, and he stepped down off the cart and lifted my bag, and took me gently by the arm and pointed at the building next door. 'Our living quarters.'

I noted the fine brick house, and it came to me then that I'd never been in a house made of brick before, but that was the past, for the man from the west of Ireland was no longer... I was Brother James Carmichael, a Jesuit and a man of God, fulla life and wonder, and I was just as entitled as any man to step inside a fine house made of brick.

'This way,' said Brother Michael, and he went up the steps and opened the door and we stepped inside.

How fine it was!

'We'll get you installed in your room then we'll find you a bite to eat,' he said, then we went up the fine wooden stairs, with beautiful paper on the walls and lamps to light the way, and we got to the top and there was a wonderful civilised smell about the place, a smell of polish and devotion, and he took me down a corridor and opened a door. A fine bed awaited me with a mattress and sheets and a pillow, and I almost danced in the hall for joy.

'You'll be sharing with Brother Klaus,' he said, and I didn't care, for I'd share with the devil himself if I had to.

'He's a German and is a bit short on the English, so you'll have to get creative with your communication.'

'That's too bad,' I said, but I was relieved, for it was one less man I'd have to explain myself too.

'He's a quiet sort, anyhow.'

'I'm sure it won't matter a bit. Where is the good brother?'

'Brother Klaus is tending to our garden. He's a great man for toiling the earth.'

'I dabble a bit myself. I'd be happy to help out while I'm here.'

'Don't be troubling yourself, brother. Now, why don't you freshen up and see us downstairs in half an hour? Cook is preparing the food as we speak.'

'I will,' I said.

Brother Michael closed the door, and I took off my boots and did a little jig before throwing myself on the bed.

Later, I went downstairs to find a table of priests, who all turned expectantly to look at the face of Father James Carmichael. I gave them my best smile, and it wasn't a false one for I was ripe with the joy of the New World.

'Brother James,' said Father Michael, 'let me introduce you around. Father Larkin won't be joining us today, he's out at Fordham on business, but the others are here.' And he led me towards the flock. 'This is Brother Klaus, who you'll be rooming with while you stay.'

Big bearded meaty fella. He stood, we shook hands.

'Brother Francis, from England.'

I shook his hand.

And on round the table we went, Brother Rudolfo, Brother Paulo and another Brother James, all polite and priest-like and saying 'It's a pleasure', 'Pleasure I'm sure,' then I was seated at the table in fine Jesuit company, the table with linen and cutlery, and all things alien to men from hovels, behind the table a fine cabinet and on the walls tremendous paintings, and, wafting above it all, the smell of bacon and cabbage from the kitchen. My head spun and I nodded politely at the gentle conversation, my finger tapping unconsciously at the side of my plate, a plate of fine china, and a nice woman came in and poured us all a cup of milk, the smell coming all the more powerful through the kitchen door, and some brother said to me, 'So you're going to rebuild the reductions in the south?', and I said, 'I am', and he replied, 'One of mankind's greatest achievements, what we did in Paraquaria', and the nice servant woman went out through the kitchen door once more, bacon smells coming in with the draft, food, meat, something I hadn't known for six weeks... and Brother Michael came to my aid, saying, 'Leave him be now til he's had a bite to eat.' He knew. I guess it was written all over my face – the panic of the hungry. Talking God is no kind of appetiser. Then Brother James, the other, asked me if I wanted to say grace, and I said, 'No', that I would never say grace as a guest of the table, and what did I know about grace apart from some old words the mother whispered in Gaeilge, and what good was that here? Instead Brother Klaus bowed his head and said something in a hard old German, no kind of language at all to be spoken over food, but then I guess it didn't matter here at God's table here in the New World where one could here German and Gaeilge and English and Hindoo and Chinese, and all that even before breakfast.

Amen.

It came then, the food. Great steaming plates of bacon and cabbage, and I thought at first I might be ill, the stomach of me lurching at the sight and the smell of it. Then my head spun and I held onto the table. There was no doubt I was gonna eat it though, and maybe a second and a third too if they gave it to me. I stayed the savage in me, the animal that rose up at the great mountain of food, and stayed the hand that would take great fistfuls of bacon and cabbage and feed it right into my poor mouth. I picked up the fork and ate like a Christian, like a good Jesuit would, and we ate in silence peppered by the soft approvals and grunts of hungry men. Nevertheless, I made short work of it, and soon Brother Michael was calling the servant woman to bring me another. I made no pretense to politeness, but picked up my plate and put it right in her hand, and told her how good her cabbage was. She smiled coyly, good Christian woman that she was.

'Tell me now, Brother,' said Brother Francis, addressing me directly in a fine polite English, 'how do you intend to spend your days here in New York?'

'I'm going to walk the city from corner to corner,' I told him. I wanted to see all of it, every corner and cranny and dark hole, I wanted to see it all.

'I'd be happy to accompany you on your outing,' he told me then.

'Brother, I find the best way to discover any new corner of the world is to get out and get lost and find your own way home.'

'Quite right. If you weren't an adventurous spirit, you wouldn't be taking the word of God to the Indians,' Brother Michael said.

'The world doesn't scare me,' I said.

'Nevertheless, you'll need to have your wits about you when you go about the city. It's no joke. There have been incidents,' Brother Francis said.

'Now, now, let's not give him a bad impression of the place,' said Brother Michael.

'Brothers,' I say, 'I had the measure of the place when we pulled up in the boat, and when we got on the cart and rode through the city, I saw it all, the terrible scourge of poverty and alcohol, and all those things that make man decrepit in his mind and in his soul...'

I heard myself say the words, and I didn't know if it was the food or the city or the fine table and linen, but I felt the spirit move in me and the priest, Brother James Carmichael, took over, coming into me, and the Word moved me and I spread it among the holy brothers.

'...and I know, brothers, that even here among the wretched and lost that God will protect me, God will watch over me; that here in the New World, for all its horrors and dangers, that a true believer in the Word and in Christ shall fear no evil...'

And perhaps I went too far, because the priests, the English-speaking ones anyway, had looked up from their food, maybe expecting me to stand on the chair and crack a fist on my Bible and cry out the good Word of the Lord.

I was saved by a second plate of bacon and cabbage, and I took refuge in it gladly.

'God save the true believers,' said Brother Francis, and we got back to the eating.

8

I went to my room that night, tired and elated, and before I slept I dug out Brother James Carmichael's books and sat down at a small desk to peruse his affairs, and in among those books I found a fine leather notebook, untouched but for a few pages, so I sat down and, compelled to do so, I took a pen and wrote it all down, about Ireland and the brother and the eating, and the boat and the sick and the dead, about young Molly and Eliza and Brother James, and the rooms of the cold Atlantic and the sharks, and every foul twist and turn of my tale I wrote, right up to New York and the mad, raucous Irish and the good Jesuit brothers... I wrote it all, then with the light of the rising morning I passed out in the bed, tired and weeping and happy.

I sleep with the angels watching over me and wake with a cold October sun coming in the window. Curtains, rug on the floor, a chamber pot... no shitting in a hole in the ground for me no more.

Germans start early. Brother Klaus awakes and we exchange a friendly nod, and he gets dressed and heads out, so I take the opportunity to lie on undisturbed; I open the window and let in the sounds and smells of the street, of Elizabeth Street, of New York, of America, and I inhale and stretch and yawn and wonder how I landed it so good. I thought about Brother James Carmichael, down in his rooms, and me lying here in my room, and thought it strange, life, how things flipped and turned out sometimes. *A strange life it is*.

I get up and do my morning business, wash and put on some clothes, not the cassock but a pair of black trousers and a jacket. There'd be time to take up the burden of priesthood when I ventured south, but for now I wanted to take things in like a man, not a priest or a peasant or an Irishman, but a man.

I go downstairs and join the good Jesuit men at the table, Germans, English and Irish all together, and we have a fine civilised breakfast of oats and tea. I was a human again. A man turns into an animal without food, and here I was, sitting at a table with linen and cutlery and fine eating, me a human being again just like the rest of them.

'They must've starved you on the boat,' Brother Michael says.

'I won't lie, brother, but it was horror. An absolute horror.'

'They say dozens aren't making the journey at all – dead and buried at sea before they even get here.'

'One hundred and twenty odd on my boat,' I tell them, and as one they drop their spoons or put down their tea and look at me. I put down my own spoon and look back, them waiting for more but it was hardly talk for the dining table. But they wait, and so I tell them all about it, all about Eliza – leaving out that she was my wife – and the kids, and Thomas and his family and the cholera and the dysentery and the burials at sea, and I even quote Brother James, about our Father and his many rooms and they seem to understand, they bow their heads all remorseful, and I heard them lift up their silent prayers and I knew, I could sense, that these men were compassionate and good and that they wished they could ease the suffering of the world, and I thought then, these old priests aren't the worst after all.

Brother Michael shakes his head. 'It's a tragedy.'

'It is,' I say. I drink my tea, sorry that I'd ruined breakfast.

'So you'll be wandering out today, will you?' says Brother Francis.

'I will.' I sense he's fishing for an invite, but I leave it alone, for I'd no wish to be lumbered with a Jesuit as I explored the greatest city in the world.

'Keep your wits about you,' he says. 'They'd have the eye out of your head here quicker than you can blink.'

Nods all round.

And I laugh and nod along, for what could they steal from a man who has nothing?

Joyously I hit the street, walking on air and high on New York. In the shoes of Brother James Carmichael I traipse all over the island, up and down again. I find Broadway, walk up its wide expanse – splendid, the fine people of New York, finely cut, with men hatted and suited and the women in their fine dresses... lovely to see, the fine women of New York and the smell of flowers as they pass, rose and lavender and what else a man like me scarcely knows, only that it makes a man turn as he walks by; and fine carriages of ornamental design I see drawn by the loveliest horses, and I hear a *tring-a-ling* and I turn, and there's a kinda street train coming along the street towards us, small boys hanging from the end of it, caps in their hands and the air in their faces, little rogues with nothing to do but get up to mischief, and yet other young boys flogging the paper, and for the thrill of it I buy one, I break a dollar from Brother Michael's own pocket just to get a look at a paper in a new land. It's fulla war with the Mexicans and the gold rush and expeditions, and I find it marvellous that I'm standing in New York in a fine jacket and with a newspaper, so I tuck it under my arm like a gentleman and amble down the street. It's a fine morning, warm, the smells of perfume, bakery, newspapers and smoke in the air, so I walk down Broadway til I find myself in the Italian district, and here the people's not so fine as up Broadway, but life is all and every manner, so I inhale it all and walk on, hearing that fine foreign tongue and the shouting and the roaring of the Italian men and women, those fine dark women with eyes of fire. From Italian streets I pass into the town of the Chinamen, and what a strange, frightening people, with their gowns and stern faces. I keep walking til I'm surrounded by Irish, I hear it all round me, the Gaeilge, and here the houses are leaning every which way, not the fine brick houses like the Jesuits' or those on Broadway, but houses of wood and nail, leaning every which direction and fulla holes, bending left, bending right, and a woman in every decrepit window, clothes flying out above the street, drunken men on the ground, drunken woman with bottles, pigs underfoot, urchins on bare feet, and a monstrous smell of filth in the air; and I asked a passerby where I was and he told me I was in Paradise, and I laughed out loud, for never was there a place on earth so far from paradise. So there were two New Yorks, then, just like there were two Irelands: one for the fine women smelling of roses and the other for the poor drunken Irish smelling of whiskey and despair. I'd never been one for the alcohol myself, but the brother liked it when he was alive, but I thought now, since I was in the New World, I'd have a drink for the brother who'd got me here and who was even now still with me. Every second building was a drinking house, so I picked one right on the square, and I went in the doors and found myself next to a great barrel, crowds round it, and a bawdy old Irish woman filling glasses. I squeezed my way through and told her I'd have a whiskey. 'No whiskey here,' she told me, only the rum. I'd never had it and didn't know what it was, but told her I'd have one just the same, and I gave her five cents and she gave me a glass, and I said 'Sláinte' and drank the rotten stuff, not for me but for the brother, and I stepped outta that den back into the square, and whaddaya know, but it looked a little more like paradise. Tremendous, I thought, and I began to understand the beauty of alcohol. And standing there in Paradise, with a cold October sun glinting and the ruin of black Ireland all round me, I heard the brother's voice speaking, but inside me, in my own head like, his words plain as day:

—Fine old stuff, that rum, he said.

'Eoin?' I said.

—It's meself, he said.

'Get to fuck,' I said, me who was even less a man for the swearing than the drink.

—You had to be expectin this to happen, he said. Sure aren't I inside you now, didn't you say it yourself in those very words?

And I didn't like it, didn't like it at all. Not one bit.

'You can hear my thoughts?' I asked him.

—Of course I can. Whaddaya think happens when you eat a man?

Jesus Christ. That's it then – years of poverty, starvation and bitterness have driven me over the edge. I've lost it now.

—Don't be goin there, now. That's only an old escape from the reality of things. You can't do away with it all by thinkin you're mad. Sure as the smell of shite in your nostrils, I'm talkin to ya now.

'Jaysus, Eoin,' I said. I stood outside the bar and scanned the crowd around me. No one was eyeing me, no one was aware I was talking to my brother who was dead cause I'd eaten him, and who seemed now very much alive and whispering inside me.

—How was I? he said.

'Whaddaya mean?'

—The eatin, I'm talkin about. How was it?

'Well, truth be told, Eoin, you were no pork chop. Sure the skin was hangin off ya right at the end.'

—But didn't I get you here? he said.

'That you did. I can't take that away from ya,' I told him.

—You didn't eat the ma too, did ya?

'Christ, no,' I said.

—Naw, I haven't encountered her, here inside ya, he said.

'Christ, would ya stop,' I told him. 'What is it you want?'

—I don't want anything, he said. It's only your good fortune that you're carryin me round inside ya, and now you've summoned me with a taste of the rum. Go n'have another will ya? I'm pure parched.

'You can fuck away off,' I told him.

'Wassat, mister?' A foul drunken Kerryman beside me turned to give me the eye.

'Nothin, friend, I told him,' and I walked away.

'You can fuck right off yourself!' he shouted.

'Eoin, you'll have me set upon.' I walked out into the middle of the square, mad paradise all round me.

—You're stuck with me now, he said. No two ways about it. Now go n'take another shot of that rum, he told me, and I understood then it was the liquor had summoned him, and he wasn't gonna let it go. So I stuck my fingers down and throat and threw it up all over the ground. As it came outta me I heard the brother curse me.

'I'll not be havin it, Eoin,' I told him. 'I'll not be havin ya gabbin in my ear.'

—Ya bastard! Is that all the thanks I get?

And I walked outta the square, the tantrum of the brother growing weaker in my ear, and by the time I was back on Elizabeth Street, his protestations were merely a whisper on the fine afternoon air.

I met Brother Larkin that evening. He was back from Fordham and was at the table when I joined the brothers for dinner. He stood up to shake my hand. Genteel fella, English, but with a certain indomitable spirit about him. He had a good look at me as we joined palms.

'Welcome, Brother James.' He clasped my hand in both of his. 'I trust you're being looked after?'

I smiled. 'Yes, Brother Larkin. I can't thank you enough for all your arrangements on my behalf.'

'Please sit.' We sat down on opposite sides of the table and Brother Michael said grace, then we got to eating.

'So you're on your way to Buenos Aires?' Brother Larkin said.

'I am.'

'A brave fellow. It was a terrible loss, what happened back then. If I was ten years younger, I might still have your fearless spirit, but old man that I am, I prefer it here in the modern world of letters.'

'Aw now,' I said. 'You're not so old as that.'

'No need to be polite, Brother. I know my place in the world now. It's my hope that you find your own.'

'I'm sure God will lead me there,' I said. *Terrible easy it was, talkin God with these fellas.*

The brothers nodded appreciatively.

'Amen.' Brother Larkin paused to go at his soup. 'Brother Declan spoke very highly of you in his letter,' he continued, dabbing his mouth with his napkin.

Brother Declan Fitzgerald, my superior in Dublin. I knew my stuff – I'd read Brother James's letters. 'Aw now. I'm sure he was too generous.'

'I knew him, don't you know?'

I didn't. 'Really?'

'He didn't mention it?'

'I didn't see much of him as I was making preparations to leave,' I said. *Christ.*

'Yes, we spent time together at college in Liverpool, not a few years before coming out here. A fine man he was... a fine, handsome gentleman. I remember him warmly.'

'Not as handsome as he was wise,' I said. *On a wing and a prayer.*

'Do you say that, Brother, because of how highly he spoke of you?'

The brothers laughed and I laughed along too. 'Now now... I'm a modest fellow myself.'

'Oh, I'm only toying with you, Brother James. So, did you get out around the city today?'

'I did. I almost walked the feet of myself. I walked right up Broadway and back down it, and found myself in the Italian streets, and then I wandered into the Chinese streets, and then I found myself surrounded by Irishmen in a place called Paradise.'

There was a strange exclamation from Brother James. 'Oh, now!'

'God save us, you're lucky you're still with us at all,' Brother Michael said.

Brother Larkin gave a strange smirk. 'The man is leaving for the wild south. I'm sure he can handle himself among the more unfortunate of his kin.'

'I had my eyes opened, alright,' I said. I shook my head to add a touch of drama.

'If there's anywhere God's work is needed, it's in the Five Points,' Brother Michael said.

'Those that are ready for it are in need of it, but most of them are not,' Brother James said.

Brother Larkin put down his spoon. 'There will always be poverty, gentlemen, no matter how we toil. It's the sad truth of things.'

'I fear you're right,' I said.

I heard a voice that was not my own. A fine-speaking fellow I was now.

'So Brother James, do you have any idea how long you want to stay with us? We've a ticket on hold for your passage south. The boat for Buenos Aires leaves every Saturday, so if you're out on the next that'll be five days for you to rest. But if you feel very strongly about it, there's no reason why we can't hold off for another week.'

I thought it over quickly. Five days was enough. I told him: 'Five days will be enough, Brother Larkin.'

'I'll send word to the shipping office tomorrow then.'

'Thank you, Brother.'

The plates were cleared from the table. I smelled lamb from the kitchen.

Later in the evening, I sat in the drawing room with a few of the brothers. Brother Larkin was early in the bed, and we sat silently save for a few scattered moments of dull conversation. In a quiet lull, I pulled my newspaper from the inside pocket of my jacket where it had lain since the afternoon. I opened it. The paper was fulla what they called the 'gold rush', the hills in California – fine-sounding place, *Kal-ee-for-nee-a* – fulla gold, they said. People getting rich and quickly. Much there to tempt a man, for sure, and it crossed my mind it did, a young man like myself, here in a new country, whole continent laid out before him, why not skip town and hoof it over to California, buy yourself a bucket and a pick and start digging, and don't stop til you've unearthed some of that fine stuff you've heard so much of in life but never seen a drop of, for it don't fall much to the likes of you. And why not, after all? Sitting here, dressed like a priest and lounging with priests, and with a ticket to head off to the wilds of the world to be a missionary to poor, unclothed and uneducated savages, savage like yourself... sure what in the name of Christ are you gonna say to them? You gonna pray for them, teach them to pray? And will you preach and say mass to them, too? What could you be preaching to them, you pig-ignorant fowl? Take yourself off, why the hell not, and dig up some gold and, who knows, maybe find a good American woman and settle down and give her a few young'uns of your own, and maybe even call them Molly and Jake, in remembrance like, for the sufferings of the past. A house, a wife, a family... be your own man, like. Aye, I said. *Kal-ee-for-nee-a*.

Then my eyes fell upon an article, bottom corner of the page, an eye-catching title if ever there was: *The Cannibal of Hell's Kitchen*. I fell to reading it, read it from start to finish, and then again, a second time.

'Jesus Christ,' I said out loud.

Four priests looked up from their meditations.

'Are you alright, Brother James?' Brother Michael said.

I nodded. 'What are the Tombs?' I asked him.

9

I got up in the morning and put on my cassock, for what I was doing would need the priest's gear. And I hadn't a care what they'd say to me in the street, for I knew what I had to do and I was gonna do it. They could swear and spit, but by God I was going out and I was paying a visit to the Tombs.

I was up early. Breakfast at seven and only Brother Klaus at the table. We ate together, and I asked him if he was going gardening, speaking with my hands, digging with an imaginary spade, he said, 'Yes yes!' and we fell back at our food in silence. And fed, I headed out into the street, Jesuit hat on my head and Bible in my hand, for a man of God always has the Word to back him up. And wasn't I thrilled to see that it was dry again, and I marvelled that there were places in the world where a man could step outta the house in good spirits in October.

I made my way down Elizabeth Street, encountering no hostilities along the way, only barren looks or indifferent, and only one man spat in my path as I passed him, but that didn't bother me none. I turned on to Howard Street, taking it all in as I went, for I had a great mind for seeing things. The pigs were out wandering, patrolling the gutters, those boisterous, dirty animals snouting through all the filth of the gutter.

Then I turned onto Center Street and soon enough I saw it, a great monstrosity of a building, squat and brutal: the Tombs, the House of Detention of Manhattan, New York, the holding cells for all those awaiting trial for their sins. What a wretched place! I stood for some moments looking up between the great pillars of its entrance. Christ, what a place to be holed up. Some went in and never came out according to the brothers. The 'devil's own black hole', Brother James had called it. So be it, I thought, for if I was now a priest, then the devil's people were my business, and I went up the steps and inside.

It was early, and inside the door I found an auld fella at a desk.

'Good mornin, Fadder,' he says.

Irish. I'm starting to see that it's here where the whole island of Ireland has moved to, here in the New World her starving millions have gathered, taken over, her good and bad alike. And wasn't it an Irishman I was here to see?

'Good mornin, sir. I'm here to see Declan Linehan.'

'Mr Linehan, is it? Will he be expectin ya?'

'I think no... but I'd say Mr Linehan could be usin a bit of the Lord's comfort now, don't you think?'

'I'd say he could. But he may well tell you where to go. No disrespect intended, Fadder— what was your name, now?'

'James Carmichael.'

'Well, Fadder James, we can go and ask, is all we can do. Follow me.'

We go in. I smell it right away, shit and sickness, and for a moment, I'm back on the boat, lying next to people whose only future is a death sentence and a swift one. I understand then the naming of the place. *The Tombs*.

'The name's Barney, sir.'

I follow the hunched little fella through the cold, soulless Tombs. He leads me down a corridor and into the gaol, the stench getting thicker, and all round me in the wall little black iron doors, not big enough for a man to enter upright, miserable little cells for dying. A guard sits in a chair at the bottom of the steps, and Barney gives him a nod as we pass. We go upstairs and the air clears some.

'Fellows downstairs have it the worst, do they?'

'Downstairs is for the black fellas,' Barney says.

He leads me across a bridge to the other side and heads down the end where he stops and rattles the door. 'Are you up, yerself?' he says.

A pause. 'Whaddaya want?'

I hear it, Irish through and through. Condemned long before he was thrown in here.

'There's a priest here to see ya.'

'Tell him to fuck off.'

Barney turns to me. 'Told ya, Fadder.'

'Give me a minute with him, will ya?'

Barney shrugs and steps back towards the rail. I look in through the hatch. He's sitting on a rotten mattress rubbing the back of his neck. Declan Linehan. *The Cannibal of Hell's Kitchen*.

'I just want a word with ya,' I say through the hatch.

'I told the other fella the same thing. I'm not lookin for redemption,' he says.

'I'm not sellin it.'

He looks up. 'Whaddaya want?'

'I wanna talk about your wife. Specifically, the eatin of her.'

And now he stands up and walks over to the door. 'What'd ya say?'

'I know what it's like,' I tell him.

'What kind of priest are you?'

'I'm not a priest,' I tell him. 'I'm here to talk *human flesh*.'

I guess he understands, cause he shouts for the warden and Barney comes over.

'You can let the man in.'

'Jaysus,' Barney says, 'but you may make a believer of him yet.'

Barney opens the door and I'm standing there with the man himself. I hold out my hand. 'Brother James Carmichael.'

'Declan Linehan.' He shakes my hand.

'I'll leave yis to it then,' Barney says, and he walks away, leaving the door open behind him.

'Sit down,' Declan says.

He sits down on the bed so I sit on a stool, my back to the wall.

67

I take off the hat and put it on the table. I lean back on the cold stone, but I hear the whisper of my brother and pull away.

'I read about you in the paper.'

He nods. 'You read what they're callin me, so?'

'I did. It's just for the papers, sure isn't it?'

He doesn't reply. I take a moment to examine him. He's had better days, I'm sure. Ill-fed, and he must be in the same clothes he was in the day he was lifted. Could use a wash. Now I feel foolish, like I shoulda brought him something. Like a bit of soap or a drop of food.

'You got anyone here in the city?'

He shrugs. 'I got some people I know, but none's been to visit. I don't blame em.' He seems to relax and leans back against the wall. 'You have a cigarette?'

'I don't.' *Somethin else I shoulda known to bring.* 'How're they treatin ya here?'

'Did ya come to talk about my predicament, Father, or did ya come to talk about somethin else?'

His eyes are lit up now and he's impatient to hear it. I clear my throat. 'I came here to talk about the wife,' I say.

He nods, slow like, waiting for more.

'I ate my own brother,' I tell him. *There, right out with it.*

He crosses his legs on the bed, leans forward.

So I tell him the whole story, about me dying in a hovel back home, and the brother dying and the mother dying, and me killing the brother and the cooking and the eating of him. I leave out the bit about feeding him to the ma before killing her. Maybe it'd be too much. Then I tell him about walking across the island and getting on a boat, and now here, sitting in New York with the only man I can tell about these things.

'How'd you do it?' he says.

'The killin or the eatin?'

'Killin first.'

'I put a pillow over his head. There was fight in him at the end, but not fight enough.'

'And you carved him up yourself?'

I nod. 'It wasn't the clean job.'

'My old man was a butcher,' he tells me, 'so I had a bit of trainin – but we'll get to that. What about the cookin?'

So I tell him about the big pot with the fattier parts for the soup, and about the roasting of the fleshier pieces on the open fire, and about the eating of it carrying me all across the land and ocean to the New World. He looks disappointed. Like he was expecting more from me. He leans back against the wall, looks at the ceiling and sighs. I feel foolish.

'I wanted to talk to you cause I hear him,' I say.

He looks up. 'Whaddaya mean?'

'I hear him talkin to me. He's in my head, talkin to me.'

'When? All the time?'

'No.' Then I tell him about the rum, and the brother crawling up from inside me and shouting in my head. This gets him. Now he's on edge of the bed, waiting, all eager. And I tell him the brother was a stonemason, and when I touch a bit of stone now I can hear him too.

'Do it now,' he says. So I do. I turn and put my hand on the cold, damp wall and caress its rough face. 'Do ya hear him, do ya?'

I hear the faint stirrings of a whisper, but I keep quiet and fondle the cold stone. Oftentimes I would watch the brother at work, holding a lump of limestone or granite in his hand, lost, just fondling the rock with his calloused fingers. Lost, away in some stonemason dream, feeling the rock, holding it, whispering to it. Now I hear it, him whispering to me.

'Do ya hear him?' Declan's over my side of the cell now.

—What the fuck are you at, at all? Eoin says to me.

'I hear him,' I tell Declan.

'What's he say?'

'He's askin me what the fuck I'm doin.'

Declan's jittery, jumping from foot to foot, chewing on a finger. 'Go on,' he says.

—Tell your fella to sit down, will ya?

'He says will ya sit down, will ya,' I tell Declan.

'Jaysus be!' Declan hops backwards. 'Ask him will I be gettin outta here.'

'Did you hear the man?' I say.

—Of course I heard him. Tell him I'm no circus fortune teller.

'He says no,' I tell him, and I let go of the wall.

Declan sits back down.

'Do you know what? Before they lifted me I thought I heard her, I did – the wife. But I put it down to the drink, for I was at it wild before the law came to the door. But I did – I heard her in me. I swear I heard her.'

This is what I came for.

'Father—'

'James,' I say.

'... James – you've gotta do somethin for me.'

'If I can.'

He leans in. 'Go to the brother's, will ya? Ask him for Maeve's locket. Will you do it?'

'You want it to talk with her?'

'Yes. Bring it here. Will ya do it?'

A trolley stops outside the door and a warder walks in. We go silent. He's got a bowl in his hand and he puts sit down on the table. 'Some eatin for ya,' he says.

The smell of it makes me retch. The warder laughs and walks out.

'Will you do it?' Declan says.

I have to know more. 'I will.'

'And Christ,' he says, 'will ya bring a bit of food with ya next time? Somethin that won't poison me.'

I nod and get up. 'I'll be back tomorrow.'

'I'll be waitin.'

So I turn to go.

'And James,' he says, 'I'd love a little taste, too.'

I nod. *Some things you just can't deny a man.*

10

I did it, too. I chased down his brother in the Five Points and asked for the locket. They were unwilling, the wife in particular, but good Irish as they were they hadn't the stomach to refuse a priest, so they relented and handed it over. And the next morning, with the locket and a sandwich and a quart of cheap whiskey (for I hadn't the coin for the good stuff) I took myself down the Tombs once more. Barney was there waiting, good old fella. 'Good mornin, Fadder,' he said, and he led me back into the dank hole.

'Will ye be turnin our man back to God now, will ye?' Barney says.

'I can only do the Lord's biddin,' I say.

'You're a great man, Fadder.'

'Aw now – I'm only a poor servant,' I say.

'Bless you, and a modest one too.'

We crossed the floor, the stench at ground level more than a man could stomach.

'Lord save us, they've it terrible down here. Can I get a look in one of the cells?'

'Go'on then, Fadder – take a gander through the slats.'

So I peek inside, and there's a black fella passed out on the mattress, the rats crawling all over him.

'Is he dead?' I say.

'Some of em go in the middle of the night. Can't be helped.'

'Seems inhuman.'

The floor is covered with a thick black slime, as if it was oozing up from the very rock. Rats claw at each other, writhing in the puddles, and that familiar stink of sickness comes at me. Without knowing it, I bless myself.

'For the black fellas,' Barney says again. He turns and walks away.

I follow him up the stairs and he leads me to Declan's cell, and this time he's there waiting at the cell door, standing peeking through the grill when we walk up.

'Good mornin to yis,' he says.

'Look, Fadder – he's waitin for ya.'

'I'm ready to confess my sins,' Declan says.

'Well, Jaysus Christ,' Barney says. 'Forgive me, Fadder. But I've just witnessed a miracle, right here in the Tombs of New York.'

Barney opens the door and I see Declan wink. His tongue is darting out, licking his lips, the thirst or the hunger on him. Barney steps back and holds the door open. Declan backs against the wall to let me in.

'I'll leave you to it, will I?' Old Barney is looking at the pair of us.

Aye,' says Declan.

I nod. The old jailer walks away.

'Queer auld fella,' Declan says.

'He's a good sort.'

'Aye, he is n'that. So – did ya bring what I asked ya?'

'I brought everything,' I say, as Declan pulls up the stool for me. I pull the bread outta my inside pocket for him, all wrapped up nice in paper with a hunk o'ham inside. He snatches it from me, a man starved, sits down on the bed and tears it open. He's on it like maggots on a dead man. I've seen the fury of hunger and I know what it's like. I watch him go at it, wolf-like, all teeth and fingers. He doesn't stop, doesn't look at me til there's nothing but paper left. Smoothing out the paper on the bed, he folds it and slips it under his pillow. He looks at me.

'They're not feedin you in here.'

'It'd fucken kill ya, the food here,' he says.

'A lotta things in here'd likely kill ya.'

'Don't ya know it.'

We go silent for a few moments. He's waiting.

'Did you have any joy with the other thing?' he says.

So I reach into my pocket and pull out a fine cotton handkerchief, and unwrap it and hold it out to him.

'Oh Jesus, Maeve.' He starts weeping.

He reaches out to take it but pulls his hand away, afraid to touch it. So I lay it on the bed beside him, and he slides away from it, like it's a thing's gonna hurt him. He tries to lift it but can't. Still weeping and with snot running down his face, he wipes himself with a filthy sleeve. 'Jesus,' he says. He sits and stares at the locket, shoulders heaving.

I sit quietly.

'I bought it for her, you know. We was fifteen – before we even got married.'

'You were sweethearts?'

'We was.'

'You musta loved her.'

'I did.'

The weeping stopped, he wipes his eyes. He still hasn't touched the locket, the gilt locket with virgin blue inlay. I reach into my jacket and pull out a bottle. He hears the rustle of the paper and his senses prick up like a dog on the scent.

'That what I think it is?'

I look out the door.

'Don't worry – they're all at it in here,' he says.

I pass it to him and he uncorks it. Sips. Slow at first, then he takes a great suck from the bottle. His face still wet with the tears but the sadness fast leaving him. He passes it to me. I hold up my hands but he insists, so I take a lick of it and pass it back.

'Wanna know the strange thing of it? I loved her,' he says.

'I've no doubt on it.'

'Jesus, I loved her. But I couldn't live with her no more. We'd have killed each other sooner or later. We was strugglin, ya know? With the wee'un and the feedin of it, and the feedin of ourselves. But drinkin's cheaper than eatin so we went at it hard. *Hard*. Nights I'd beat her or she'd beat me... she could put it away, she could. One night I woke up with a knife at my throat. She'd have done it too, she would've, only the wee'un started screamin. Hungry it was. I wasn't gonna wake up like that again. So one night I came back and she was well-lit, and she tried to skull me with the fryin pan and I lost it... I belted her in the side of the head, she went down n'cracked her skull on the side of the table. I dunno what happened, but she was dead before she hit the floor. Finished, she was. I started drinkin. I drank myself into a hole and back out again, til about three in the mornin I decided I had to do somethin. My own father was a butcher, so I took the knife and sharpened it.'

He's still pulling on the bottle and I see him disappear back to that night.

'How'd you go about it?' I say.

He gets up, all animated like. 'Stand up will ya?' he says.

So I stand up. And he lifts my chin and draws a finger across my throat. 'First I took her head cause I couldn't have her lookin at me. Her eyes were still open, those fucken beautiful blue eyes... so I took her head.' And he does it again – sweeps the finger in a graceful arc across my throat.

'And the arms and legs,' he says, and he shows me how to break the arms before making the cut, and he marks out the sweep of the cut down my chest and under the arm, and the same with the legs. 'And that's your basic butchery done, and after that it's all down to the sharpness of your filletin knife,' he explains.

Then he goes on to point out where all the best cuts of meat are on the body, using the edge of his palm to mark out the direction of the cut and how deep to go. Maps it all out for me, he does, and I get a chill, for now I'm the one under the knife, and I feel it all – each time he slices at me with his finger it's like I'm being carved up. I take the bottle from him and take a sup.

'And if you've the heart for it,' he says, 'you can take the tongue.

Good eatin in the tongue, though it takes a strong stomach to cut it out o'the head. Takes will.'

He tells me how he took the parts of her he couldn't eat down the river – the hands, feet and the head, and the bones too – and dumped her in with a load of rocks. And I get a detailed explanation of the preparation, how he dipped the parts of her in boiling water cause it makes it easier to remove the skin, and how she was butchered then cured, the meat dry-salted and left for four days before he got to the smoking of her. It was the smoking of the meat that set the law upon him, cause the neighbours were well aware they'd never money for meat, and since she was gone a week, not sight nor sound of her, they put two and two together and called in the law. He'd only got to eating part of her thigh before he was arrested and thrown into the Tombs. Now he's lit on whiskey and describing the taste of her, eyes wide.

'...and those thighs, Jimmy,' he says, licking his lips, 'the finest thing I've tasted in my whole life. Those thighs, Jimmy, like the white thighs of holy Mother Ireland...'

And he starts groaning, disappearing in his mind between those thighs. And myself, with no knowledge of women, I take refuge in the bottle.

'Aye,' he says, 'white thighs and blue eyes,' and without realising it he reaches down and picks up the locket, and he starts shuddering.

'Maeve, Jesus,' he whispers. I hand him the bottle. Eyes fulla hatred turn to look at me, and I hear her, I know it's her by Christ, she speaks low and hard and mean, the bitterness preserved for all eternity.

—Ya ate me, ya filthy bastard.

Such violence there is in the voice, I lean back against the wall.

—Ya ate me, ya bastard, before I could take the knife to your throat.

'Maeve, my love,' Declan says, and he's weeping again, 'it was either me or you.'

—And aren't we fucken delighted it was me, she says.

I'm leaning back against the wall, my hands on the cold stone, and now I hear it welling up in me, a laugh, not out loud but it's there in my head. Eoin. He's laughing.

—Aren't you the man, he says.

'Now, Eoin...' I say.

'What?' says Declan.

—Birds of a feather, eh? Eoin says, and his voice spills outta me. Declan's looking at me like, *Christ, what are ya sayin to me now?*

—Two great men yis are, great men for the murderin, Eoin says, my own brother's words pouring from my mouth, and now the two spirits strike up talk between them.

—You as well, is it? Butchered, were ya? Maeve says.

—By my own brother, Eoin says.

—Two bastards yis are is right, Maeve says. Two murderin bastards.

'Jesus, your wife has a tongue on her,' I say to Declan.

He's weeping but he's laughing; he looks insane, and probably he is and I am too. Now Eoin is getting pushy with the drink and has me grabbing at the bottle.

—Gimme a sip of it, will ya?

—Get away to fuck, Maeve says.

Declan throws his head back and sucks hard on the bottle.

—Fuck sake, gimme a taste, Eoin says, and I'm up over Declan and then we're on the floor tearing lumps outta each other, except it's not me and it's not Declan, it's my brother and his wife, two old drunks on the floor fighting over the whiskey bottle.

—Get off to fuck, she shouts, and I get a belt over the head with something hard and cry out.

It's not long before the guards are in the door and I'm pulled off Declan, me a priest, rolling round on the floor with a cannibal, two cannibals the both of us, possessed by the ghosts of our own misdeeds. A line came to me then, dredged up from the Bible, some terrifying thing I'd fallen upon on the bed of sickness on the death boat over while people died in their dozens round me: *I said in mine heart concerning the estate of the sons of men, that God might make them manifest and they might see they themselves are beasts.*

Later, I came to understand the beauty of that moment.

November, 1847

11

We sailed into Buenos Aires on a dark, dry day, beginning of November. That city put the fear of God into the two of us. I had a companion now, a young English brother called Theodore. I was almost exposed back at Fordham, when it came out I hadn't a word of Spanish to my name. Brother James Carmichael, it seems, had. He never mentioned it and I hadn't given it a thought. I explained it away by coming up with an imaginary bout of typhus which I'd contracted on the journey over the Atlantic, from that moment losing a considerable degree of my mental faculties which I could in no way explain, and the brothers, who surely thought I was shitting them, had no choice but to go along with it. So they dragged a poor young brother from the library who'd a knowledge of the Spanish tongue and told him he was to accompany me on my trip south. Despite an early onset of the travel jitters which plagued him from the moment we stepped onto the boat in New York, Theodore soon got into the spirit of things, that is, until we reached Buenos Aires. Not that I was at all comfortable myself in that hole – I never knew such savagery existed, me who'd killed his own ma and brother, which for me was an act of mercy, but down there, in that city way south of all the known world, we encountered a different type of ruthlessness.

There was a civil war, or so it was explained to us on the boat by a New York tobacco merchant who'd occasion to be in those parts often enough, business taking him there, where he bought vast quantities of the leaf and shipped it back to New York. There were two sides warring for the city of Montevideo on the other side of the river, he said, the Blancos on one side and the Colorados on the other, or the reds and the whites, both of them bent on destroying the other and doing a very good job of it too so far as we could see. In the streets of Buenos Aires, a fella called Rosas, an ally of the whites, was shooting anyone he thought was against him. And not only shooting, which was the decent thing to do, war being the general state of affairs, but this fella apparently liked a bit of suffering, for his men were doing all kinds of things that have no place on this green earth, like cutting off heads or taking the living heart out of a man, or burning people in the streets. Me and Theodore saw it ourselves. We were warned about going out after dark but we didn't listen, and we saw things, things that no man need see in this world.

Our second night in Buenos Aires we were sitting in the office of Oliver Rackham, a Jesuit from Anglia who lived like a prisoner, gone with the fear. Oil lamps lit the place and a handsome library towered behind the man, his desk littered with books and papers. Me and Theodore sat on the other side of the desk, tea in hand, Rackham giving us the gist of what was expected of us in the jungle.

'We brought heaven to earth out there a hundred years ago,' he said. 'By the grace of God, we made the impossible possible. San Ignacio was the cornerstone of the Manzana in Córdoba.'

'And what condition is it in now, Brother?' I said.

'Well, I haven't seen it with my own eyes, but I believe it's gone somewhat the way of all things here, that being a fast and frightening return to nature.'

'You mean the crops have gone to ruin?' said Brother Theodore.

'It's more than that, I'm afraid. You see, the Franciscans were kind enough to take on care of our estate, but there is only so much they were able to do. Dedicated as they are, their manpower is thin. San Ignacio has received no care these ninety years since we were expelled.'

'So there's nothing at all left?' I said.

'The buildings are still standing, according to the reports I've received, but they will require considerable work. We'll be sending some paid labour with you for the first few months, but over time we'll expect you to populate the reduction as in the old days.'

'Converts?' I said.

'Naturally,' said Rackham. 'But most of the Indians were converted a century ago. Your task will be to entice them from the towns, the estates, and in some cases down from the mountains, back to the reduction, back into the bosom of the Lord Jesus Christ.'

'There are still Indians living wild?' Brother Theodore said.

'As I hear it, yes. After the expulsion, many went back to the jungle and remain there today, living in small but tight communities. They may be easier to bring down onto the reductions than those in paid work on the big estates, ranching or cultivating tobacco, or in the pay of the tea merchants.'

'How will we find these communities?' I said.

'With the help of a few natives, of course. We'll supply you with the necessary guides.'

I'd a good idea what it'd be about, the missionary work, but foolishly I hadn't considered we'd be venturing into the jungle in search of poor savage Indians. I pictured building a few huts for shelter, maybe teaching them a few words of the Queen's English, saying the odd Our Father or Hail Mary, or telling of the fella Jesus Christ who fed the poor and comforted the meek. But chasing Indians in the jungle was another thing altogether.

'How likely are we to meet foul play?' I said.

'What do you mean "foul play"?' said Rackham.

'I mean, getting a spear in the back or an axe in the head,' I said.

Outta the corner of my eye, I saw Theodore sit up straight.

'Those days are gone,' said Rackham. 'Sure enough, the early brothers had it hard, and some of them were even killed, but that was a hundred and fifty years ago. The land is much tamed since then.'

'I don't get that impression looking out into the streets, Brother

Rackham,' said Brother Theodore.

When we'd arrived the previous evening, we'd passed a body tied to a lamppost and missing the head only two hundred yards from the house.

'To be sure, Buenos Aires is going through a difficult spell. There is much to fear here. But outside, in the country, they don't suffer the inhumanities that we do here, God save us.'

We fell silent. We had turned our ears to the street, for while it was quiet, the tension was deafening, and all manner of things could be imagined if you only listened.

Oliver Rackham lived in a house at Moreno Street with a staff of one. We heard the maid above us now in her quarters, stealing over the thin wooden floor.

'It's a wonder the brothers are still here at all,' I said.

'We feel we're on the brink of a breakthrough here in the New World, Brother James. Reports have come to us that the ban on our ministry in lands under Spanish rule is soon to end. That is why we cannot abandon our post here, and that is also why you are here, dear brothers, in order to pave the way for a resurgence of the Jesuits here in the Argentine Republic. A phoenix from the ashes, let's say.'

He smiled, or he tried to. It wasn't entirely convincing, his reassurances lost on even himself. I looked at Theodore, he looked at me. Neither of us was entirely sold on the task.

'Look, let's have a look at San Ignacio of old, shall we?' Rackham said.

He got up and went to the shelves behind him. 'I have the deeds to all the properties here, and some basic plans and financial information. You'll find more detailed records at Alta Gracia should you need them, but this'll be enough to get you started.'

Rackham pulled out some books and papers and laid them on the desk. He unfolded a large plan and laid it on the table.

'Here's your plan of the reduction. Church here...' He pointed to the map. '...courtyard adjacent with residences and stores, a well at the centre. Next to that you have the farm outbuildings, where most of the animals were kept – not the mules, of course. Did you know San Ignacio used to produce over half of the mules used by the reductions here in Córdoba?'

'I didn't,' I said.

'Incredible breeding program,' Rackham said. 'Of course, population in the reduction was almost five thousand at its peak. We won't be expecting you to reach that kind of output again.' Rackham ran his hands over the plan. 'Here's the windmill – probably in a great state of disrepair – for production of flour. The workshops also have several looms; they were completely self-sufficient in clothing. They grew their own cotton, of course.'

He then opened a ledger.

'At the time of expulsion the brothers were tending to over nine hundred peach trees, about half that in quince, pear and walnuts... the list goes on. They had an annual production of twenty-five tonnes of wheat and corn, much of which was sold. The Guaraní also collected about a hundred tonnes of yerba maté a year, across the six reductions that is. It's a fine earner.'

'I'm sorry – the *who*, sir?'

'The Guaraní. The locals, natives. I thought you'd be better informed of these things, Brother James.'

'Ah yes. Of course, Brother Rackham. It's the pronunciation, see.'

'Am I to understand you don't have a word of the Spanish tongue?'

'I suffered a serious bout of typhus on the boat over, Brother. It seemed to do an injury to my faculties.'

'Is that so?' He peered over his eyeglasses at me. 'How mysterious.'

'How much help will we have to begin with, Brother Oliver?' Theodore asked.

'We can send seven men to help out for a month or two, but no more. You can understand that without an income the Jesuits just don't have the means to support paid labour. It is imperative that you start to build your flock immediately.'

'Five thousand souls you say, Brother?' I said.

'Praise the Lord.'

'All we need is five hundred. With five hundred we can move heaven and earth.'

'Bless you, Brother James.'

I grinned. I think I even inspired Brother Theodore, but I hadn't a clue what I was getting into. I mean, I hadn't a fucken clue, God forgive me. I was fulla shite and I knew it.

12

Thirty-six hours after landing in Buenos Aires we left Rackham, and found ourselves on a boat going up the Rio de la Plata, the River of Silver, me and Theodore and our two guides, Diego and Anuncio, brown as the earth and of the Spanish tongue, who would see us upriver to our new home. Those two fellows steered our boat, Anuncio up front and Diego at the back, the boat long and thin like a cigarette and cutting easily through the water at the gentle urging of the oars. Anuncio wasn't a talker but Diego gabbed away to Theodore. Diego was a man of the river. I'd seen it myself, back home, men who lived for the ocean, lived and breathed the water, weren't no men at all on land, all dark and shadow when they came onshore but who came alive again when they pushed the boat out. Diego was one. His face lit up the moment we stepped on the boat and he grinned all the way upriver, never letting up, and he talked to Theodore, Theodore reporting to me the gist of the conversation as we went.

'Diego says we have a week's travel ahead of us,' Theodore tells me, Diego looking at me and grinning, so I grin back.

'Ask him what he knows of the place,' I say.

Theodore quizzes him in their common tongue, and I see a sadness come over Diego.

Theodore relays the information. 'He says there's a great emptiness there now.'

Theodore is hitting thirty but I got a year or two on him. Sparse hair on his youthful face and a keen air, even if he's still scared at the turn his life has taken. I'm not much better. Boats pass us going downriver, faces stare at us across the water, some brown like Diego and Anuncio, impassive and unreadable, the weight of a continent behind the eyes; others, whiter like us but not so white, men I will come to know as the guacho, men whose only purpose is survival. I feel mistrust in them as we pass. On the banks of the river dirty naked children and big brown women splashing in the water, the children at play and the women washing, also living and waiting and watching, and those black eyes follow us upriver, unknowable eyes, all the children grinning like Diego, 'Hola hola!' they shout and we see them at every turn as we venture upland.

Diego says something to Theodore and the two of them start laughing, and Diego sticks in his oar, now left now right, pushing us on up the Rio de la Plata.

'Diego says you look like a guacho.'

I grin, Diego grins.

True, I haven't seen a pair of shears since I left Ireland two months ago, and why would I, for I'm a new man in a new country, wild and free and living.

'*Guacho,*' Diego says, and laughs like one of the river children.

We all laugh together. Not Anuncio, he's up front, sure and silent, the oar dipping left, long and slow, then right, and the two of them, Diego and Anuncio, have the rhythm of it solid, the boat making no waves, just sure and steady upriver she goes. Boatmen. Rivermen. I watch Anuncio from the back; he's thin and wiry, arms like barbed wire all knots and tension, no stopping him as he paddles on. I wonder what they'd make of the Atlantic, these two, put them in a boat off Donegal and see how they'd fare, but I know they'd make it no matter, cause sailors are sailors, river or sea. They know water.

Those fellas get going they do, pushing us up into the continent, and in four days we stop at a bend in the river called Rosario, little more than a collection of huts by the water's edge, a village of sorts. It's dark, and our cases are pulled off the boat and up the bank to a mud hut, where a small man comes out and greets Anuncio, speaking softly, and Diego drags our cases inside and comes out grinning, those great white teeth shining in the dark. Me and Theodore, we hang back waiting, and soon our host turns to us, shakes our hand and beckons us inside.

Candles burn softly within, and a small woman, tiny and black and clad in a long cotton robe, turns from the fire and smiles and we are bid to sit. Plates are put in front of us laden with beans, and we tear into them, me and Theodore and Diego and Anuncio, and we eat silently in the low light beside the mumbling river. Our hosts don't sit but lurk in the shadows and watch us fill our bellies. The night is cool, fresh; a light breeze comes in the open window and out the door at my back. I sit opposite Anuncio. I look at his face, not old by any means but lined, probably got a few years on me, the face of a worker, all day in the sun at some mean task, the face of a man who knows who he is. He doesn't look up, just lifts the food from his bowl to his mouth. His hands, hard and bony, grip the wooden spoon as a child would, as if brandishing a hammer.

I empty the bowl and sit silently for some minutes. Theodore says something to the hosts, probably a 'Thank you', and the woman emerges from the shadows and smiles and nods, and as she reaches over my shoulder I smell her, all sweat and earth and fire. Anuncio finishes and gets up and steps outside and our host sits down in front of me. He says a few words to me in the Spanish and Theodore answers.

'He asks if we're going to the missions,' Theodore says.

I nod.

He and Theodore fall to more talking.

'There's nothing up there now, he says. Nothing but grass and wild horses,' Theodore tells me.

'I was told we would be met by the Franciscan caretaker,' I say, and Theodore translates.

'He says maybe there's a priest there, but no people, no crops, no animals. Only fallen buildings.' Theodore looks at me intently while he says it all, and I realise he's looking for reassurance. Confidence is what he needs, from me, Brother James Carmichael, fake priest and charlatan. But what fears a man who has seen hunger, true hunger, and the death of all he knows and cares for?

I smile. 'That's why we're here,' I tell him. 'That's what we've come to do, to rebuild the reductions. And if we have to build from scratch, then we'll build them even better than before.' And for a moment, just a moment, I even believe my own shite.

Theodore smiles and relates my words to our host, who nods solemnly. I can't interpret his response, so I don't try. Tiredness comes over me.

Our host says something and gets up, and takes me by the arm and leads me to a room and points at a mattress.

'This is where we'll sleep,' Theodore says, following us in.

Two straw mattresses on the floor, and what of it, for a man who's been sleeping on a blanket by the river for three nights needs nothing else. I nod and smile and hold out my hand. He shakes it and nods.

'Gracias,' I say, my first word in the Spanish tongue, and he says, 'De nada,' and I understand, and I think, *Maybe this foreign tongue won't bring me much trouble at all.*

Theodore looks at me and I look at him, and we peel off our robes and lie down in the dark, the earthy smoky dark, and I thank Christ for the smoke cause it'll keep the flies away, eaten alive the past three nights. It's cool, and I pull the robe round me like a blanket, feeling its rough hew against my neck as I pull it over my shoulders. It smells of sea and salt and sweat and earth, but somewhere below I smell him, the priest, him now below in the ocean but his odours still there, following me all the way south of the world and up the Rio de la Plata and the Rio Paraná into the jungle.

I smell him, salt and piety, as I drift off to sleep.

I wake in the night, startled by a large bug on my face. I brush it off and sit up. It's dark, but a little moonlight makes its way in the window. Theodore is snoring softly next to me, face turned to the wall, his robes pulled up round his head. I turn my ear to the night. I hear the river below, its insistent murmur, and above it the crickets, the *cigarra*, twitching and scraping. It's a music of sorts, a music for souls robbed of slumber. I listen to it awhile then stand up. I go outta the room and out the front door, and round the back to the weeds by the river for a piss in the bushes. The music around me stops. A ways upriver I see the glow of a pipe so I stand still and watch, under a tree two forms becoming clear, one is certainly Anuncio, for I see him squat rigidly just like he does on the boat, and next to him a companion, must be our host. I slip between the grasses to watch the scene, the two men, studied, silent, puffing on the pipe they pass between them on the bank of the Paraná. I move upstream towards them and crouch now under the canopy of a low-hanging tree to observe. The scent of their tobacco drifts downriver towards me, a strange, sweet scent, intoxicating and delicious, and the glow of the bowl lights Anuncio's face as he draws on it. Old man river, old river men, smoking the music of the night, inhaling the river, barbs of sweet tobacco on the nose, warble of the water, scratching in the air, a cool breeze on my neck, the sky above, and the moon's whisper soothes... I feel I've awoken in a dream, a dream of the south, the south of the earth, and I wondered if you poked a hole in the earth all the way through was Ireland there on the other side, me here now on the other end, upriver on a dark continent, maybe the anti-Ireland; over there the people white and here black, there winter and here spring, there field and here jungle and with music on the night air. What music in Ireland but the howl of the night wind and the rattle of the rain on your walls? And the smell of shite and of the dead and dying, and here only the smell of beans and sweet tobacco. It was true, I was here in the far pole of the earth, far from my home country.

I get up off my screaming knees and take a spill down the bank, cursing softly. When I get up, the two faces are peering downriver at me, and so that I don't look like a madman I walk over. My host slaps the earth next to him so I sit down with the two men under the tree, and my host passes me the pipe and I take it from his hand, him whispering words in his strange tongue, smiling softly, and I puff on it and sputter, for I never was much of a man for the leaf. I pass it back but he insists gently, patting me on the back, laughing, so I have another lick at it, sucking on it, burning my lungs, that strange sweet fire, and I cough some more.

'Si, si,' he says. 'Si, si, si.'

'Yes,' I say, '*Si*,' and he chuckles, and even Anuncio breaks into a half-smile. 'Si, si...'

'Beautiful,' I say when I stop coughing, the two of them nodding, *si si*, and the cool air blows off the river and I nod with them.

'Irlandese,' says my host, and I nod. 'Yes, Irlandese,' and we're all in agreement somehow that this is just fine.

Somewhere out behind us an ass brays. 'Burro,' I say, and my host gets to giggling and so do I, and we're all looking at each other nodding and smiling. 'Si, burro,' my host says and claps me on the back.

Not too bad this.

I fall quiet, the occasional whisper between my two companions only another layer of the music, the song of the Paraná and the pious crickets and our friend the *burro*, sweet tobacco and river smells and damp on the night air, and moonshot trees and whispering grasses and holy stars, sweet sweet the night.

'Paraná,' I say, and let it hang there on the air, my companions saying nothing, them knowing the intent of that word, a note in the music of the night and nothing more, just three syllables cast upon the river's song to dance over the moonsilver water and burst like bubbles in the greedy air.

13

Grasses long and uncut, a tumbledown wall. A donkey wanders. From the riven jungle, a spire pokes up amid a sea of green.

The long trip upriver and across land, ten days on mules and here we are, the New Jerusalem in the jungle, and I tell ya, make no mistake, what is here is proper gone. Gone the great works of the brothers of past centuries, gone the flock, their sanctuary swallowed, gone the crops and animals. The land untamed, wild, unrevived. Civilisation, gone.

We get down off our mules, me and Theodore, and wild-eyed we survey the Estancia San Ignacio, our rightful inheritance and spiritual estate.

'God love us,' I say. Strange that God should come to me, but he does. *We'll need something way out here. If not God, then something.*

Our Franciscan guide is watching me. Brother Paolo has accompanied us from Alta Gracia, one of the brothers whose lot was the care of the Jesuit estate here after our expulsion. He explains himself to Theodore, who in turn explains it to me.

'He says it was unfortunate, but they just didn't have the resources to look after it. They were spread thin looking after Alta Gracia and the other estates, the university being their main priority, and San Ignacio was let go to ruin.'

'Brother Theodore, I can see this undertaking is going to test my faith in the Lord.' So I say then fall silent, one arm on the back of my mule.

Our Franciscan brother gestures towards the estate. We leave our mules to graze by the walls and we squeeze through the gate.

We pause inside. Theodore whistles and Brother Paolo mutters a few words in Spanish. Aye, it's a wreck of a place, gone all to hell, but I can see it, I can, through the weeds and the trees and the creepers and the bushes, what it was in its glory day, and at that moment a little sun breaks through the clouds and lights up that forlorn spot, wild with weeds and growth and animals rustling in the grasses, and I see it for the sanctuary that it once was. A little corner of heaven on God's green earth. Now a shitehole.

Brother Paolo speaks.

'He says these must have been the living quarters over here,' Brother Theodore says. Brother Paolo is pointing to the back, where there's a fine little colonnade, covered and shaded, roof caved in everywhere, but in its day a fine abode, I'm sure.

We wade through the grass to the back where the cells are and we push open the doors for a look inside. There was a room here once. Not now. The jungle has invaded, crept in through the windows, birds nested in the corners, the chirping of baby birds; a bed there too, given birth to its own little jungle of sorts. The frame is good, solid, the craftsmanship of the Jesuits of old. She's still standing. There are cupboards there also, probably rotten through, shelves on the walls, a solid wooden floor. A little holy icon still hangs above the bed, a faded and haloed Christ. A porcelain jug and bowl on the dresser, there from the day they were abandoned.

Brother Paolo says something in the Spanish, no doubt a commentary on the state of the place.

'I think it's a fine room,' I say. 'I'll be taking this one.'

A small bird flies in, panics, and flies right back out again.

'Sorry, little fella,' I say after him. I hear him frantic outside the window. 'Let's get a look at your room, Brother Theodore, will we?'

We find the kitchen and get a fire going for tea. Theodore rolls up his sleeves for a bit of cleaning while I help Brother Paolo unload supplies from the donkey. Maize and wheat flour, cured meats, fruit conserves, potatoes – as rare-looking ones as ever I've seen – cakes of manioc, or at least that's what they tell me, vegetables, corn, several varieties of tea, and a *bit-o-this-that-and-the-other*. Supplies, so we can take time to get our own gardens up and running.

We drag water up from the river and get the pot boiling, and me and Theodore drag the last of the provisions inside. Brother Paolo sets about fixing us a cup of tea, explaining things as he goes.

'Brother Paolo says this is the local tea.' Theodore slaps a sack on the workboard. 'It's called yerba maté. He asks would you like to try some?'

'I'll give it a shot,' I say.

So the brother fires up a pot of the local brew and unpacks three small gourds, silver straws in them – straws for the tea, God almighty – and pours us each a cup of the brew, and we go out and sit on a broken bench looking at the overgrown yard. Evening now, maybe going on eight, and we watch the colours soften and the sky go red-purple, and we're silent for a few moments, an unspoken something between us, a feeling that we're strangers in this here place, guests, not yet masters of our new home.

The sky turns a deep violet and I sip on my tea, a bitter earthy brew. Theodore's peering into his, curious, wondering what the hell he's drinking.

'Queer enough,' I say.

'Not sure how I feel about it,' Theodore says.

Then Brother Paolo goes off on one, holding up his cup, pointing now at the mules, now at the jungle, explaining about the tea.

'The brother says it's gathered from the mountains and carried down here on mules,' says Brother Theodore, 'and there's a good quality and a poor one, but this is the good one. The Indians drink it from morning to night, and it's the reason they work like donkeys, for the energy it gives them. And it's healthy too, he says. Apparently, it became so popular with the missionaries that they prefer it to their own tea.'

I slurp on the bitter brew. 'I'd say we won't be long getting used to it.'

Brother Paolo nods and smiles.

We sit and chat in broken turns as it goes dark, the sound of the jungle all round us, cicadas, birds, the whisper of the grass and the trees, above us the brilliant sky, diamond-lit like the west of Ireland, and as I sit and peer up at it Brother Paolo rises, takes a bedroll from his mule, says a few words in the Spanish tongue and wanders off under the eaves to find a place to lay his head.

'I may just do the same,' Theodore says.

'I'll sit out and watch the sky for a bit,' I say.

Two weeks after our arrival, five men showed up with Anuncio and Diego at the head of a mule train, leading a couple each of horses, donkeys, goats and some chickens, and sacks of temporary provisions, tools, seeds, cloth, utensils and a whole host of other stuff, the purpose of which was to get us on our feet. We set the mules loose in the courtyard and they soon had it cleared, and I got to work on some of the tougher weeds with a scythe I'd dug outta one of the sheds and cleaned up with a pot of oil and a sharpening stone. The horses and the goats we set loose in the animal yard to much the same effect, and within a fortnight we had the compound looking respectable enough. Our first week was spent working on the living quarters and the kitchen. The birds were expelled from the rooms and we'd a couple of half-decent beds for lying in. Things were shaping up.

The five men who came with Diego and Anuncio were guachos, surly men and quiet and who smoked from morning to night. But they knew the land and they worked. First, they got to repairing the barns, and two of them worked on re-setting the walls of the wells; five days in and they were drawing water, both holes. The roof over the living quarters was repaired and the windows re-hung. None of us went near the church. This made Theodore uneasy, but I insisted we were to get daily life in running order before we set about organising the spiritual one.

Diego and Anuncio stuck around too, helping where they could. Every day they came back from the lake with baskets full of fish that were cooked over an open fire in the evening, wonderful fish laced with spices, hot spices but tasty, and so much fish that we ate two or three of them to a man, as much as we could eat night after night. Nights like this we sat round the fire, the company talking in that rough Spanish tongue, Theodore sitting quietly, joining in where he could, and me listening, picking up words here and there, *hombre, burros, pez, arroz, cigarillo*... all those words that danced round the fire on nights like these, and soon I was picking bits up, 'Muy bueno', and 'Non, gracias', and 'Soy cansado'... I liked that word, *cansado*, nights it swam fishlike on the air, so when we were *cansado* we ate and lay down, and soon we were *descansado*... the Spanish tongue flitting like little fishes round the fire.

Like this, it went for a month or so.

Now we'd horses and donkeys and we set them upon each other, and I'd little knowledge of rearing animals but you set two animals together soon enough you get little babies of one sort or another, and the donkey got riding on the mare and soon Diego informed us that she'd a baby *mula* on the way, and there was much hooting and clapping among us.

It was coming into summer – winter in Ireland and summer here in the anti-Ireland – and not long after we'd settled on the estancia, Diego returned from Buenos Aires with news that in another fortnight the guachos would be pulled from San Ignacio and sent to Santa Catalina to begin work there. What they'd done in the six weeks they'd been there had been something; the place was starting to look like a proper working farm. The animal yard was running smoothly, with chicken coops and troughs and stalls for the horses, and outside we'd fenced off grazing lands for the mules we hoped we'd be raising a year down the line. We'd rehabilitated some of the fruit trees; most of the peach were done for but we'd twenty or thirty still strong, and a few quince and pear, enough for our own purposes, and we'd planted potato, tomato, beans, chilis, and all sorts of other produce. But it was clear to both me and Theodore that it was too much work for the two of us. Diego had returned with his family, a wife and two children, who would stay and help out round the estate. The wife was short, strong, and I'd no doubt she could help out, but the two sons were still young – eleven and thirteen – and their usefulness would be limited. Anuncio would stay with us too, but he was a single man with no family to speak of, no wife and no sons. We'd need to start recruiting, and soon.

Before they left, the guachos put the church into shape. The roof and wooden floors were repaired. The pews were fixed and the doors repainted, the walls whitewashed. We'd need artisans to retouch the icons and the paintings round the walls but that would come later. Paths round the church were repaved and the bells were put back in working order.

The last night before the guachos would leave us, before we sat down to supper, Brother Theodore rang the bells, and we all gathered together to bless the rebirth of the reduction. I asked Theodore to say something but he insisted I do it and wouldn't relent, and so I threw together a blessing, dredged from the mutterings of the ma and pieces from history, gleaned as a child, and I gave my best as we all stood together in a circle, the sun down, arms crossed and hats held in front of us, and I said,

'Lord, we are gathered here today in the far corner of God's green earth, some of us far from home and family but in a bounteous land of plenty, where, by your grace, we have found new friends, and, with time, we hope they become family...'

I said the words, and Theodore translated them into the Spanish tongue, and, *Who knows*, I thought, *maybe I'm a natural at this priest business after all.*

'...and with your own blessing and grace, we pray for the success of your earthly abode, made wholesome by your word and your light. We pray, Lord, that you spread your wings of protection over us – *gettin a bit carried away, for sure* – and accept this testament to your own glory and good will.'

And saying so, I spread out my arms, gesturing to the fine sanctuary that we were building here in a wild and savage country.

'Amen,' said Brother Theodore.

Brother James himself would be proud. Yes he would.

'Jesus, Diego, but she's a great woman,' I say, the two of us taking a break from the digging. 'Buena mujer.'

We're watching Jacinta, Diego's wife, root around in the potato field.

'Si, si,' he says. 'Muy buena mujer.'

Then he goes on to explain how among the Guaraní, the women do the field work.

'Si?' I say. He nods. 'In Ireland,' I tell him, 'it's the men do it.'

'No, no,' he says. 'No, no bueno.'

'No?'

'No, no.' He shakes his head.

We're definitely in the anti-Ireland.

'What do the men do, Diego?' I say.

'Men talk to God,' he says.

'Only this?'

'This only.'

'Quare fellas yis are, Diego,' I say.

'Que?'

'Muy bueno, Diego.'

'Si, bueno,' he says and grins.

Then we get to talking about women, and he asks me why I have no wife, and I tell him he knows the score, I'm a priest and priests don't take wives.

'No bueno,' he says.

And it hits me, it does, the sacrifices required to lead the life of a priest, a life dedicated to God, a life of prayer and kneeling before the

Lord and doing good for your fellow man. A quare life indeed.

We watch Jacinta's rump come up among the green, big womanly hips in her white cotton dress, the dirty soles of her feet and bare brown calves, strong calves and sinewy, the hard legs of a working woman.

'A great woman, Diego.'

Later that afternoon, I find Theodore sitting against the wall in the shade, so I sit down next to him and he passes me a gourd of water. I sip on it and pass it back to him. He looks tired but happy. Diego's two boys, Santiago and Nicolás, have taken a break from their labours and are chasing each other through the grass beyond the fields. The children can work, after all; once their mother tells them to get doing something, they do it. Diego and Jacinta have disappeared. The horses have sought out the shade of a walnut tree and pick at the grass. We watch the scene with a detached contentment.

'I never saw this as my path,' Brother Theodore says. 'When I left England for New York two years ago, I had only scholarship on my mind. I love study and always have, and I always believed that my place was in the library. But this, this is a different kind of worship. When I left New York, I was scared, and when we arrived in Buenos Aires, I became terrified, but now... now I go to sleep every night with a gentle joy in my heart, weary but joyous. I never thought I'd say it, but I think I can be happy here.'

He turns his head and smiles. This the first time we've communicated like this, as people, not priests.

'Aye,' I say, 'there's a life here for us, there is. What say we cast off the old robes and find ourselves a couple of women, have some wee'uns and raise them here as cousins?'

Theodore's head comes up off the wall, a shocked look on his face. I laugh. In relief, he laughs too.

'In truth, though,' I say, 'I think we've done well for ourselves. This place can be a home. Don't you think?'

Brother Theodore nods. 'I'll go wherever God calls me to. But I pray he keeps me here.'

Anuncio came back the next day from one of his forays into the woods. He liked to go alone and returned after a day or so, his mule laden with sacks of yerba maté. So that night over dinner round the fire, with me, Brother Theodore, Diego and his family and the guachos, I brought up the possibility of a trip into the jungle to seek out the tribes living there. We spoke haltingly, half in English and half in Spanish, Theodore pitching in where necessary. Anuncio was reluctant. 'No, no.' He shook his head. 'The people don't want it. They are happy in the jungle. They don't want to leave.'

I listened to his pleadings and tried to show patience. 'I understand Anuncio, I do, but don't you think they would live better here? We have animals, wheat, corn, fruit... look what we're building here.'

Anuncio held my gaze across the fire. 'People in the jungle eat good – eat fish, fruit, plenty of tea. They don't need the Jesuit.'

'But they'd be safe here, Anuncio. No bandits, no wild animals, no hunters. Safe.'

'And the children can grow up here in God's love, with the church, and grow in Christianity,' added Brother Theodore. 'And learn to read and write.'

I saw a flash of anger cross Anuncio's face, the face of a man hitherto stoic and inexpressive. 'The Guaraní are not Christian!' He said it with a raised voice, startling everyone round the fire. His eyes were wide, defiant, so I let him cool off a bit before I spoke again.

'Maybe we could go to meet them, Anuncio, or one of us, at least – just me. Let me come out with you and meet the people, just to let them know we're here. We don't want to drag anyone down here against their will, but let us meet them, please, as a gesture of friendship.'

Anuncio was silent for a while, before his features softened into an expression that I could take as a 'Yes', or at least a 'Maybe'.

'Vale?' I said.

He didn't answer. He didn't want to do it, but I could see he would.

14

Personally, I wasn't bothered about converts, but if I was to prove I was who I said I was, then I would have to, at very least, make some kind of an effort to entice people into the reduction. For I was a missionary, after all. Brother James Carmichael, Jesuit missionary, minister to God's unanointed, saviour of lost souls. That's why I'd come – to restore the glory of the Jesuit mission here in the Argentine Republic. So I planned the day of departure for the hills, pushing Anuncio every step of the way, and five days after we'd first discussed it round the fire, we were at the gates of the estancia at six one morning, ready for leaving.

The morning was fine and cool, everyone already up and about, and they gathered there at the gates to see us off. The mood may have been lighter were it not for Anuncio's nervousness. He wasn't angry anymore, but maybe he was afraid of his fellow men and how they'd react to the presence of a priest. For all I knew they hated the Jesuits. If I'd learned a little history, as I did soon enough, I might have understood better how Anuncio felt that day and the reasons for his unwillingness. But he got up on his mule and gave it a kick and it took off, and I hopped up on mine and set out after him, and in the cool morning we left the sanctuary of the estancia and headed west.

'Go with God!' shouted Brother Theodore.

I tipped my cap, a simple cap of the guachos, leaving my big Jesuit hat behind so as not to spook the natives.

We heard the cries of the children behind us as we disappeared out behind the reduction, lost to the trees.

We crossed the Santa Rosa heading out across the plain, Anuncio in front and me behind, and for a good hour or so we didn't speak. I felt good, with a breakfast in my belly and fresh air and the morning sun on my back, so I whistled and grinned and tipped my cap to the birds, and scratched my horse behind the ear and told her what a nice girl she was. And when I grew tired of the grinning and the horse, for she wasn't so very talkative herself, I gave her a kick and we pulled up beside Anuncio, and I tried to light up a bit of conversation to glean a little more knowledge of our trip.

'So two days you think'll take us up there?'

'Two days,' Anuncio said.

He was dressed in the cotton of the Indian, all the ones I'd met anyhow, and he'd a wide straw hat on his head to keep the sun off. The land was, in turn, dense with thick vegetation or dry and barren. We'd trek for an hour through jungle-like foliage, then come across an old mule track which we stuck to for a bit, then we'd come across a dry plain covered in rock and scrub. When the treeline thinned, we saw the mountains in the distance, the Sierras, then we found ourselves back in jungle. Not a man, woman or child we saw as we traversed that land. Occasionally, Anuncio got down off the horse and I was advised to do the same, and when I asked why all he said was, 'Sacred land.'

I knew not to ask.

We stopped at sundown and made camp for the night. We'd trekked for twelve hours with a break for lunch. Anuncio chose a spot beneath the trees by a river, setting up two hammocks in a matter of minutes. Fine thing, the hammock! Would never work in Ireland, ye'd get blown on your arse in minutes, but here – here it was tremendous. Before I got myself up in the hammock, we fed and watered the horses then cooked up some beans. We'd bread with us from the estancia, and we sat down to a meal by the fire, me and Anuncio. Our bellies filled, Anuncio boiled some water for the tea, the yerba maté. It was strange stuff to me, but here I was, out in the jungle with a native, and Christ, I was gonna drink what I was given. So he filled the strange little gourd and we passed it between us, first him then me, and back again, and like this it went, the cup passing between us, and sitting there by the fire drinking tea, I felt a peculiar intimacy grow between us.

'You're not married, Anuncio?'

He shook his head, and didn't answer for some moments. 'My wife is dead,' he said eventually.

'I'm very sorry, Anuncio.'

He peered at the fire, the gourd cupped in his two hands.

'What happened?'

He inhaled long and slow. 'Killed by soldiers.'

'Jesus, Anuncio...'

'Raped and killed.'

I said nothing. What can you say to that? We sat quiet for a bit. He passed me the gourd.

'You never had children?' I asked him.

'My wife was pregnant when they killed her.'

I closed my eyes. Perhaps it was better I just shut up. I took a sip of the tea and passed it back.

'You, family?' Anuncio said.

The question gave me pause, and for a moment I was caught between two men: the man from the West of Ireland who crawled through bog to get here, and Brother James Carmichael, whose history I knew, but when it came to it I couldn't fob it off on this man, who'd just told me about his dead wife and unborn child. I couldn't.

'All dead, Anuncio,' I said. 'All dead from hunger.'

He looked at me, uncomprehending.

'No food. In all the country, there's no food. Thousands, millions dead. My mother, father, brothers, sisters, all dead.'

And for the first time, Anuncio looked at me like a human being. He nodded solemnly. Then, reaching into his pocket, he pulled out a small pipe, and I recognised it as the thing I'd smoked in Rosario by the river.

He held it up, as if he needed approval.

I grinned and shrugged. 'Sure,' I said.

So he plugged the pipe with his strange tobacco, the sweet smell of it reaching me where I sat.

'What is it, Anuncio?'

'Javorái.'

'Javorái?'

'It's how we speak to our gods.'

'You can speak to the gods by smokin it?'

'Si.'

He took an ember from the fire and inhaled on the pipe, holding the smoke in his lungs for several seconds, before blowing it skyward. I smelled it on the warm night air, orange and pine and clove, then he passed it to me and I took a long draw on it, too long, cause I started coughing and spluttering. Anuncio laughed at me, the first time I'd seen him laugh.

I passed it back, my lungs on fire, and Anuncio passed me the tea. Cool now, it soothed my throat. We swapped like this, the tea and the pipe, til my head swam... the gentle *wibble* of the river, the spark of the fire and the muttering of the horses, the cicadas all around, a wall of sound, intense and hypnotic, the rustle of leaves the plop of a fish, a river trout, or maybe a dorado or a salmon – the salmon of wisdom come to pay a visit, eyeing us from out the water, saying, *Suck on the citrus pipe and speak to the gods, and listen to the song of the cicada and hear the depth of the jungle, jungle that swallows all ills be it death or illness or ill-will, for nothing hovers out there but the absence of memory...* that would be the message of the salmon of wisdom, I thought, had it leapt from the water then.

Plop!

Back again.

'You like it?' Anuncio takes the pipe from my hands.

'Si, Anuncio, si... I like it. I like it too much.'

And he laughs softly and knowingly.

'Brother Theodore, does he like it?'

'No, Anuncio, no – he doesn't like it.'

And we laugh like two naughty children. *No, Brother Theodore is priest all the way; he has no schtick with the salmon of wisdom.*

'I can feel the jungle all round us,' I say. 'I *feel* it.'

Anuncio nods. 'The jungle is big.'

'The jungle is *heavy*, Anuncio.'

I lie back. The starpricked sky above my head, planets, galaxies, I feel the weight of it all, even the black emptiness of the sky, I feel it all press down upon me, the universe upon my chest, and somehow I feel fine.

Anuncio groans, rises to his feet. 'Time for sleep,' he says.

'Yes, Anuncio. Sleep.'

'Goodnight.'

'Goodnight, Anuncio.'

The glow of the fire illuminates the lined contours of his face, the rest of him swallowed by the jungle at his back. I hear him climb into his hammock as I stretch out beside the fire, my cap under my head, and as I feel my own eyes closing I hear it again: *Plop!*

The salmon of wisdom says goodnight.

We arrived at the village the following evening.

We'd been following the bank of the Rio Durazno for some hours when we chanced upon two fellows in the jungle, though I suspect they didn't much chance upon us, for it seemed to me they were waiting. Such a sight I'd never seen, nor ever will, for they wore nothing only a loincloth to cover their privates and had bindings on their upper arms, one wearing a necklace of animal teeth, both of them with bows slung across their backs. Jungle men with a fighting spirit, and me wrapped in my priest's cassock – I suddenly felt like an impostor. And I was.

Anuncio slid off his mule and greeted the men. I followed his lead and got off the beast, and Anuncio chatted briefly to his two companions in their native tongue. He turned and gestured to me, the two men nodding. They then turned and walked away into the jungle.

'Come,' Anuncio said.

We followed them through the darkening jungle, light fading but alive with sound, cawks and screeches and hisses and maws, and beyond, a human sound, of families, of community – the sound of living. The smell of cooking. Meat smells. The cry of a child. Laughter.

And so I came to the village, saw them, all the living people, all dark skin and nakedness, the women even with the paps out, all ages, breasts and thighs and hips, and me son of poor Catholics, praying folk, a son who'd never seen more than a woman's forearm in his puff.

I followed Anuncio, and no one stopped to look at the priest, the Irishman, the white man, no one stopped to marvel at the foreigner. Only a few children no higher than my knee who gathered to see the man in long dresses, but to the rest I was just another in a long line, come with bread and words and empty prayers. Seeing them go about it, life and all its little duties and obligations, I realised immediately, without doubt, that I had nothing at all to offer these people.

We stopped outside a hut and one of our escort nipped inside.

'Who's inside, Anuncio?' I said.

'A priest.'

'Jesuit?'

Anuncio smiled and shook his head. 'Our priest.'

Anuncio's companion came back out of the tent, behind him a small man, bent and old with brown skin like leather. He looked up at me and there was something in his eyes, a curiosity, a puzzlement, a flash of recognition, that I may have seen or may not have seen at all.

'Brother James, this is my grandfather,' Anuncio said.

Thus I met Silverio Cato.

15

The old man led us inside and we waited for him to sit down. When he was seated, we sat round a small table on the floor. The walls of the hut were bare and simple and it was cool inside. An old woman with sagging breasts came in the door behind us and placed a pot on the table and the now familiar gourd, and Silverio said a few words to the old woman, who left. We sat in silence, and the old man spooned tea into the gourd and filled in with water and we waited for the tea to steep. Eventually, he raised the gourd to his lips and sipped, before passing it to Anuncio on his right. Anuncio drank and passed it on, and the gourd did a full circle back to the old man before he spoke.

'What brings you here, padre?' he said.

'We've been tasked with rebuilding the Jesuit missions here in Córdoba,' I told him.

He sipped on the tea and passed it on. 'Many years you've been gone now. What brings you back?'

'We believe the Spanish king is about to reverse the decision that expelled the Jesuits from crown lands. We're here to pave the way for a return.'

'And the chancellor has not objected to your visit?'

'The chancellor in Buenos Aires was told of our arrival. He made no objection. Or at least, he was told not to.'

The old man wore no jewellery like the others, but instead was decorated with markings in ink from his shoulders down across his chest. It was this that I was now staring at.

'And what do you hope to achieve by coming here today?'

'I hope to convince you to come and join us in the reduction.' I heard myself say it, and I heard the lack of conviction in my voice.

'You know our history here?' he said.

'I'm ashamed to say that I don't.'

'So let me tell it to you,' said the old man. 'Long before the Jesuits came, or the Spanish or the Portuguese, or the Franciscans, or any of the others, we were here, the Guaraní. We lived alone ourselves, sometimes fighting with each other but mostly in peace, and we made our homes and had our children and things were alright with the world. Then, about two hundred years ago, the Spanish came, and in the beginning we fought them off but they had cannons and rifles and they killed us in large numbers, and so we were forced to live with them. To make peace we offered them our daughters, and we worked the land for them and they gave us nothing in return, but we kept on because they had more lead than they needed to finish all of us. But soon the daughters we gave them were not enough, they wanted more, so they came in the night and lifted our women from their beds, all those they could carry, and those who resisted were raped and murdered and left for us to bury. Despite all this, we continued to work for them, but they didn't want to pay us for our work so we became slaves. Enslaved by the Spanish, the Viceroy of Brazil saw that he was disadvantaged, and so he sent his mercenaries to go south and take us as slaves too, and those of us that resisted were killed.

'Then came the Franciscans wearing the face of our saviours, and some of us went with them into the missions, and there we worked and were fed, but not paid, and so, in their own way, the Franciscans enslaved us too, not with a whip or a bullet, but with the word of God and the saviour Jesus Christ, and when we had been seduced by the word, the Jesuits came, whispering more sweet words, and more and more of us listened, because anything was preferable to slaughter by the Spanish and the Portuguese. But all-powerful as Jesus Christ was, somehow he still couldn't protect us, for the mercenaries still came and dragged us away by the hair and tied us up, and marched us off to work the fields for them, and if we resisted they cut our throats and left us to stain the earth with our blood.

'Many times we rose up against them, our oppressors, but with spears and bows we had no hope of defeating their bullets and cannons. We were wiped out in greater and greater numbers, and the Jesuits and the Franciscans, though they tried to talk to our slave masters, nothing they said had any effect on those men.

'And one hundred years ago when the Jesuits were expelled from the country, even knowing that their flight would leave us helpless, they walked out on us, and we were left to the mercy of the Spanish King and the Portuguese Viceroy. In Paraquaria, we were kicked off our land and told to go to the Rio de la Plata, and in Brazil we were swept up as slaves by the mercenaries, and here we abandoned our land and fled to the hills so that we would not suffer the same fate.

'So you see,' Silverio Cato said, 'we've always had men come here, men of God, a god we don't understand, but we know now the way of those men is not our way and never will be. And so I ask you again, padre, how is it you come to be here and what is it you think you can do for us?'

All this he said as he watched me intently, but without judgement or malice or ill-will. He told me his story and watched me solemnly and waited for my reply. I dug my thumbs into my palms and tried to hold his gaze. I was not a Jesuit, not a Franciscan, not a priest of any sort or other and I longed to say it, but instead I uttered vague and noncommittal words that I hoped would pass as some kind of answer.

'We are here to try to build a life for ourselves and our fellow men,' I said.

Silverio nodded. 'We have no objection to that, and no one of the Guaraní will try to stop you in your endeavours. In the early days some of us fought the priests, some of our people even took a pride in killing them and took their heads as trophies, but that was long ago. While we have never learned to live with the Spanish or the Portuguese, we have learned to live beside the priests, even if our ways are different.'

'Is there nothing at all that the Jesuits have given you?'

'You misunderstand, padre – many things the Jesuits gave us: we learned to make fine things with our hands, not only weapons and tools but works of art too, and we learned reading and writing and the different tongues of your people, and we gained the knowledge of different crops and plants and herbs, medicines that complement our own remedies, and for all this we are thankful, but what we never gained from anyone of them was protection against oppression. No one stood up for us, but one.'

'Who?'

The old man stood up. 'We will show you, padre.'

We headed out of the village and into the jungle, the bow-legged old man walking out ahead with his staff, a stout bit of wood wrapped in red ribbon and with a gourd tied to the top end, following him only me and Anuncio, the others staying behind in the village. It was dark now, and we followed the steps of Silverio, the old man picking his way through the jungle with ease, over stump and bush without pause. A little moonlight filtered down through the trees and behind me Anuncio carried a burning torch, and with the whole weight of the jungle around us we ventured deeper.

Eventually, we came to a hut, not much more than a lean-to of sticks and twine Silverio Cato swung the door open and we stepped inside. Anuncio followed me in, the light from his torch falling on the walls, and in the flickering light I saw a horrific thing, a monstrous thing, and as I stood staring at it Anuncio lit some candles and the hut came alive, the walls adorned with animal heads and furs and all manner of things that once lived, and on the back wall, not an animal but a human skeleton, arms spread in the gesture of Christ and wearing the cassock of the priest, his shining skull eyeing us like some terrible harbinger. In the candlelight it looked like he was grinning. I stared at it in horror. The thought crossed my mind that I was about to die, and when Anuncio put his hand on my shoulder I jumped.

'Don't be afraid, padre,' he said.

I was, I was afraid. For no matter how many dead I'd seen in Ireland and even those that I'd buried with my own hands, I'd never seen anything like this. Silverio took me by the arm and ushered me forward.

'You are safe here,' he said. 'But we want you to see someone, and know who he is. This is a man, a priest who we still worship here today, who our people still revere, for he is the only white man that ever fought and died for the Guaraní. His name was Giuseppe Zucchero.'

'A Jesuit?'

'Yes. A Jesuit and a warrior.'

Silverio lifted a bunch of dried herbs from the small altar in front of the god-awful figure and lit it, placing the smoking bush in front of the dead priest.

'This is how we honour his memory.'

I stared at Giuseppe Zucchero, the skeletal remains of him hanging there like a malevolent angel, and I wondered what deeds had caused such reverence among the people that he hung here still above the altar of the old shaman, bones cleaned and polished, a makeshift crucifix of wheat tied to his chest. Below him, on the table, were offerings of maize and dried meat, and a single fish swam in a bowl of water.

I smelled a familiar citrusy scent, and I turned to see Anuncio on the floor, tamping the weed into his pipe.

Silverio Cato sat down next to him so I sat down to complete the circle. Anuncio took a candle and lit the pipe, sucking on it before passing it to his grandfather, then the pipe was passed to me.

'I know, given your customs,' Silverio said, 'that this may be difficult for you to understand. But this man was very important to us.'

I drew on the pipe and passed it to Anuncio.

'But this man was a priest,' I said. 'Doesn't he deserved to be buried like a Christian?'

'In some ways, this man was closer to our gods than yours.' He gestured up at the altar. 'This is what he would have wanted.'

'How do you know that?'

'Because he was more than a priest,' Silverio said. He took the pipe and puffed on it and then blew the smoke right at me. 'And you too are more than a priest.'

'What do you mean?'

Silverio reached behind him and lifted a large gourd, and unplugged it and I smelled what it was, and I thought, *Christ Almighty, not now*. Silverio raised it to his lips and swallowed. Then he passed it to me and I pushed it back towards him.

'I can't.'

But he pushed it into my chest and looked me in the eye and said, 'Drink.'

I looked at Anuncio, and if I had any doubt the old man meant it, Anuncio dispelled it with his eyes, so I lifted the gourd to my lips and swallowed, tasting the acrid bitterness of the brew, me with a head fulla the funny tobacco and now booze in my blood, and I heard it, soft at first but growing, the voice of Eoin, prodding, mocking, saying:

—What are ya at now, ya prick, sittin in the jungle in the voodoo shack with a dead priest and smokin the jungle bush and boozin now too, aren't you the fella...

His voice grew louder in my head.

'No, you are more than a priest,' Silverio said.

'I am just a man,' I said. My head swam.

'You are *avaporú*,' Silverio said.

'What?' I looked at Anuncio.

Anuncio's eyes widened. 'He says you are a man who eats men.'

—They got ya now, ya flesh-eatin hoor, said the voice in my head.

16

They had me. With a head fulla smoke and the drink too, the lies just weren't in me. So I kept my mouth shut.

'You're two men,' Silverio says. 'Is it not so?'

—Two men, is that what ya are? *Eoin*.

I say nothing, so Silverio stands up and goes to the altar and comes back with a basket. He sits down and opens it, and reaches inside and pulls out a rocky, black lump. He holds it up for me to see.

'This is the liver of the man that killed my brother,' he says. He places it back in the basket and pulls out another. 'This is the kidney of the Portuguese who dragged six of our people away to Brazil thirty years ago. When he came back for more we were waiting, and we killed him and three others. We ate the rest of him.'

—You're in good company now.

'All of him?' I say.

'All the parts of a man that are good to eat. But I don't need to tell *you* what those are.'

—Aye, you know eatin alright, don't ya? Eoin says. Ate my arms, my back and legs, even ate my hole, ya dirty hoor ye…

And despite myself I grin, and Silverio sees and passes the gourd. I hold up my hands to push it away, but Eoin's at me again. —You'll take it and you'll drink it if ya know what's good for ya, he says.

So I take it and drink, Eoin giving it, —Oh aye, that's the man.

Silverio laughs. 'I can hear him.'

—What's that now?

'Your brother,' Silverio says, and I nod. I'm past the point of lying, and since I'm in the company of a man who eats folk, I decide to get it all out. Confess, like.

'I ate my brother,' I say, 'to escape from Ireland, cause he was dying and I was dying and one of us had to live, and I decided it would be me.'

Silverio nods, eyes glinting.

—Thought it'd be you, did ya? Eoin says, and quietly I tell him to shut it. But he's lit now on jungle beer and probably the smoke has him off on one too, and he isn't letting up. —Tell the old witch doctor to pass the ale.

Silverio laughs and passes me the gourd. So I take a lick of it and hand it back. 'That's the last you're gettin',' I tell Eoin. He swears.

'Your brother likes the beer,' Silverio says, smiling. I nod.

'He was always a fiend for it.'

'You need to learn how to control him. His spirit can work for you if you know how to keep it silent.'

'His spirit?'

He nods. 'Each man has his own spirit. The spirit inhabits every corner of him – it exists in every hair and every drop of water in the body. It's in him when he's born, and stays with him for a short time after he dies. Long ago, our ancestors discovered that this spirit could be eaten, ingested, absorbed. We can steal a man's spirit, and thus his powers, by eating him. Everything a man is and can do, we can assume for ourselves by eating his flesh.'

I listen intently to the old man, Eoin buzzing away in my ear.

'What was your brother good at?' Silverio says.

'He could build a fierce wall,' I tell him.

—You foul bastard, I could do more than that, Eoin says.

Silverio holds up his fist and clenches it, and I feel Eoin choke.

'Your brother doesn't know when to be silent,' says the old man. 'If you know how to use it, you can assume all the skills of your brother. You only need a trigger.'

'What's that?'

'Something that was dear to your kin – in your brother's case, the beer. Just a little taste will waken him, and then you will find yourself equipped with all the skills that he possessed. But all the weaknesses too. It takes a long time to master these things. This man,' says Silverio, picking up the Portuguese heart from the basket, 'was one of the greatest swordsmen I have ever seen. And he loved gold more than all other things. So I keep a little gold coin in my pouch for those moments when I need to fight, and I put it in my mouth before I draw my sword. But this man's weakness was the smell of a woman, so if there's a woman nearby, or even sweet-smelling flowers, he is diminished. But there are other things we can use to increase the effects of eating a man's flesh.'

'Like what?' I say.

'You've heard enough today. When you're ready, you will come back and see me and we'll talk more about these things. Anuncio will guide you here when it's time to return.'

Anuncio nods.

Silverio stands up and retrieves several gourds of beer from a shelf on the wall, placing them into my hands. 'Get used to living with another human inside you, because he will never go away. Drink, and learn to control him. Discover his strengths and weaknesses too, for you will always be susceptible to them. So when it comes time to eat flesh again – and it always does, for a man who has eaten flesh is never sated – next time you will be ready to be master of your guests.'

I hear Eoin deep down, struggling, shouting, but whatever the old man had done shut him up.

'Those who are awakened by alcohol or other things come with their own dangers. That is why you must drink,' Silverio says. Then he laughs.

Thirty years on this earth and me never a drinker, and now I was being instructed to start. Strange enough it all was, me only trying to be some kinda priest.

The next morning, Eoin was alive and well and singing, as me and

Anuncio cavorted through the woods on horseback, passing a gourd of Silverio Cato's maize beer between us. We stopped for lunch under a large oak, heating manioc cakes and beans given us by the tribe, and we ate and we drank and we sang, Eoin too, and then we got to talking about killing and eating men.

'How many men have you killed, Anuncio?'

'Seven,' he says.

'Did you eat all of em?'

'I ate three.'

—Pair o'sick bastards, Eoin says.

'Why did you eat only three and not the others?'

'We eat only the powerful ones. If you kill a strong man, it is good to eat his heart. Then you have strength of two. But if you kill a coward or a weak man, you do not eat him. He will not make you stronger, only weaker.'

—Hear that? Lucky one of us had some balls. *All opinion, the brother*.

'These men you ate – you took only the heart?'

'Not only. We can eat all of his flesh. If he is strong, we eat the muscle. If he is intelligent we eat the brain. Some shamans eat the penis, if the man is sexually powerful…'

I blush. —You're only a half-man, Eoin says.

'… or the eyes if he sees well. Tongue, if his words are sharp. We eat many things,' Anuncio says.

'So if I find a very intelligent man and eat his brain, I will become very intelligent?'

—Jaysus…

'If you know how to control the spirits. You must learn the art of avaporú. You must know the power and how to control it.'

'Can you teach me?'

'Silverio will teach you. He will call you when it is time.'

I nod. 'How many men has Silverio eaten?'

'I do not know. You cannot ask this. I can tell you these things, because you are avaporú and you must know. But the more men you eat the wiser you become. You will learn when to stay silent.'

So I shut up for a spell and drink, and listen to the whistles and chirrups and scratches of the jungle, and Eoin shuts up n'all and we all listen together, not two men but three – no! Not three men, but six, for I was two and Anuncio was four, and I listened intently to see if I could hear Anuncio's other spirits but I heard nothing, only scratches in the trees and the presence of Eoin, who was perhaps learning to be still, or was it me that was stilling him, willing him to be silent and do as he was told? I didn't know. I felt I was getting there. All I had to do was keep getting drunk. Soon I'd master it.

We arrived back at the estancia several days later. Brother Theodore met us in a state of childish excitement, having received a family of seven into the reduction only a day after our departure. The family had fled a distant farm due to reasons they hadn't disclosed. Theodore dragged me off to meet them immediately, and perhaps I was a little too keen in my reception of them, for I fell down at their feet and kissed the earth, and told them that truly we were building God's house here on this earth. Even Theodore was surprised. Of course, I was wild drunk on maize beer, me and Anuncio having hit it in the morning due to lack of clean drinking water, and so we arrived back at San Ignacio more than a touch cut.

'Are you alright, Brother James?' Brother Theodore said. He took me by the elbow and lifted me from the ground.

'Yes, Brother. It's been a difficult few days. I'm merely joyous to see you all.'

—You're fucken cut son, Eoin said.

The bastard brother. Hours later still hawkin in my ear.

'How did it go? You know, with the mission?' Brother Theodore said.

'I'll tell you all about it later,' I told him.

And we all greeted each other affectionately, before Anuncio drifted off with the new family to get acquainted.

We sat down altogether that evening for supper. Diego and Brother Theodore and the father of the new family, Juan, had spent two days finishing our dining room. A long, spacious room next to the kitchen which up til then had lain unused, had been cleaned out and repainted, and the three men had repaired the enormous mahogany table, which now sat centre of the room and easily accommodated the fourteen of us round it. Yes, we ate well and happily on rice and vegetables and chicken, with a breeze coming in through the window at my back, me at the head of the table, Brother Theodore at the other end, occasionally sharing a look of satisfaction and pride at the fruits of our labours there in the jungle.

Later I sat outside with Brother Theodore, the two of us drinking tea, and we discussed my foray into the jungle to meet the Guaraní.

'So are they open to coming down to us?' he said.

I inhaled meditatively. 'It's going to be difficult. We'll need to persevere. The tribes there have been hurt terribly by their experiences in the past.'

'Like what?'

So I told Brother Theodore what Silverio Cato had told me, about the slavers and the Spanish and the priests leaving and all the whole story. He listened with sadness.

'That is a terrible tale,' he said.

I shook my head remorsefully.

'Do you think we can convince them to join us?'

'With God's will,' I said.

—You dirty, filthy, drunken liar, said the voice, faded and deep down, almost inaudible.

'God willing,' said Brother Theodore, nursing his cup in his hands.

I awoke the morning after our return shortly after daybreak and looked outside and saw rumps in the field, the rumps of women and children, rising and falling with the toil, the toil of peasants, of working people, and something about it made me think of Ireland and my father and mother, and the rump of my father as he came up lifting a sod or with a spud in his hand, or the arse of my mother as she stooped to examine the sow, and to hell with it, I put on my boots and I went out there and got down in the dirt with the women and the children and spent the day with my hands in the soil, smiling and digging, throwing clods at the children, amusing the women, stopping for lunch or for a drink of milk in the shade, and the menfolk came to look at me crawling around on my hands and knees, and right quare they must've though me, us, the Jesuits, men who didn't take wives and who did the fieldwork. Sometimes I would come up, head above the wheat, and find myself staring at the big rump of one of those fine women, and the haunches of their thick brown figures could be seen through the white cotton of their dresses, their thick arms and shoulders glistening in the sun, and maybe it was the scent, the aroma of their sweat reaching me on the air, but I'd think about touching their thick flanks, their hard, fleshy flanks, hard and brown, and soft too, for they worked but they were still women. And when I thought about touching those thick haunches I would stir, there would be a stir in my groin, a twitching, and the lad would start to poke up, me who'd never had a sex thought in his thirty years, never knew what it was or wanted it or looked for it, but now here in the sun with these thick brown women smelling of earth and toil and motherhood, I was feeling a man's feelings, thinking man thoughts... or was it something else? Was it Eoin's feelings, Eoin's thoughts? Eoin was a drinker and a carouser, and I'd heard it said he'd knocked one up when he was eighteen but there was an awful scandal and it was quieted down and no one ever spoke of it, and me not all that close to him I never asked. Eoin, they said, liked the women, liked them all, even the married ones. Me here in the field now, looking at brown rumps under the sun and my groin twitching – was it me or him? Jesus, I wanted to touch those women, feel the hardness of their calves and the softness of their backsides, and I wanted to push my nose into their folds and inhale their odour...

Christ almighty. I knelt and blessed myself.

17

the waters of the lake were heathen cold, and why in the name o'christ was I out fishin at this ungodly hour anyway? I couldn't tell if it was dawn or dusk, for there was a silver mist sittin over the water like a whispery skin, little smoky eddies that rolled and twisted, and the sky above me fierce heavy like, a back-sittin sky on the shoulders, me under it wonderin when in christ in would let up off me. —a quare mornin for fishin, I said, me alone, for there was no McKibbin in his boat, his auld knackered rowboat, time-served and sturdy, daily on the water scoutin for salmon on her was McKibbin, not there today though, just misty auld me, misty-eyed me, and but for me there were none other. and no salmon either by the looks of it, for my basket was empty, and I looked out sore-like in the direction of my line, where below the lure swam cutshimmer through the dark water, the fish shy-like below, that sly auld salmon of wisdom just waitin and watchin, oh yes, a sly one her, won't come up for any auld lure, she must be teased with prayers and soft whisper and fairy word, and I had, I'd whispered on the lure the words that were needed to hook the girl, and I knew it was only time was needed to reel her in. so to help things along I sang an auld birch song, a rambunctious auld Sweeney song, sung sweet the swirlin eddies, and whaddayaknow but the sky came up off my back and across the water I saw the wall my own brother'd built from the lip of the lake up the rollin hill where the auld widow Biddy had her home, a home with no fire but plenty of fish, and they said she'd eat them raw when the auld fella came back without the firewood, drunk on the firewater he loved so, so taken was he with the sweet fire of the poitín.

I dunno what Biddy was eatin, but it wasn't the salmon of wisdom, for the salmon'd not be caught on her hearth, but I'd have her, cause I knew the songs and the fairy whispers, the prayers that'd take her up outta the water. and so the sky lifted up off me and me free to cast n'draw, out and in and out, and soon I was tired so I laid the rod on the earth and had a bite to eat, a bit o'pork and a husk o'bread, fine eatin on a cold mornin, and I looked out over that lake clean over the glassy water to the other side, my eyes followin the wall, straight it was, by christ he could build a wall the brother if he could do anything, straight as the shaft of a longtail up the side of the hill into the sky, a great wall it was. so I turned over on my back and craned my neck and looked at it upside down, still straight as pike, but now the lake above me and wall droppin towards the sky like a stair into the grey, but there was no denyin it, whatever angle you took it from it was a straight feckin wall, pardon me, missus. I rolled over on my belly and ate the last of the bread there on the dewgrass, and sat up and scratched my head and marvelled at how the auld drunk of a brother could see straight enough to put up a wall like it, bless him.

no bitin this mornin, nah, the line pure idle, so I reel her in and hold the lure in my hands, and maybe she's not the one for the girl of wisdom, so I swap her out with somethin more pure-like, less frisky, less of an *erin-go-bragh* in the water more of a *settle-down-sally*, less swim more sail, easy now, just let that song sing and the salmon'll do the swimmin, so I put her on, my lazy little silver girl who goes crystal through the water on the pithy song, and I give her the words as it comes to me then, slivers of roewhisper, on the air or I dunno from where, but I hold my little silver girl to my lips and whisper it slow,

spitsilver girl with spin-crimson tail
cosmhuil do ghnúis ergna iarn-ól
spear-like through the water, songspun
do rosg rogormadh mar ghloin

mar oigreadh seimh snúadhamail;
slow and winterlong the song
that calls the sunwise salmon
who sleeps below...

a shimmy sung on crystal whispers it was, whispered it I did into the ear of my little silver girl before casting her out into the lake. out she went, the silver of her sleek spine broke the surface of the grey water, her red tail deep disappeared, down deep where the salmon sleeps. *oh girl, I wish I could hear you sing...*

down she went and the mist swirled, frantic now, spun eddies on the surface of the water, thinspun eddies like whispering mouths, terrifyin for a simple man like me, but they tell me the salmon doesn't come easy, but come she did, for I felt her on the line, she pulled and darted and whipped, but that auld fairysung magic had her, the silver girl had her – *christ, I'd like to hear you sing silken-like* – whipped and slithered she did til her head crested, dark hair riversleek, shoulders like polished blackwood, comes up and looks me in the eye before dartin below, but I've a good line and she's not goin anywhere, and I'm up on my feet sure, reelin her in til she's on the rock on her hands and knees, riversleek tresses, salmon-pink silken guise, and eyes, *christ-a-man*, eyes look at me and she's the girl, *do rosg rogormadh mar ghloin*, blue-silver all a-go like, not for a man like me to be stood over her, so I sit down assfirst on the grass. swims up to me she does, tressed and salmon-like, shouldersung and hipslither, me all agape, me never seen the cold shin of a flesh woman in my puff, now she's crawlin up on me salmon sung, I can smell weed and dandelion and woodsmoke and salty rashers, and is that the smell of a woman? sure I've never been close enough to know... she's dark as the water and she crawls up on me, —afraid? she says, —only moments ago you were singin me songs, and I say, —you're quite the woman, like, and she sniffs at my hair and my face, the locks of her clingin now to my own neck like river grass, grippin me cold-like her black tresses, and —ever heard the song of the river? she says, and —no, I tell her, —the river that laps at the belly and washes a man clean? she says, and her hand slides between my legs and *woowee-jaysus-love* where ya goin, slow now, but no, she's up on a man all riverlike, and what can I do but I grip the haunches of her, those hips like a mule's, hard and hardenin the muscles, wrap a man clean and squeeze the life outta him, *ooh-wee* and the great backside slides into the two palms of my hands all wet and quiverin, *there's somethin for a man*, I'm thinkin, *isn't that what all the fuss is about*, my own brother Eoin they say he's a man for it, he'd know what to do, me all ham-fisted and shiverin, and the tit's at my chin, she pulls the gown down now and slides one of them into my mouth, —there's life there for a man, she says, and I know there is, cause the man is alive, and I suck on the brown tit of the salmon of wisdom, no wiser me but there's fire in a man, then she spits in my eye and licks it off and I taste her salmon breath, while the hand is down into the trousers and takes the haft of me, and —jaysus no, I say, and she says, —you took yourself down the river and this is where it leads, she says, —into the river with ya, and she sits on me and I slide in, a river alright, slide in and sail upstream, me and the salmon of wisdom on up we go, cold and wet and clingin to the water's edge fore we lose ourselves, but I'm already lost, she has me, so I pull at those haunches and bite into those brown shoulders, and a tongue slides into my ear all the way in, right into my head, and I hear the song I whispered to my own silver girl, comes back to me now on gypsy breath, soft at first, sad, then low, til coldwild she's screamin in my ear, and a river runs from her and the waves explode over me, *sweet-fucken-christ* I see it, once a great flowing ocean from between her thighs, and I close my eyes and open them an age later and it's just me, me by the lake with my trousers round my thighs and belly sticky, and I wept out loud for the salmon of wisdom, me a man who sat by the lake his whole life and never knew the true nature of the salmon.

That's how I woke, woke in the bed of my small cell, undershorts round my thighs and belly sticky and a great pain in my groin, and outside the night cicadas fibbed and hummed, fibbed, and I wept the salty tears of a man lost on a bleeding continent surrounded by a dark, unending ocean.

February, 1848

18

Me and Anuncio travel to Córdoba high on maize beer and smoke. 'Studying', it's called, Anuncio showing me the spirit ways, the ways of the flesh-eater, the way of the avaporú. We're on the horses, and we take a smoke and Anuncio says to me,

'Close your eyes.'

Eoin's going on in my ear: —Gonna listen to the brown fella, close your eyes on a fucken horse, ya fool?

I do as Anuncio says, close them, the horse under me at a steady pace, footfall fine and the breath heavy, I can feel the lungs of the horse fill between my legs, and, if I listen closely, the beat of his enormous heart in his chest.

'Don't listen to the horse,' Anuncio says.

'How do you know what I'm thinkin?'

'Listen to yourself.'

'How do I do that?'

'Start with the breathing,' he says. 'Just listen to your breath – in and out.'

So I do, *in out, out and in*, the sun on my back and the great beast beneath me.

'Breathing,' Anuncio says, and he's on it cause I was back thinking of the horse, so I get back to the breath, *in and out*, and soon it's my own lungs I feel, Eoin nagging away all the while, but the more I feel the breath the more he starts to settle, and he says, —Any quieter and ye'd be asleep, but that's the last thing I hear him say, cause he quiets right down. I'm way down in my insides feeling the heart pump and the blood flow, the taut muscles soften, and I know the horse is underneath me and carrying me but it's like we're one, and I still feel the sun but it's shining right through me, I feel it course through my insides all warm like, and then it feels like my body is separating, all the wee pieces floating away, tiny little bubbles popping in the warm air.

'Yes,' Anuncio says. 'Now ask your brother something.'

'What?' I say.

'Something only he can tell you.'

And what can I ask him, but I ask about putting up walls. And it comes outta him, it does, in a great river: —In the fingertips, son, feel the cuts and the crags and the course of the granite, or the cold clamminess of the fieldstone, mucked with earth and moist with dew, a great pile of rock to be fingered and clawed and caressed, there it is, not in the eye or the level but in the hands and fingers; thus the stone talks to ya, tells you where it will lay, how it will slumber in the bedrock – embrace the sandstone or the granite, and sometimes a polished auld sea stone, watershorn of its edge, for walls need eyes too, how else would they keep watch over the field...

A great mad diatribe comes outta him about stone and walls and building, and I feel the madness of it as if it was my own, so I jump down off the horse as we're passing a great boulder next to the track and I embrace it, press my cheek against it, claw it with my fingers, inhale its cold odour, feel it pulse like something living, and I know then unmistakably the artist that my brother was.

Anuncio comes down off his horse, sits down behind me. And when I come up from the rock, having filled my senses with its arid wisdom, I turn round to see him smiling at me, and I get it now, what he's been trying to teach me for the last two months.

'When we get what Silverio asked for, we'll go back to see him,' he says.

A hundred kilometres in three days on the horses, and we arrive mid-afternoon at the Colegium Maximum, sweaty, hungover, probably still drunk. I've been summoned by the Father Provincial, the brother in charge of the oversight of the six estancias of Córdoba. We are greeted by a Franciscan at the gates of the university, a great sprawling building in the centre of that fine town, not frightening like Buenos Aires but welcoming, a place where people live and love and work. The brother helps me down off the horse, me a little unsteady, and he looks at me with concern.

'Are you alright, Brother?' he says.

'Must be the sun,' I tell him. 'And the travel.'

I hear Eoin laughing deep down, not entirely mastered yet, the brother: —Sun. Lyin prick.

'It's hot weather for travel,' the Franciscan brother says.

'It is,' I say. 'Do you have somewhere we can stable the horses while we're here?'

'I do. Follow me.'

We set the horses up with a bit of hay and some water, and the Franciscan sends Anuncio off with another Guaraní to find something to eat. He goes, and I see the drunk twinkle in his eye as he leaves.

'Brother Rodrigo thought you may have arrived yesterday,' says the Franciscan.

'I saw no advantage in driving the horses into the ground,' I tell him. 'I'm sure one day either way'll make no great difference.'

'I suppose you're right. Brother Rodrigo will want to prepare lunch for you, so I'll take you to get cleaned up and I'll inform him of your arrival.'

'Thank you, Brother.'

I cleaned my face and made myself presentable, and some forty-five minutes later I was led into a parlour where, seated with a book in his hand, Brother Rodrigo Rubio-Salamanca sat. He closed the book and took off his glasses, and stood to shake my hand.

'Ah! Brother James Carmichael, is it? The missionary who knows no Spanish,' he said dryly.

—Cheeky cunt, this one, whispered Eoin.

'You've heard of me?' I said.

'Brother Oliver in Buenos Aires told me of your meeting,' he said. 'You made a fine impression, I can tell you, even if you don't know the local tongue.'

'Did I? I'm pleased to hear it. How is Brother Oliver?'

'I can't say he's happy in the city. You know what's going on there, don't you?'

'I saw it with my own eyes.'

'Terrible thing.'

'It is.'

'You must be hungry. Follow me.'

'Three months you've been with us,' said Brother Rodrigo, when we'd sat down after dinner and I'd given him an account of the estancia in its current state. 'You're still a long way off achieving full potential.'

'It's very early yet,' I said.

'Clearly. But we had Brother Jacob here last week from Santa Catalina. He informs us that almost sixty Guaraní have joined him on the estancia, working men and women, and he has already planted twenty-five squats of wheat and has cleared six acres of land for maize. With all due respect, Brother James, your reports of a few pear and quince trees just don't impress.'

'Our mules are breeding happily,' I told him.

'Yes, you said. But please remember, the money is in the crops. Alta Gracia is introducing tobacco to its crops this year – good money in tobacco. You must diversify, Brother James. Think big. The Jesuit operation here one hundred years ago was an economic powerhouse. We can only spread God's word to the continent if we have the economy to back it up.'

I nodded. 'Yes, Brother Rodrigo.'

'Tell me more of the families that joined you already,' he said.

'Nice folk. The children are young, but the parents work hard. The native women really know their way about a field,' I told him.

'The children aren't working yet?'

'They do their bit.'

'You must get them into the field. These children need to be started young. God knows they don't get any discipline at home. Get them out and working, Brother, and by the time they're sixteen they'll be a real asset to you.'

I took a hard look at Brother Rodrigo. I saw now what he really was; he wasn't a missionary here to spread the word, he was a numbers man, an accountant. He wore the garb of the priest but he was a pen and paper man, here to balance the books. Make sure nobody was outta pocket. I didn't despise him, he was far too plain a man for that. But a look round the room where we'd just eaten told me that he suffered no hardships, was not accustomed to such and did not foresee any in the future. He was fat and contented.

With the benefit of my new learning, I wondered how it would be to eat such a man. More eating on him than my brother, for sure, and tastier, I imagined, all the good eating he got here, like the turkey he'd just treated me too only an hour before. Probably was fond of the pork, too, and no doubt treated himself to steak whenever it pleased him. Tastier yeah, but what would he bring me? What powers would eating a man like this bestow on me? The power of numbers, the power over coin – is that something I needed? Maybe he had other strengths too; he could speak well, certainly – did I need the gift of speech? Maybe he had his tongue up the Pope's arse, or whoever's it was landed him this fine position here in Cordoba, while our brother down in Buenos Aires was afraid to step outside the door. Could I eat a man who liked to get his tongue up arses, had a gift for licking holes? Maybe I could. But did I want to?

'You mentioned a trip up into the jungle, Brother? Tell me more about it.'

'Yes, Brother Rodrigo. I went up into the hills above the estancia with my guide, Anuncio – a good man. We visited a tribe of Guaraní who'd been settled there for some time.'

'And were they receptive to you?'

'They were very kind and hospitable. But as to moving down to the estancia, I didn't feel they were ready and willing to make the jump. They seem happy there.'

'It is easy for the simple to be happy, Brother James. All they need is a fire and some rice and they won't lift a finger. You're here as a missionary, are you not?'

'Yes, Brother.'

'And what is your primary purpose as a missionary?'

Condescending prick. 'To spread the word of God,' I said.

'And spread it you will, Brother...'

I breathed in, and deep down I felt Eoin rise up. —Don't like this cunt at all, he said.

'Nor do I.'

'I'm sorry, Brother?'

'Nothing, Brother Rodrigo. I'm just tired. Sometimes I talk to myself.'

'Yes, well. As I was saying, I trust you were fully equipped with the tools of the missionary when you completed your training. And if your tools are not sufficient, there are ways that we can help you,' he said.

'What do you mean?' I said.

He pursed his lips. 'I am confident you won't need any assistance, Brother James. You seem like a capable young man...' —*Fat prick.* '...and we have every faith in you.'

'Thank you, Brother.'

Brother Rodrigo picked up a glass of wine, sipped from it and put it back on the table, dabbing the corner of his mouth with a napkin. 'You'll be staying the night with us, yes?' he said.

'No, Brother – actually, we'll be leaving right away. We have some business to attend to outside town.'

'Business?'

'Nothing I'd trouble you with.'

'I can't say I understand, but very well.'

'There was one other thing, Brother Rodrigo,' I said.

'Yes?'

'Could I have the use of the library for an hour?'

The Franciscan led me outside where I found Anuncio sitting, back to the wall, drinking tea. He sat with his usual stoic gaze, philosophical, unforgiving. He looked up at me as I approached. He seemed to intuit the results of my foray into the library, nodding, yet asked anyway.

'Did you find it?'

I looked round me before reaching into my robes.

Anuncio looked at the book, eyes revealing something of the value which it held for the old shaman.

'Silverio will be well-pleased,' he said.

'And you? Did you get what you went for?'

Anuncio lifted his hat from the grass to reveal several gourds, the contents of which were calling out to the both of us. I'd never been a drinker in my younger years, but now, with the things I'd learned and the quest to silence my brother, and the heat and the new pace of life and just the good old buzz of that maize beer, I was getting a taste for it.

'Get the horses, and we'll get shiftin,' I said.

We set off from the Colegium, day's work done. We'd camp for the night on the edge of town, drink ourselves happy, maybe smoke a little jungle leaf, sleep like jaguars and be back in San Ignacio in a couple of days. I liked the town but was more comfortable at the estancia. Perhaps it was the fugitive in me, perhaps the farmer, but I was eager to get back. Anuncio led us out through the fine streets: low, pretty houses, some brick and some mud, not a bad living at all, better than Ireland in every way, and in the windows of the houses linen curtains fluttered, all colours, red and white and yellow, and heavy Guaraní women stood in doorways, sweeping or shooing children out from under their feet into the street; guachos passed us in the road barefoot, smoking and peering out from under wide hats, walking in twos or threes, sometimes on a mule, or Spaniards on horses in fine coats high up off the road, looking down on the rest of them, but not me or Anuncio cause we were up on horses too, eye to eye with them. And when half a dozen militia passed us as we turned outta town, I saw Anuncio slow, come to a stop, and I came up beside him, his face ashen, him a black man and the colour just sucked outta him, ghosted. I stopped.

'Anuncio?'

He couldn't speak.

'Tell me, Anuncio.'

Nothing. He turned the horse around and went right back after them.

19

We tailed them through town. They stopped at a pulperia for an hour then got back on their horses, and we followed them due south where, out five hundred yards ahead of us in a small copse by a river, we saw them get down and make camp for the night. Anuncio got off his horse too, and so I followed, and that's when he told me.

'That's the man who raped and killed my wife,' he said.

I looked at him. I can't say he had murder in his eyes, that's not how he looked. He looked at peace. But I guessed there would be murder.

'Wait here,' Anuncio said. 'And watch.'

'Where ar—?' But he was on his horse and away.

So I tied my horse to a tree and sat down. It was getting dark, sun dropping down behind the treeline, but I watched the copse in the distance, a small fire soon sending smoke up through the trees and the occasional whinny from a horse, and I watched til it was dark and the only thing I could see was the crackle of the fire.

Anuncio came back several hours later. He sat down beside me without saying a word. We sat in silence for a spell.

'Anuncio,' I said, 'you know I'll do what I can to help you, but there are six of em. There's two of us.'

'The others will sleep like the dead,' he said. And he pulled out his pouch and showed me what was inside.

I don't know what time it was, maybe two or three in the morning, but Anuncio left me and snuck down to the camp to dump his strange brew on the fire, and minutes later he fell in beside me again.

'What if it doesn't work?' I said.

'It will work,' he said.

Ten minutes later he handed me a cloth, and took another and wrapped it round his head covering his mouth and nose, then took me by the arm and we crept down towards the camp over the grassy hill, thin night above us and the sound of the cicadas all around, the night soft and alien and afraid. I followed Anuncio down to the river, where we entered the water up to our knees and crept upstream, pausing when we saw the horses, which were tied to two trees about thirty feet from the fire, and we left the river and snuck up through the brush and came up behind the camp where the men lay on bedrolls scattered round the fire. Anuncio looked at me and pointed to one on the outside, the closest to us but in between two others – our man. The heavy stench of whatever Anuncio had thrown on the fire stole in through the cloth round my face, a stench like the jungle weed we smoked but with something else, something fouler; it stuck in my throat and my head felt heavy.

Anuncio flicked his hand, directed me towards the bedrolls, and I crept up on one side and he the other, and we came up next to the three men laying side by side, and no hesitation we took him by his two arms. I looked down at the soldier on the other side of him, his eyes on me, looking at me like he was awake but kinda sleepy, scared the shit clean outta me but he didn't move, no shifting outta him, too far gone on Anuncio's jungle poison... still, his eyes froze me rigid they did, til Anuncio shoved me and we got to pulling and dragged that militia fella from his bed. Anuncio untied one of the horses then we trussed up the guy's hands and feet and tossed him up on the saddle. Then we walked him right outta there, no shooting, no protest.

We just kidnapped a man.

Anuncio's by the river getting water for the horses. I'm sitting in front of the soldier, him looking at me. It's high morning, hot, and we're in the jungle about twenty miles outside Córdoba in among the trees, quiet, far from anyone anywhere. The soldier's trussed up, gagged and sweating like a mule. He wants to kill me, but there's fear too in his eyes. He doesn't know what's happening. He was kicking some earlier, but he's settled now cause Anuncio has him tied up good and he knows he's not going anywhere. A cool fella this one, doing a good job of keeping his fear down. He eyes us, watching.

Anuncio comes back up from the river, so we take the gag off the soldier to water him. A torrent of abuse falls outta his mouth, he spits at Anuncio, so Anuncio slaps him, ferocious like – *crack!* The palm of his hand against this fella's sun-roughed cheek. Stuns him. He gags him again. Soon as the gag's on the guy recovers, starts thrashing and kicking, so we step back and leave him go, rolling round like a savage on the ground. We watch. Hands tied and gagged, he wears himself out. We wait. Sweating and grunting, he gives up, rolls over on his back and stares at the sky through the trees. We all sit quietly.

'Friend's just trying to give you some water,' I say in my muck Spanish.

He swears.

So me and Anuncio sit, wait and watch. He sits up. He's black with dirt now; it cakes the lines of his face that have filled with sweat, dirty black creases across his leathered face and beard clogged with clay. Still murder in his eyes, though.

Anuncio takes the gag off again and the fella keeps still, so he lifts the water to his mouth and feeds it to him til he chokes. Anuncio sits next to me. The soldier stares bloody murder.

Anuncio smokes, and having nothing else to do, I drink some beer. I'm curious to know what Eoin makes of all of it, so I summon him for a bit of talking. He emits a low whistle. —Some shit you're into, he says.

'Isn't it, brother.'

Soldier looks at me. Anuncio knows the score.

—Gonna kill him?

'I suppose we have to now,' I say.

—I suppose you do. Looks like a hard bastard.

'Not much fight in him with his hands tied behind his back.'

—Aye. There wasn't much fight in me when you put the pillow over my head.

Eoin's lost some of the fire he had before. More sedate in his outlook.

'Water under the bridge, brother.'

—Gonna eat him?

'I reckon we will,' I say.

'Who's he talking to?' the soldier says, looking from me to Anuncio. He's spooked.

'The last man he ate,' Anuncio says.

Proper spooked now, he is.

'*Que?*'

'He eats men,' Anuncio tells him. 'Eats their hearts.'

The soldier spits at him, spits at me, so Anuncio lifts a rock and nails him on the side of the head with it. He spills over, sits up, blood running down his cheek into his beard. Now he asks us what we want with him, but my friend's letting him stew, and I can see Anuncio eaten with the hatred, he wants to kill him now, but the guy needs to understand first. Needs to know. Anuncio turns him over on his belly, pulls off his boots, then his trousers and his undergarments and throws them into the bushes. Now the fella loses it. He sits up and slides away from us.

—Your friend's gonna cut his balls off, Eoin says.

I say nothing, but I know he's right.

Anuncio sits down and keeps smoking, and the guy's slithering away towards the bush, so I get up and grab him by the feet and drag him back. I kick him in the ribs.

—You're not the same man at all, Eoin says.

I guess I'm not. I'm two men now.

The guy starts growling, a strange animal howl, face a mess of blood and muck. I sip on the maize beer and feel strangely peaceful.

Anuncio gets up and walks into the trees and comes back with a big stick fresh broken off the tree. He stands over the soldier. He looks at me and I know what he's asking. I'm alright with it. So I get up and take the fella by the shoulders and turn him over on his belly and he starts squealing. Anuncio takes the stick, that sharp end just fresh broken and shoves it into the guy's arse. Sticks it up there, rips the guy open, pulls it out. Screams murder, the soldier does.

—Jesus-fucken-Christ, Eoin says.

Blood pours out his arse and he shits himself. Anuncio tosses the stick away. The guy spits and screams, but he's weeping too. Knows he's gonna die. Doesn't wanna die in the jungle bleeding from his arsehole.

We sit down, let him empty it all out. He weeps into the earth.

'*Porque?*'

So Anuncio tells him. He sits down next to him, whispers close into his ear, says all those things that've been sitting with him for years, the rage and the shame and the blue-fucken-murder and the hate, pours it into his ear like tar.

—Can't say he hadn't it comin, Eoin says.

'*Por favor...*'

But the time for begging's long gone, and Anuncio lets his words seep into the soldier before he gets up and sits on the soldier's belly, then he takes that big Indian knife of his, long as my forearm with the big bone handle, and he grips the balls in his hands and slices them clean off. We watch the guy go off. He screams, eyes hopping from his head, frothing at the mouth, but the blood is leaping outta him and he starts to pass out. Before he goes though, Anuncio takes the soldier's head in his hands and squeezes him tight, and says, 'Nothing of you will be left on this earth.'

And he caves his head in with a rock.

We stand over the bloodied body as the last of him leaks into the soil. I pass Anuncio the gourd. He takes a swallow and passes it back.

'Help me cut him up?' he says.

We're not long at the job. Two men working on a body get things done pretty quick. Anuncio cleaves the limbs from his torso with his machete, and I get to work carving them up while Anuncio opens up the chest. I see it all come out: lungs, kidneys, heart... Anuncio parcels each in some old sack we're carrying and wraps them up nice.

'For eatin?' I say.

He shakes his head. 'I can't eat the man who killed and raped my wife.'

'Isn't it custom to eat your enemies?'

'Enemies we kill in battle, yes. Brave enemies. Not animals like this man.'

'And those?' I point at the organs.

'For Silverio.'

'For what?'

Anuncio shrugs. 'To keep, to work magic.'

The old man and his big basket of body parts.

I look at the leg I'm in the process of cutting up. Anuncio is watching me and he knows what I'm thinking. 'You eat,' he says.

And I want to. Yes, I do. Now I've gained control of the brother's spirit and can call upon it at will, I want more. I wanna eat this man to see what power he gives me. And not only him, I want others too. I wanna keep eating.

'I'm gonna eat him,' I say.

Anuncio nods.

So we finish the cutting and we dig a hole, and in goes the head and the hands and the innards and the rest, Anuncio's got his parts and I've chosen mine, I'm gonna eat the ribs and part of the thigh, cause he had good strong legs this fella and it'll give me strength, so we fill in the hole and cover it up, then we get a fire going. I'm gonna cook him on stone, so I get a big rock and toss in on the fire, and in about forty-five minutes the thing is hot enough, so I put my steak on there, cut nice and fine like, the scent of seared meat filling the jungle. I give it just enough on each side so it's perfectly done, little bit reddish in the middle still, then I sit back and eat the bastard. I eat his flesh and I drink maize beer, and I'm thinking, maybe I shoulda said 'no' outta respect for my friend, but Anuncio is alright with it and drinks with me. It comes back to me then, the taste of the brother, except this meat is richer, more aromatic, the soldier better fed. The brother's meat was tough and bitter but this rough old soldier tastes the part, not bad at all. Missing some salt is the only thing. I eat the leg then the ribs, and when I'm done eating we drink some more and smoke a little too.

I am sated. Quiet within, quiet without. The jungle round me goes silent, breathes with me... *in, out*. Sweet repose after a full belly, but Anuncio's not hanging around and wants to get moving.

'The soldiers may track us,' he says.

I want to sit and breathe the jungle, but Anuncio's not having it.

'Let's move.'

Alright, then. We pack our horses and bury the fire, and cover all traces of our presence, and before we go, Anuncio spits on the grave of the soldier, and what can I do, but I nod solemnly. *We'll talk soon enough*, I'm thinking.

And as we canter away towards San Ignacio, me full and sleepy and peaceful on the back of my horse, I know it, sure as that bastard is dead in a hole behind us, I know it: I am an eater of men. I am avaporú.

20

We went straight to see old Silverio Cato. Anuncio had his gifts and I had mine, and we found ourselves sitting in the hut of the old shaman, and one by one Anuncio took out the organs he'd harvested from the soldier. They were rotting already, the heat of summer having gone at them hard, but it didn't rattle Anuncio or the old man. He unwrapped them, laid them out on some clay plates, and put them in front of the altar where the body of the dark angel Zucchero hung. Heart, lungs, kidneys, he laid them all out, then set about praying over the altar, some kind of chant, me and Anuncio sitting in silence behind him.

When he was done, he turned and sat down with us, and I understood it was time to hand him my offering. I placed the book in his hands, and he ran his hands over the dry leather cover of the tome and closed his eyes. When he opened them, he looked at me.

'Do you know what this is?'

I didn't know, but I could guess. I'd had a look at the book after I'd located it in the library. It was some kind of botanical work or collection, with sketches of plants and trees, some of which I could recognise from my time here, some of which were unknown to me, and alongside the pictures were formulas, recipes. It was a book of medicine. Perhaps something more.

'No,' I said.

'Some of what is in this book you will need to know,' he said. 'The avaporú has particular needs that other men do not – one of those needs is a knowledge of plants and their uses. Other spirits live in you; the more spirits live within you, the more difficult it becomes to control them. Plants and herbs are the keys that nature gives us to help us control the spirits. You will need to learn how to use them.'

'How long will it take?' I asked him.

'It will take as long as it takes,' he said. 'The knowledge cannot be rushed.'

'I have duties at the estancia also. I cannot be here all of the time.'

'You come when you need to. You will have to decide, sooner or later, what your true mission is. Are you really a priest?" he said.

'No.'

'Then sooner or later you must stop pretending, and do what you have come here to do.'

'What is that?'

'I do not konw.'

And neither did I. But I suspected it involved eating more men.

'Now you've eaten another, it's time to teach you a few things,' Silverio said.

Silverio mixed up a brew, showed me how. We drank it and I fell ill right off, and came down with cramps that I thought would cause my stomach to rip open. This went on for an hour, or it felt like it, but when the cramps passed and I stopped sweating, I ate the paste he gave me and passed out on the ground and came round in the jungle, sitting by a fire with my brother, the soldier, and a great scaled animal like a lizard, longer and bigger and with a huge mouth of razor teeth. In its mouth was a human arm, its teeth laced with flayed flesh. Blood dripped from its jaw. I could smell its rank breath across the fire.

—What in the flyin fuck are we doin here, Eoin says. —And who's that fierce fucker?

He points at the big lizard fella who's chewing on the arm.

—His name is Teyú, the soldier says.

—And you? What's your name? I say.

—Antonio.

—You the rapist? Eoin says.

Antonio says nothing.

—I think we need to get it outta the way, Eoin says. —If we're gonna get along n'all.

—I think you're right, I say.

Antonio nods. —I did. I raped. Many women and girls. I'm a soldier, that's what we do. I have no regrets, nor am I sorry for what I did.

—Maybe you should be, Eoin says.

—Maybe you shouldn't be pointing any fingers, Eoin. You're no saint yourself. Maybe you didn't rape any women, but you certainly fiddled with a few married ones from what I heard, I say.

—That what you heard, is it? he says.

—Aye.

—No harm in it, he says. —I didn't have a knife at anyone's throat. This one did.

—Wanna go at it? Antonio says. He speaks with a Donegal accent, like Eoin's and my own.

—Enough, I say. —He's a rapist, you're an adulterer, let's forget about it.

—And you, brother? What do we call you? Cannibal?

—Avaporú, the lizard says.

—It speaks, Eoin says.

The lizard tosses the arm from its jaw and looks at me. —What do you say, avaporú?

It, too, speaks like a muck savage from the West of Ireland.

I nod. —I'm a cannibalist. I eat men.

—Maybe if ye'd ate a woman or two in your time, you wouldn't be so fucked in the head, Eoin says.

—Like you, dirty dick?

—Ah, go away...

And then we all get to giggling, stoned like, and look at each other across the fire and smile, and Teyú the big lizard blows on the fire and it turns green, and the green leaks up into the sky and now the sky's all green flecked with purple, and Teyú starts to sing,

—do rosg rogormadh mar ghloin
mar oigreadh seimh snúadhamail...

—Hey, I say, —I know that one. That's the song of the salmon.

—That's the song of the gypsy, Teyú says.

—Who's the gypsy, now? Eoin says.

Antonio starts rubbing his thighs all perverted like and whistles through his teeth.

—Oh aye? Eoin says. —Quare one, is she now? So how do we get her round the fire with us?

—Naw, she's not for the likes of us. The gypsy's no jungle woman. Wouldn't be caught dead sitting round a dirty fire with a cannibalist and a rapist and one who fiddles with married women, Antonio says.

—Yeah? And just what kinda gypsy is she, too good for the likes of us? Eoin says.

—I have to find her, I say, it coming to me then. —I have to find the gypsy.

Teyú laughs, the stench of raw meat wafting around the fire.

—I'm right, I say.

—You're right, Teyú says. —You need to find the gypsy.

—Why?

—Because the gypsy has knowledge you require.

—What knowledge?

—The knowledge that every avaporú seeks. The wisdom of the Book of Dying, Teyú says.

—Hold on a minute, Eoin says. —If it's only an auld hoor with a book you're after, I'll get ya a hoor with a book.

—I'll find you two hoors with two books apiece, Antonio says.

And we laugh, Christ, we laugh like fuck and roll around, Teyú the big bastard lizard singin the song of the gypsy, and I lie back and think of strange gypsy women with books, next to me Eoin thinking of hoors reading books with their legs spread, and across the fire Antonio's thinking of writing a book on all the hoors he's raped, gypsy or otherwise, and Teyú, well, he's thinking of eating hoors.

—What's your story anyway? Eoin says to Teyú when we all get done laughing. —What are you all about?

Big lizard Teyú Yaguá opens his mouth wide, and inside we see a great valley teeming with bountiful trees, and animals of every kind cantering and galloping through the lush grasses, and above it there in the green sky a blue sun and all around a song like a celestial music which makes us weep. All this, we see and hear inside the mouth of Teyú.

—People pray to me, and I provide, Teyú says.

—What, like a god?

—Like a god, Antonio says. —The Guaraní worship Teyú.

—And what do they pray to you for?

—Meat and tea and long life, Teyú says.

— Quare fella. Isn't he? Eoin says, looking at me.

I smile. —Slow and winterlong the song that calls the sunwise salmon who sleeps below, I say.

—Fuck's that now? Eoin says, but hearing the words, Teyú has opened up his mouth again, and I see the valley and its joyous bounty, and for no good reason I crawl over the fire and into his great maw, scrambling down towards the valley, but it only gets darker and the valley recedes, and I'm only crawling deeper down into his belly cause I can smell the great stench of rotten human flesh, and under me the dissolving bones and teeth and the skulls of his feast, auld Teyú, well eaten on men and women. The god of the avaporú, auld lizard head, deathbreath – how deep is this belly anyhow? I keep on crawling till I find myself in the hole I crawled outta, that auld hole in Donegal, bog walls and a fireplace, empty pot on the cold fire, and who's there but the ma, still sleeping, so I pull the shawl up round her and lie down in my own corner, straw for a pillow, dry cowshite the mattress I lie on. I close my eyes, and when I wake up I'm lying on the ground outside old Silverio Cato's hut, the sky above me blue again, covered in shite like I've been rolling round with the pigs right enough, and Anuncio's looking at me, laughing... he's laughing now alright, me head to toe in shite.

'What happened?' I say.

'You made some new friends,' Anuncio says. And he points to a pig pen off in the distance.

'You mean I was in there?'

He nods, laughing.

'And you let me?' I said.

He holds up his hands, *Far be it from me*, as if to say.

'Jesus Christ Almighty,' I say, and me a man of the cloth, head to toe in pig shite.

The door of the hut opens and old Silverio steps out and looks down at me, not laughing like Anuncio, just looking at me all serious like, and I look back.

'So, who did you meet?' he says.

'I met Teyú,' I tell him.

And he just smiles. Like that's exactly what he wanted to hear.

21

I started to lose all interest in the estancia. I was there in body, doing my best to engage with day-to-day duties, but in spirit I was elsewhere, head in the jungle, or in old Silverio Cato's hut putting together his strange brews, and I thought about Teyú and strange gypsy women. Women – that was the thing was eating my mind. Mornings I went out in the fields and puttered about on my hands and knees just to get a look at those Guaraní women crawling around, rumps in the air; possessed me, it did, the thought of gripping their ample buttocks in my hands, and I knew it was Eoin or Antonio, their ways bleeding into me, the brother an adulterer and Antonio a foul raper of women, and hard as I tried the methods Anuncio and Silverio had taught me, I just couldn't keep the thoughts down, they were too strong in me, and they rose up mornings when I would take to the fields, or evenings, Christ, when I lay down in my bed by starlight, gentle sounds around the estancia, and if there was the laughter of women, my poor unused member would swell between my legs til it was knocking off my belly, and I'd lie there in pain and rage til the urge became too great and I'd have to pull the prick off myself, lying there in the bed of despair, me a man who'd never known a woman.

I made opportunities to walk by them in the kitchen or when they washed the clothes, just so's I could smell the sweat of their labours; that earthy, acrid smell made me hard, and I'd inhale it before finding a quiet corner somewhere where I could beat the bishop, as I'd heard them say back in Ireland, and beating the bishop became a daily thing, often several times in the day, me prowling round the estancia like a filthy dog in heat looking for women to sniff or eye or get close to.

One night I broke down in tears and prayed. I prayed for the foul organ between my legs to behave itself, to do my bidding, to submit to the will which I tried without success to impose upon it, but I soon discovered that the wayward pizzle submitted neither to God nor man, and so I was condemned to wander the corners of the estancia with a furious hoary animal between my thighs. Eoin started referring to it as my ladle: —Your ladle needs dipping before you do yourself some damage, he told me, and to Antonio it was a cudgel, and many's a foul thing he instructed me to do with my cudgel. Try as I might, when it came to the women, I couldn't shut the two of them up.

To mix up matters, around this time, there wandered into the estancia one day a single woman with a young daughter. Salome Yaguarete her name was, and we came to learn her husband had been killed in a farming accident, at least that's what she told us, being a little coy she was as to the nature of her predicament. Salome was younger than the other Guaraní women on the reduction, age like my own perhaps, but as short and hard in body all the same: thickset, heavy-thighed from labour, generous bosom, mother that she was. She was a simple sort, and you could never be sure if she understood what you'd said. Even when they spoke to her in the Guaraní tongue she'd a strange air about her, but this dreamy way of hers gave her the look of purity, in her eyes a dull, warm and sweet look, and the first time I looked into those brown eyes of innocence I knew I was going to suffer for her.

Brother Theodore accepted Salome Yaguarete into the embrace of our estancia with his usual joyous abandon and I met them outside the kitchen as I was coming back from the fields. Wound up I was from watching the women plough the earth in the morning sun, the old devil on my back and Eoin and Antonio howling in me, and when Theodore called me over those brown eyes had me right from the off.

'Brother James, would you believe it? The Good Lord has sent us more believers! Meet Salome, and — who's this?' He looks at the young girl.

The girl is shy and hides in her mother's skirts. 'Teodora,' the mother says coyly. She looks at Brother Theodore, then to me, then at the earth.

'Praises,' I say, having nothing else to say, but I'm looking at the mother, trying to catch her eye again, and my own eyes drift down to her bosom, heavy, rising and falling with her breath, then on down to her waist. The daughter has her arms wrapped round her mother's leg, and the thin cotton of her dress is stretched tight over the ample thigh, so that I see the curve of her inside leg all the way up into the holy darkness between her thighs, *Christ save us*, and Eoin is getting all hot, saying, —Boys, I never saw a sweet dark angel like the one I'm seein now, and Antonio's howling a dark animal anger, the wolf out, and I'm trying to keep it down, keep them down, and it's all too much and I start sweating.

'Brother James?' says Brother Theodore, looking at me queerly.

'Ah? Yes! Welcome... you're alone, are you?' I say. '*Tu es solo?*'

Confused, she shakes her head and looks at her daughter.

'No, no,' I say. 'No husband? *No tienes marido?*'

She shakes her head. Then she gives us the story about the accident. My heart melts. *I'd like to hear you sing, singswum silkenlike*, it comes back to me the dream, the dream of a woman climbing up on me and making me howl and the river and the lake, and an ocean between dark brown thighs, and Christ my heart is going ten bells...

'Brother James?'

I snap out of it. 'Yes?'

'I was asking where we'd put them. Perhaps in the room behind yours?'

'No! I mean, yes. Of course. Perfect for them...' My outburst alarms everyone.

'Alright then. Let's show you to your quarters, and then we'll get you something to eat, shall we?'

Salome looks at me as she goes, smiles softly, and takes her daughter by the hand and off they go, and Christ I watch as she walks away.

Brother Theodore's joyous and ardent conviction infects everyone. New faces coming in, and not only Salome and her daughter, but another family also, two days after. The numbers growing, our family expanding. It occurs to me that if it continues like this I won't have that old bastard in Córdoba on my back about not hitting the numbers to sustain the 'economy' of the reductions. Old prick. If things keep going like they are, we'll be the equal of Santa Catalina or Alta Gracia in no time. We might even get things back the way they were a hundred years ago.

'Isn't it wonderful, brother,' Theodore says, catching me after a morning watching Salome at work, her taken to the fields like a true Guaraní and working the earth with her hands and her back, and didn't I just crawl up next to her in the soil, getting on my knees, just so I could smell the milk and sweat of her dark brown body.

'No, padre, you mustn't,' she'd said.

'Oh yes, I must,' I said. And I took potatoes from her hands, her fingers brushing mine, and—

'Are you listening, Brother James?'

'What?'

'I said we'll need to start building new accommodation outside the walls. The main building can no longer hold any new members.'

'Of course. We'll get Diego on it right away. Maybe now we're showing signs of growth we can get the labourers back for a month.'

'Well, that's what I wanted to talk to you about. I've arranged to start out for Alta Gracia with Diego this afternoon, to ask them if we can borrow some manpower for a spell. That means you'll have to say mass this evening, and for the next three days.'

'It's mass day?'

'Sunday. Yes.'

'Brother Theodore, I think it's best if you leave me do the runnin—'

'I insist, Brother James. I've been waiting for an opportunity to get out to do some ornithological studies in the jungle. We've been here for six months, and I still haven't had a chance.'

Him and his bloody birds. 'Brother Th—'

'The arrangements have all been made. There is no problem, is there?' Brother Theodore, high and happy, is looking at me all expectant – how can I say no?

The voice of Eoin rises up behind his laughter. —Fucken mass? How ya gonna say mass, ya rare prick?

Six months here and I've not given a single service, cause I've been at the helm, Brother James Carmichael, designating work here and there, running around, keeping on top of things. As far as I was concerned Brother Theodore was here to the priest's thing, like praying and mass and confession n'all that. What do I know about it? But it's true, ya gotta let the horses run free once in a while. Then there's Salome...

'Sure, Brother Theodore. You go plead our case in Alta Gracia. I'll keep things running while you're gone.'

'Thank you, Brother James.' He gives me a great smile.

'Enjoy yourself. Enjoy the birds.'

He rushes off to pack his bags.

'Welcome to mass,' I say later that evening. Like that's even a thing priests say. My flock look up at me, puzzled and bemused.

'*In ainm an Athair, agus and Mhic, agus an Spioraid Naomh, Amen.*'

More confusion. I'm just saying what I heard the old ma say for years, me having an antipathy towards church in general. Julio, Diego's young one, who's altar boy for the service, is looking at me pure confused; his routines are all shot, doesn't know what he's doing, cause I dunno what in the name of Christ I'm doing. Poor kid.

'We are gathered here today...'

And I ramble like a fool for the next twenty minutes, no idea what I'm saying, and at one point I tell them, 'So I'll tell you a little story...', and I ramble on about two brothers who were dying and condemned to eternal suffering, and the one, realising he wouldn't make it gave his life for the other brother, so the other brother got to leave this life of misery and enter the kingdom of heaven.

—You sick bastard, Eoin says. *No controlling him, not with my mind on other things.*

"And the moral is,' I tell them, 'there's a fella in the sky waiting for us all, and he'll do anything to save our souls, cause he's like a brother who'll lay down his life for us with no thought at all for himself because he's his father's son...'

—You're a pure gobshite, ya are...

And on and on I go, spouting all the shite that comes into my head: '...and the Lord shall save us and turn us around, cause he never turns his back on us cause his back is strong like the holy dove's...'

Pure dribble runs outta me and I've lost the flock, they're looking at me pure panicked, like, *What's happened to the padre, has he lost it?* and yes, he certainly has, cause now he's talking about holy mules and even holy swine, God's own beloved. So I figure it's time for the food, and I gesture young Julio to get the bread and I dig out the wine, and I bluster through the holy sacrament – *hoop and whistle, give us our gristle* – course I don't say it, but I'm thinking it, and I hold aloft the Holy Juice and give praise, and the congregation are all standing, *Yes, we give praise*, nodding and repeating what I say like fools, 'And this is my body,' I say and I eat the Holy Cake, 'And this is my blood,' I tell them and I imbibe of the Holy Juice – *Ooh-wee!* goes Eoin – and I step forward to deliver it to the souls of the flock. 'Take my body,' I say and place the Holy Cake in their mouths, feeding the five thousand, or twenty in this case, but then Salome comes up and kneels before me, and suddenly I notice the sweltering heat of the church, the walls closing in round me, the roof descending, the buzz of insects, beads of sweat running into my eyes, and she's kneeling there and looking up at me, big brown eyes of innocence, pleading for my body, so I feed her the Holy Cake, the tips of my fingers brushing the warm saliva of her tongue, so close I feel the warm whisper of her breath, and I see her bosom rise and fall, —She wants a stab of the Holy Ladle, Eoin says, and I hear the groans of Antonio deep down, and between my legs I feel the ladle twitch – *Christ almighty, not now* – me standing at the front feeding them with the Holy Cake and the lad twitching on me, so I dish out the last of the cake and dash in behind the altar, before the faithful get an eyeful of the suffering of our Lord.

'In the name of the Father and the Son and the—'

—Sweet sufferin Jesus, would ya get the fuck on with it! Eoin says.

And I wrap it up double-quick, giving the holy sign of the cross and blessing the believers, and when they've all backed out the door in confusion, I rush to my room to indulge in a touch of self-worship at the holy thought of Salome.

'I think I found the gypsy woman,' I tell Silverio on the next trip to his abode.

'If you met her, you'd know,' he replies.

'She has me under a spell.'

'A man has two heads, padre: one is in communication with the higher, and one with the lower. Be careful not to confuse the two,' he says. 'You know what I'm talking about, don't you?'

'Yes,' I say. 'But this woman has somethin about her. I think she's the woman I dreamed about.'

'There's only way to know for sure.'

'How?'

'You must find Kurupi and ask him.'

'Who's Kurupi?'

Silverio tells me about Kurupi – like Teyú, one of the gods of the Guaraní – who lives in the abode of the spirits. I have to go find him.

'You know what you have to do,' he says.

22

I prepare a 'trip south', as I come to think of it. I have all the makings, Silverio has me well-stocked and versed in the arts of preparation. *Caapi* is a fickle girl. Gotta be handled nicely, doesn't like sloppy work. She needs to be fixed up right, so I wait for dark, when I can sneak into the jungle to do my cooking. The estancia sleeps early, about half-eight, and by nine o'clock everyone's down, so I sit at the desk and check my satchel, make sure it's all there, everything I need for the pot. A single candle burns on the desk, and while I wait, I write in my book, pouring it all out onto the page, about the jungle and caapi and the Indians, and about Indian women and women who smell like earth and milk, and dreams of gypsy women who crawl up on me from the water, pour it all out I do, and that notebook bequeathed to me by Father James Carmichael is starting to swell with the fine adventures of a wandering mick from the West of Ireland.

The flame flickers at my movements making shadows dance on the walls, and I hear the sounds of the estancia: a door creaking, hushed voices behind walls, animals stirring. Jungle sounds too, the cicada over all, and unknown cries and whelps. I lay out my makings on the table: my chacruna and my barks, the punga and the ayahuma, and the ilex that is Silverio's own addition to the brew, it's all there, so I wrap it carefully and back in the satchel it goes, and when the estancia goes quiet, I snuff out the candle. Darkness lives, with a little starlight coming in the window and the moon not out yet, so I take my iron pot and duck outside, me in my bare feet like a native, over the courtyard and out the gate I go, and round the back and into the trees.

I've chosen my spot, about five hundred metres other side of the church, deep in, where far from human eyes I sit under the blue jacaranda, dig a pit and prepare a small fire. Lovely, out there. Night sounds and dull air, and a blue veil above my head lit by starlight and whispers in the dark. *Simmerin, nightlike, under the jacaranda.* I build the fire and light it up, rustles from the jungle as the fire sparks, and the flame lights the tree up purple, me under the purple cowl in the dark night of whispers. I place three rocks round the fire and set the pot on it, and add the water and the chacruna. I let it boil and simmer and take its time, then I add the bark, and while I whisper to the brew a little friend shows up, a capybara, a big lumpen rat-like thing, friendly sort, sits down beside me by the fire, and I knew something was coming out tonight that's why I put a pear in my pocket, so I take out the pear and slice it up and give him a bit – the little fella loves it. *You're alright little fella, you're alright. Sit by me awhile, tell me a story...* And I sit there and cook up my brew, and I imagine what kind of tale the lumpy capybara might spin for me, a tale of dried leaf beds and lapping rivers and night smiles, so I blow him a kiss and keep feeding him pear and we decide that we'll be friends. I call him Lumpy: 'Lumpy'll be your name, fella, and it's a very fine name, so don't let it get you down.' Me and Lumpy eating pear and cooking *caapi* and having a fine old time of it out here in the jungle. 'Know what, Lumpy? Ever had a taste of the *caapi*?' And I consider feeding him some, but he's an animal and doesn't need the holy brew. Sees it all already, he does.

Me and Lumpy under the blue-purple jacaranda, whispering to the night, and soon we'll be whispering to Teyú, and maybe Kurupi if he comes out, and I'm sure the boys will be there too, singing songs round the fire, talking of women and pricks and maize beer, talking of cudgels and ladles and sticking them places and the best places to stick them, and where a man might best dip his ladle without trouble or woe. These are the things the men are talking about round the fire, and soon I'll be round it with them, and they'll be asking about Salome, and when I might have a stab at her, seeing what she does to my auld priesty-prick.

I add the ilex. Stirring and singing, singing and stirring, and whispering to Lumpy who's still there at my side, taken a liking to me he has, or maybe he just likes the pear and knows a good thing when he sees it. Auld Lumpy. I feed him the last of the fruit. *Let's see if you stick round when the food's gone*. Stirring, stirring. The mixture turns pulpy, the caapi thickens, another half-hour and it'll be done. Caapi. Female. Has the spirit and heart of a woman. Fickle, testy. That's why her embrace is so bittersweet. She takes you deep places, buried places hard to crawl outta, where the animals hide, Teyú and Kurupi and *who-knows-what*, even capybara is down there in a man's soul and that's why he likes us. Capybara is a part of a man like the rest of them. Drink the caapi and soon you learn all about it. Animals, spirit guides, down deep and listening...

Boiling for hours now, the caapi thickens. I raise it off the fire and let it cool, Lumpy still by my side, and now and again eyes peer from the darkness, friends, shy ones, won't approach the fire but like the company all the same, even if they'd rather sit back and enjoy it from a distance. Just fine by me. We're all friends here.

The caapi cools and I strain it off, and I've got my brew ready to go, so no hanging about I drink it down, Lumpy watching, knowing what it's all about, seen it before the lumpyboy, knows what men do in the jungle. It's not long before I'm retching, spilling my stomach out into the earth, and that's when he flees, he knows what ghosts rise from a man's belly, so he scarpers off into the jungle, *See you soon auld Lumpy friend...*

My guts spill onto the carpet of the jungle. I am cleansed, ripped open, emptied. And then I'm being dragged down into myself, down to the place inside me, away deep where another me sits under the blue jacaranda, one who is not confined by the constraints of time and space but can flit here and there, talk to the dead, talk to the animals, and find out about all things in the jungle if he knows who to ask or what to ask. Yes, all things are known to men and beast alike.

I blink my eyes at the sky, the sky green above the blue jacaranda, but there's no fire and no Eoin and no Antonio, but Teyú's there... I can't see him, but I hear him breathing and I can smell his breath, auld Teyú rasping in the dark, —Teyú? I say, and he chuckles auld Teyú does, —I'm looking for Kurupi, I tell him, and Teyú says, —Where you find the women, that's where you find Kurupi.

So alright, I wander off into the jungle, can't see but the jungle knows the way, and the jungle whispers in my ear and I wind through the trees, the eucalyptus and the ivy and the mimosa, only one path through the jungle when it comes down to it anyway...

I come to the hut, a lonely hut in the jungle like Silverio Cato's, all hung with vine and orchid, dark and queer, and I open the door and it's empty inside, smells musky like a man all goat and semen, but there's no Kurupi and no women, no one and no thing.

I go back the way I came, green sky above, back to Teyú where there's now a fire and Teyú's chewing on a nice thick meaty leg, and I tell him, I say, —Kurupi's nowhere to be found, and he says again, —First you find the woman, then you find Kurupi, so I tell him, —I found the woman already – the woman is Salome, but Teyú doesn't reply, just goes on chewing on the leg.

I lie down on the earth and when I wake up it's morning, and I'm rolled up by the fire and it's cold but my pot is there, so I tidy up and bury the fire and leave a little quince for Lumpy, and make my way back to my room as the first light wakes the believers.

23

I spend the morning in the fields, hands down and arse up, and occasionally I rise to watch Salome crawl through the rows of potato in her white cotton dress. Her little girl, Teodora, is skipping through the cabbage patch beyond the spuds, waif-like, joyous, oblivious. Blessed thing. She's younger than Diego and Jacinta's two boys, only six, and now we've a family arrived only two days ago with a boy of five and a child only six months old, and the three older ones of the Ocariyu family that arrived a month ago. Eight children now, fifteen adults, our enterprise still growing slow but steady. Building has started too. I can see new homes rise from the ground beyond the fields – small, simple mud huts but homes nonetheless, homes which'll house those families who do the farm work. Salome will probably move out there too when they're done. I don't want her to; I like having her other side of the wall, hearing her sing soft in the night to the child, or rising with a tired and happy yawn in the morning, or sometimes I hear her whisper out the window and I don't know if she's talking to the birds or the trees, or Christ, maybe she's singing soft little words to Lumpy. Maybe she talks to him too or one of his fat little friends. She's wild somehow, Salome. Feral. Of the jungle.

I rise up on my knees, sun on my back, blue sky above scattered here and there with cloud. I breathe in the earth, the warm scent of the jungle beyond, Teodora humming and giggling somewhere, and the boys Santiago and Nicolas chatting loudly as they lug a basket of carrots between them. The chatter of the builders drifting over on the breeze, a whiff of tobacco smoke, a horse snorts; Diego shouting at his wife, his wife shouting at him, then the two of them laughing; Brother Theodore, hiking up his robe to step over the mule shite to collect their feed buckets, more comfortable in the church than in the field and that's just fine with me. Then a little cry from Salome. I get up dash over and fall on my knees next to her. She's gashed her finger with the trowel.

'Jesus, what have ya done?' I say.

'Nada,' she says.

'No, no – come with me,' I tell her, wrapping a tissue round her finger, and I take her by the hand and lead her towards the store room. Next to the kitchen we got a small room for supplies, and I take her in there and she rests against the table as I dig out the bandages.

'Gimme a second here,' I say, and I dig out the little box of medical supplies and open it on the table next to her. 'Gone and opened your finger, you have.' I take her hand, hard and calloused and dirty with earth, and now blood pooling in her palm, so I clean it down softly as I can, rubbing it with a wet cloth. A speck of blood has fallen between her breasts, which rise and fall as she watches me work, her breathing heavy.

—I'd be questioning your dedication to the priesthood right about now, I hear Eoin whisper. Right on cue. Any opportunity for a bit o'filth.

'I'll just clean this up a bit,' I say, blabbering.

She looks at me, mildly amused, or confused, I dunno. Breasts rising softly, the smell of milk and papaya off her.

I rub her finger with a bit of iodine, she winces, I flinch, then I take a bandage and wrap it tight around her finger, holding her hand just a little too tightly.

'Gracias, padre.' A little smile.

I feel it now, no hiding it, the prick between my legs wakening.

In ainm an Athair, agus and Mhic, agus an Spioradh—

I'm trying to fight it, she senses it and looks down and sees it, the swelling between my legs, pressing against the pants. She puts her hand to her mouth, looks me in the eye, then reaches out and pinches my prick gently between her thumb and forefinger.

'Jesus!' I cry. I step back, then freeze.

—Don't be letting the side down now, Eoin says. —This is it, you gotta whip the ladle into her now boy.

—Swing that cudgel, Antonio says, and I can feel the heat rising in the two of them.

Still frozen, I watch as Salome lifts up her dress and drops her undergarments, and slides up on the table and opens her thighs, and I see it for the first time, thirty-one years on this earth and I see it for the first time, the tuft of thick curly bush, the holy darkness between her legs, and I look in her eyes and she has the look of the jungle, the gaze of Teyú, hungry and implacable, and she holds out her hand and I take it, and she pulls me towards her.

—Good man yerself, Eoin says. —Give her a stab of the Holy Ladle.

—Beat her with the cudgel...

I fight down the voices of the pair of them as Salome opens my trousers and takes a hold of my prick, swollen and cudgel-like, and opens her legs wide, the smell of the ocean now, and she guides me in and coils her legs round me, the sweet embrace, brown eyes and wet lips which I taste and suck on, the smell of milk on her neck and the earth in her hair, and I hold the dark vine-like flesh of her legs and bury my head in her breasts, and I drown in the perfect river lapping at her belly.

'People are talking,' Brother Theodore says to me a few days later.

'About what?'

'About...' He can barely say it. 'About Salome... and *you*.'

'What exactly are they sayin?'

He's too timid for confrontation, but it's his godly duty to address it. 'That, you know, you're always around her when she's in the fields, or helping her at her other duties, or carrying things for her.'

—Gonna tell him ya stuck her with it, are ya? Eoin says.

'I dunno what you're suggesting, Brother. All I'm doin is helpin one of our sisters here at the estancia...'

—Dipped into her right good...

'...a woman with no husband of her own to help her out with her daily duties...'

—dipped right in the honeypot and stirred up the ladle—

'Well, that's just it, Brother... do you see yourself as a replacement for her husband?'

—So sweet and sticky...

'Of course not. How can you even suggest it?'

Brother Theodore gives a nervous little cough. 'I'm only telling you what people are saying. I think it's best for everyone if you... *spread* your support a little more evenly around all of our brothers and sisters.'

—Is he sayin what I think he's sayin?

'I appreciate your lookin out for me, Brother Theodore. But I can assure you there's nothin to what people are sayin. Maybe you should just ignore foul rumours. God knows the truth.'

—Now that's just low...

Brother Theodore nods. He doesn't look sold on the matter, but it's clear there are more eyes round here than what I imagined. I'll have to stay low.

I wake up in the morning next to her. The smell of milk and papaya and warm sweat and sex. It's still dark, so before I go I push my nose into her thick, black hair and breathe her in. Milky, with a smoky air. She stirs but doesn't wake. I take a last nose around before climbing outta her small, single cot, and I pull the sheet up over her shoulders. Over by the wall Teodora's sleeping night-heavy, and I climb into my trousers quiet like and put on my shirt, and before I go I sit on the chair in the dark and listen to the two of them sleep, the sounds of repose, sleep whispers and a low moan, the twitch of an arm, maybe the shadow of a dark dream. Ever since I started drinking the caapi I see shadows at night, the shadows of thoughts, they move round me as I lie in the dark and I see them now, purple and red over the head of Salome, green over Teodora, like smoky night messages from the place of dreaming. If I sat and watched, I'd see pictures there too, but it's getting on, so I get up off the seat and peer out the window, make sure no souls are wandering, and when I see it's clear I nip out the door and follow the wall to my own room and slip inside.

I'll have to get up soon, but I lie for a while, no sleep, just watch the blue trails drift up off me, not like smoke but fine and misty like, dark as the colour of the Atlantic where Brother James Carmichael lies, down there in his rooms, his resting place, where the dark tendrils of God seep down to the depths and embrace the faithful, all those who died and never made it to the other side, now held in the eternal cold embrace of the Lord. So Brother James Carmichael would have it. That's what he would say. But he's not here, not here in his estancia at San Ignacio, preaching to the faithful of the Holy Catholic church, preaching the good word to the savages of the New World. He didn't make it. He died at sea, and was reborn, avaporú, first as two men and now three, and how long before he becomes four, and five, and seven men? Or women; how long til I eat a woman? That's what I'm thinking as I lie in bed. Or a child... or, Christ, a baby? Where does it stop? But these are dark thinkings, and I turn my thoughts to the woman lying on the other side of the wall, Salome, dark and holy and smelling of papaya, and what happens now for me and her – stay here and sneak back and forward every night, her already with a child... and if she gets knocked up again? Brother James Carmichael and his lover, a bastard in her belly, the little bastard of a priest and an Indian girl, Hiberno-Guaraní, the first ever perhaps, and what would the world make of that? What then... run away, go to California and dig for gold, and build a house by the river and make more little bastards, little Irish-Indian bastards, the seeds of the New World?

Great man you are, Brother James Carmichael. A fine thing you've made of yourself. But then, aren't you happy? Or, if not, can't you sense a happiness just over the hill, peering out from the jungle, calling you gentle, like the fat little capybara might holler at you from the undergrowth... can't you hear it, soft on the night air when everyone's asleep, a whisper, an absence of sound, and contained in that absence the things men desire, and don't you know that a man's needs are simple... can't you hear it? Aye, it's there. Try n'grasp it and it flits away, so don't try, just be silent and listen. Let it find you.

With these fine thoughts, I start to drift off, and those old blue wisps become stronger, my eyes close and I sink, the old whispery wisps wrapping round me, and pictures come, not jungle pictures but sea pictures: a boat, Teyú in the water swimming by, me rowing, and up ahead of me the shore, Salome there and Teodora, and in her arms what looks like another child – my child? I dunno, I keep rowing, soon I'll get there with Teyú by my side... it's only plain sailing after all.

24

'We need you to go to Buenos Aires,' Brother Rodrigo says to me next time I'm in Cordoba.

Not what I was expecting. I was expecting a warm welcome and fine praise, our little enterprise in the jungle now grown to forty-five people and no need even to hassle the jungle Indians, them happy in the hills. We grew all by ourselves, families drifting in from the surrounding areas, hearing about our holy works, families evicted from farms or just wandering, looking for work and a roof. Forty-five and growing, and we're well proud of it, but this fat accountant is still picking.

—Maybe we'll eat the fat prick after all, Eoin says.

—Eatin him'd be like eatin poison ivy, Antonio says.

'Can you pass the gravy, Brother?' I say.

He looks over his shoulder at the servant, who lifts the ceramic bowl, circles the table, and dresses the turkey handsomely with the rich sauce. Eats too well, this big tub of Jesuit lard.

'We have a brother coming from Madrid to oversee further expansion of the reductions around Cordoba and beyond. Brother Rackham would like you to meet him off the boat. He'll be assuming direction over San Ignacio and the other estancias after his arrival. You're in a good position to bring him up to speed on developments thus far.'

'What makes you think we need intervention in the estancias?' I'm losing patience with the fat clown.

—Let's eat the bastard, Eoin says.

'Brother James, population in some of the estancias pre-expulsion was 1500 or more. While we don't envision a return to those kind of numbers, we do expect the reductions to grow to at least sixty percent of what they were in those days. You've had half a year now. We can't say that you're making the progress we expected of you.'

'And have the others?'

'Well, no. None have. That's why we're bringing someone in.'

'Brother, might I suggest that you come see the estancia for yourself? I promise you'd change your tune if you only saw it with your own eyes.'

I'll get him on the road in. Fat bastard'd be travellin with an escort, so we'd have to confuse them somehow, set them running, maybe stage an attack, a highway robbery to set the horses fleeing... then, when he's isolated, chase him down and run him off his horse, hogtie him and get a fire goin, and he'd start to put two and two together and get all jumpy. Take out the big knife, lay it down by the fire so's he can see it. Round about now he's gonna start weepin, so maybe we take the gag outta his mouth so he can beg and plead for his life, and plead and dribble snot and make a dog of himself, then we'd take him and lay him out and start peelin back the layers, the robe first, then his underclothes, til he's laid out all fat and white and flabby, mound of sweatin pink flesh gatherin dirt as he rolls around on the ground, hands tied behind his back and gettin filthy, the muck smeared across his face as it sticks to the tears and the snot. We'd have to wipe him down, ceremonial like, and maybe tie him by his feet and hang him from the tree, have to be a strong tree mind, fat prick that he is... and let him swing there for bit, flailin and swingin, til he got all pink with the blood coursin round his body, face red and filthy. The time would come and I'd pick up the knife, and I'd take it to his throat and hear him beg, then I'd say the last rights, 'This is my body, take and eat of me...' and I'd slice his throat and bleed him like a stuck pig, the last gurgles of him lost to the great heaviness of the jungle where nothin stays in the air for long. Bleed him out then cut the rope and drop him to the floor, and put those knife skills you've learned to good use. Soon after, the eatin—

'More turkey, Brother?' he says.

'No, thank you.'

'Well, I think we're beyond that,' he says. 'No need for me to be dragging myself out into the jungle, now is there?'

—Fat shite only drags himself from his bed to the table, Eoin says. *We'll have to find another way to eat him.*

'A shame, Brother Rodrigo. So when is the new brother expected to arrive?'

'In three weeks' time. You'll be at the boat to meet him. You're going to travel to the city in the meantime, stay a few days with Brother Rackham and take a good look at the direction of the estancia going forward. Of course, any steps towards the development of the reductions will have to be run by Brother Xavier when he gets here.'

Brother Xavier. Maybe we'll eat him, too.

I'll be leaving in a few days but I say nothing to Salome. We're lying in bed around two in the morning, she's stroking my chest, whispering little sweetnesses into my ear, soft so as not to wake Teodora, now in Spanish, now in Guaraní, but it doesn't matter which language she says it in, these are the kinda whispers which make a man melt in the darkness, fingers in his hair and lips on the lobe of his ear, shiver sounds dripping into him liquid-like from warm lips.

'Es tranquilo,' she says.

'Si. Estoy feliz.'

'Si?'

'Si.'

This simple our exchange, but we haven't need of more.

'Me amas?'

'Si.' Just that.

I revel in the silence. Even Eoin and Antonio are mute; nothing to say, for they've no heart the pair of them to disturb the quietude. Rare the moment, and I retreat into the silent core of me, listening to her breathe and feeling the touch of her on my skin, buried safe down, alone but not.

'Mi cielito...'
'Si?'
'Que vamos a hacer?'
'No lo se.'
'Quieres familia?'
'Si.'
'Podemos familia.'
'Si.'
'Lo quiero.'
'Y yo.'

A finger probes my ear, then my lips, then my neck. Chest and nipples. Belly. Balls. My prick hardens.

I'm goin to the city,' I tell Brother Theodore the next day.

He nods. 'Perhaps it's for the best.'

'What does that mean?'

He blushes. Shakes his head and moves off towards the church. I'm standing holding a chicken. A live one, and it's flapping and spitting, trying to break free from my grip.

'What are you flappin for? We're gonna eat ya later. Stop twitchin.'

—Your cock makin trouble? Eoin says.

'No trouble,' I mutter.

—Seems like everyone knows you've been wavin your cock about here and there, stickin it where it don't belong, pokin it in places where it shouldn't be.

'Fuck off, Eoin.'

I head out to the jungle with my caapi. Never been south in daytime, but right now I feel like I need the journey, need to see Teyú and find out what's going on, find Kurupi too, so I can see what to do about Salome and if she's the gypsy and if I really need to eat her. I don't want to eat her. I don't. But Silverio said I had to eat the gypsy woman, and if that's what I have to do, then how can I argue with the spirit gods?

It's hot out there, so I walk out a mile into the jungle and strip off and light a fire, and naked as the day I was born I hop around the fire and chant, willy swinging, and I drink my caapi and fall flat next to the fire. Soon I'm heaving the contents of my stomach all over the jungle floor, and when I start tripping over the other side, I thrust my hand into the fire and keep it in there.

July, 1848

25

Oliver Rackham sits by the window in the twilight, curtain parted a fraction, him peering out into the street. He sits with the gait of a hunted man. Oliver Rackham is a prisoner. All the people of Buenos Aires are. The Jesuits face no persecution, yet Rackham sits like a man awaiting the bailiffs or the headhunters. His shoulders twitch and his hand claws at the back of his left ear which is red raw from the scratching. The man is losing his mind.

'They hung a man from the tree outside only two nights ago,' he says. 'And the night before that, they found a man on the corner with no hands and feet.' He closes the curtain as a figure passes in the street below, then opens it a touch to watch the figure retreat. 'There are only butchers on the street at this hour. Stepping outside after dark is a sure sign you won't see morning.'

'I'm not sure sitting at that window is doing any good for your nerves, Brother.'

'I need to see what's going on out there. I want to know when they come for me.'

'Nobody's coming for us, Rackham. We have the protection of Rosas himself, don't we?'

'Anything can change overnight. Captains who were favoured last week are being beheaded this week, and even those in high society can be disappeared for a single word in the wrong ear. Nothing is certain.'

'I think as long as we keep our heads low, we'll be fine.'

'I need to get out. As soon as Brother Xavier arrives, I'll ask to be sent away from this godforsaken city.'

I sip at the heavy burgundy wine that Rackham has produced. His face is red and swollen and I can see he's been heavy at it. *Like Eoin in his day.*

—Easy, son...

I smile. Company is lacking in this dark house, and I let the voices rise up in me, their intentions made strong by the alcohol. Antonio likes to sit in the dark and brood. This atmosphere suits him just fine. The more I drink, the denser his silence. Eoin just gets testy.

—Tell this morbid wretch to close the curtain and sit down. Prick's makin me nervous.

'More wine?'

'Hmm?' Rackham turns to the glass next to him on the sideboard. It's empty, has been for some time. He lets off scratching at his ear and picks up the glass. I stand and fill it, and sit down.

'Why don't you go up country?' I say. 'Up in Córdoba there's no such strife. And on the estancia there are no worries at all.'

Rackham sighs. 'We'll see how long that lasts. Once Rosas wins the war, he'll spread his terror all over the country.'

'How do you know he'll win?'

'Who can defeat a fellow like that? There's not a man in the country would say a word against him, so a-feared they are. He's got the country by the throat.' He closes the curtain and turns to face me. 'I've even thought of fleeing across the river to Montevideo.'

'Aren't they under siege?'

He nods, swallows hard. 'How much worse can it be? Either decapitated here, or dying of starvation over there.'

'Come and sit by the table, Brother. Forget the outside for a bit.'

He stands up, not reaching his full height, and hobbles over. He sits down and places his glass on the table, and resumes the scratching of his ear.

'Do we have any further word on our brother's arrival?'

'Nothing. After not showing yesterday, I'm risking no more trips to the dock. I've paid a fellow down there to keep an eye out for him. I trust he'll make it here. But I'm not risking my own neck running around after him.' Rackham's face is in shadow, but it doesn't hide the twitching that has travelled from his shoulders to the side of his face. 'Do you smoke?' he says.

'No.'

'Do you mind?'

I shake my head.

He takes out a tobacco pouch and a pipe and stuffs it. I smell it across the table: rich, sweet, grassy. He takes out a match and sparks it, and *phap-phaps* on it til it glows. He flicks the match and discards it on the table, and the room fills with the tart aroma of pipe smoke.

'It's not something I ever entertained,' he says, 'but since being here, I've needed something for my nerves.' He looks over at me apologetically. 'This country has given me only vice and terror.'

'We all need somethin,' I say.

—Now you're talkin, Eoin says. —I never thought I'd hear a priest speak sense, but there's a smart one among them after all.

Antonio is humming softly, some Spanish rhythm, the tone of it gently teasing the inside of my head. Voices. Always voices. Rackham has disappeared in a cloud of smoke. A man in hiding.

'Just what would happen if we disappeared across the river?'

Rackham's head turns and he eyes me through the smoke, surprised and wary. 'How do you mean?'

'Who'd come lookin?' I'm not thinking about him. I'm thinking about me and Salome, of course. And Teodora.

'I'm not sure anyone would. Not during wartime. Maybe after.'

Time enough to disappear. Take refuge in Montevideo, by the time war ends a few years from now we'd be gone up country. Or just go straight to Brazil. Away from war and savagery and killing.

—Sounds easy, Eoin says. —A family, just like you want.

Antonio says nothing but he's thinking about Brazilian women. Hoors from Porto Alegre.

I drink and listen to the hum of the two voices in my head.

When I get up in the morning, Rackham is curled up on the sofa by the window, a glass of wine beneath him on the floor. Light creeps in through a crack in the curtain and I pull it closed gently not to wake him. The smell of stale smoke hangs in the room with a musty odour of sweat. The man must be living in here – eating, sleeping, working when the mind's on him. He truly is a prisoner. I go down the stairs and settle myself at the table in the dining room below a picture of Christ on Gethsemane. The housemaid, a plump Guaraní woman, comes in with a smile, her hands folded in front of her.

'Buenos dias, señor.'

'Buenos dias.'

'Vas a comer?'

'Si.'

'Señor Rackham?'

'No, señora. Más tarde.'

'Si, señor.'

She disappears into the kitchen and I play with my nice cutlery, not like the stuff we have up in San Ignacio – wooden, rough and workingman. Light filters in through the lace curtains from the street outside. Figures pass, voices hushed. A city living in fear, a city of brute tension. No doubt there are bodies to be disposed of this morning. Corpses. The Mazorca will have made sure of it.

The housemaid comes back and places a plate in front of me, the scent of milk off her, and I think of Salome, up outta bed she is surely, dressed, white cotton over her black body, on her knees in the field as we speak, hump rising in the warm sun, and I think of her hard haunches and my manhood stiffens under the table. The housemaid waits.

'Algo más?'

'No gracias, señora.'

She goes out to the kitchen and I cross my hands in my lap outta bare habit, and I lower my head and I say grace: 'Father, Son and the Holy Ghost, whoever eats fastest gets the most,' and I imagine Teodora

178

giggling at the end of the table, and Brother Theodore eyeing me with disapproval. *Sure, why not?*

A good Indian breakfast it is, manioc cakes and beans, and eggs just for the foreigner, so I shovel the beans into me then nibble at the manioc cakes the way Teodora does, round the outside then in, like there's some delicate secret at the heart of the cake you must approach with care, softly towards the inner sanctum lest you burst open the heart and let it escape. I giggle as I munch at my cake, then I grow bored and dip what's left of it into the egg and scoop it all up. When I'm done eating I sit back and sip at the piping hot tea. They know how to eat, these Indians. We did too, in Ireland, except we'd no food. I stand up and go to the window and peer outside. The street's quiet, few souls around.

'Algo más, señor?'

I turn round, the housemaid at the table behind me.

'No gracias.'

She smiles, and clears away the table, leaving my tea. I pick up the mug and go into the sitting room. But then I decide I'm not gonna sit, I'm gonna go out and do something, and I decide to go to the docks and see if I can't find Brother Xavier coming in off the boats. I'm not gonna be a prisoner in this house too.

Priest-garbed, I hit the streets. Fine streets they are, not New York fine but maybe Dublin, and I could say for sure if I'd ever visited. It's a fine city though, Buenos Aires, but soon I notice it on the cool air, a kinda tepid metallic tang... it's fear, it's horror, the horror of disembowelment and severed tongues and burning flesh. It's in the air. Antonio knows it, the soldier, his senses are on alert, those bloodhound soldier senses, he's awake, and I hear the word, not from him, not uttered from his mouth, but from somewhere deep below: —Sangre. *Blood.* City's been bathed in it for a long time now and I can sense it in the people who pass in the street and in their choking suspicion.

The morning is good and clean and, down the docks, the air comes in off the water fresh. All round, conspicuous by their inconspicuousness, armed fellows, Mazorca, those paid to cut throats and sever hands.

'Can I help ya, Father?' says a voice behind me. Irish.

I turn round and see a boy sitting on a crate, must be sixteen if a day, cap on his head and chewing on an apple.

'Don't wanna be messin with those boys, Father.'

'Do they trouble you?'

'I'm too quick for em, Father.' He grins and takes a bite of his apple.

'Where you from?' I say.

'Cork.'

'Cork, now?'

He nods.

'Long way from home.'

'Aye.'

'What are ye doin here?'

'Makin a wage, feedin meself.'

'Good man.'

He turns and flings the apple core into the water.

'You know where the boat from Bremen comes in?'

He points across the water to the far dock. 'Over there. May be in today, may not be.'

I nod. 'I'll go n'wait all the same.'

'Keep your wits about ya, Father.'

I cut north. It's bustling, guachos and Indians and Germans and everything else, all lifting and carrying and slinging and hustling, and I marvel at the New World, where men of every stripe are seen together and work together and break bread together, and I think of Salome and the little Hiberno-Indian child growing in her belly, and how'll he come out, or she? Black? Brown? Yellow? Who knows, but isn't it grand here in the New World where it matters not.

I find a crate and sit down and look at the water and the boats and whistle softly, an alien sound in that city, me a whistler in a city of blood, and no boat comes in so I pull from my cassock a Bible I've lifted from the house, and I open it at a random passage, falling on John, and I read:

'The world cannot hate you, but it hates me because I testify that its works are evil.'

And I think to myself, *The world isn't all that bad, for I've a job and food on the table, and now I've a woman and soon there'll be a child, and after there'll be a house with a roof and a fire and a place for us to bed at night, and who knows, maybe a little money later to make us comfortable, and I'll cast off the priest's garb and be a man, a man with a family and a real man. That's what's comin.*

But I'm making my way home and I find my way to the Plaza, and I realise my stupidity, seeing the awful truth of it, that the works of the world truly are evil, and I despise it all, Buenos Aires and Rosas and the Mazorca, and the eyes closed to it, men and women alike, the officials and the priests and the doctors and whoever else, all those eyes turned from the horror. I look at the rows of human heads on spikes, eyes open, mouths portending awful truths ripped from them in their final moments. The heads on display, the bodies scattered across the city or buried in shallow holes, men cut up and dumped on the street like offal, like discarded parts outside a butcher's. Some of the heads have kept their top hats, a testament to the depravity of their killers, ghoulish props for the entertainment of base men. I look round me and dotted about the square I see them, the cutthroats, scarlet jackets on their backs, the colour of the regime, they meander and mingle and they admire their own handiwork and behind them the people of the city cower, averting their eyes, and I hate them both, the murderer and the murdered. I hate all of them and I feel sick in my stomach, and I hate the city and the country too, and the boat that brought me here and New York, and even Ireland and my own dead brother and mother, those that spawned me and kept me alive and brought me here, all of it sick, evil and unnatural, and I understand those words finally: *I said in mine heart concerning the estate of the sons of men, that God might make them manifest and they might see they themselves are beasts.*

That night I drink with Rackham, broken prisoner of Rosas, and we get drunk on priestly wine and spew hell, hell for Rosas and Argentina and the Mazorca, and hell for the land we sailed forth from and hell for the boats that brought us here, and hell even for the Franciscans and the Merovingians and the Jesuits, hell for the priests who talked God and could change nothing, and hell for God too, for what did it all come down to if it didn't come down to God. I fed Rackham wine and loathing, and we laid a big bag of shite at God's doorstep and swore him out of it, and before the night was over Rackham was throwing curses at the Good Lord that would have brought hell upon us had there been a big fella in the sky for to hear us. Rackham swore and cursed and pointed thin fingers, then passed out on the sofa red in the face and sore at heart, and I threw a blanket over the fellow and put on my jacket.

Curfew since passed, I slipped out in the darkness dressed in black and I crept through the streets unseen, only Antonio and Eoin for company, Antonio intoning, —*Sangre, sangre*, and Eoin, high on wine and fear, for he was a never a man to put life at risk, saying, —Fuck are ya playin at, get in off the streets ya bare savage before you get us killed, and on and on he goes in my head. Antonio: —*Sangre!* he says, and 'Blood' is the name of the night, so when a carriage passes on the cobbled streets under the dry sky and the scalpelmoon, I slip into hidden corners and watch them pass, Rosas's butcher boys, I follow them at a distance cause I've no appetite for dying, and soon enough I catch sight of a carriage with the evil omen about it, and I follow it from the shadows, the smell of death on it, one fella cracking the whip up front and another hanging off the back, but it's what's inside that interests me, and I keep after the carriage through the fear-heavy streets til the carriage pulls up by the sidewalk and a corpse is flung from the back. It pulls away again and clods off down the cobbled road.

I've seen it all already, me a man not long gone thirty, and there's nothing else that'll scare me in this world. I approach the body on the street in the dark and I roll the gentleman over on his back to get a look at the fella. Still warm he is, not long dead, beaten black and blue, whatever his offence he was paid back a hundredfold, and he's got the grin, true enough, the grin of a man whose pain on this earth has come to an end. And I know what I've to do, so I roll up his sleeve and take out a razor and take a slice of his arm, and I eat it straight, no need for cooking, for I'm no longer afraid of flesh. What need has a man to be afraid of the dead anyway? None, for the dead are meat and bone only and the taint of lingering soul. I chew on his arm meat, —*Sangre*, Antonio says, knows it and Eoin too, and now I am four men. And soon I'll drink the caapi and visit the jungle, and we'll sit round the fire, me and Antonio and Eoin and this new fella, and he'll divulge all his soul, the high and the low alike.

But I'm not finished, for there is still work to do before daybreak, so I traipse the cobbles and the shadows below the scalpelmoon, hungry and alive and more than a man, for men who are one alone are only men but men who are legion are something more. I find them, one then another, and I take a cut and eat of the flesh, and before night is over I am six, and tired and sated I return to Moreno Street, where I slip inside and close the door, silence inside and out, the snore of the drunk and the whimpering sleep of the afraid the only noise disturbing the afflicted night.

26

Auld Teyú Yaguá, hungry again – he's chewing on Antonio's leg right up to the knee. Antonio doesn't mind, he's smoking a cigarillo and admiring the new folk. It's getting crowded round the fire. We're six now, and I sit down on a log and look around – *sctap!* – could be the sound of a twig splitting in the fire but it's Antonio's shin, snapped below the knee as Teyú eats clean through it. Antonio smiles. There's no pain or grief in the jungle. It's the survival of the fittest – eat and be eaten. I look over at Eoin. He's missing an arm. He's sucking on a coca leaf, and I've seen the Indians at it, sucking on the leaf – gives them power, a shot of *erin-go-bragh* right into the vein. Eoin waves his stump at me, tries to say something, but I can't hear him over the chatter. Stumpy Eoin. The fire flickers, us night-sunk among the trees, me and mine own. Through the canopy above us the fire-green sky, around us the sound of gypsy night whispers. Still with the gypsy on my mind, she comes back to me now, me in the grip of the caapi, I hear some far off diatribe, tonight a night of haunting. But while around the fire, what is there to fear of haunting? The red spitshiver of flame drives away all who would encroach: the banshee, Macha, the Morrigan, don't like fire they don't, and besides, who's coming near us when there's big fucken lizard sitting there, smiling and chewing on limbs and whispering black spells? Teyú is inviolable, and so are we. We, the six. And why stop there... we can be ten, or twenty. We are myriad, multitudinous. Infinite. Auld Teyú Yaguá knows. He doesn't ask questions, he just eats. Eat all of us, he will, Father of the world. Deus ex hominus.

Yeah, getting busy round the fire. Two men and a woman I've eaten this night, and Eoin is quizzing them on the particulars of their getting here.

—I was dragged from my bed three nights ago, says one gentleman, polite sort, well-dressed, and talking too in my own Donegal accent... all of them, mind, talking like muck savages. Eat a man and imbibe his spirit, but he takes on yours too. —and tortured and beaten, and forced to watch them cut out the tongue of my patron, and then they cut out my own and left me to bleed to death.

—What's your name, friend? I say.

—Gregorio, he says, and he goes on to tell us he's a merchant, or he was, exporting fine linens from 'Merica down to the New World. —The fine ladies of Buenos Aires do love their linens, he tells us.

—Which arm's your countin arm? Eoin says.

—What now? says Gregorio.

—Which hand is it you use for countin your money?

Gregorio holds up his right hand.

—Best watch now, Eoin says, —for that greedy big fucker there is comin for your limbs. He points at Teyú.

Gregorio says no mind, cause before he was tongueless and now he's whole again, and he'd rather lose a hand than his tongue. Teyú bows his head at Gregorio's wisdom. See? Avaporú reunites and reconstitutes. People made whole under the gift of flesh. I have saved them. There's Gregorio, and then there's Aniceto, a caudillo from the province. Rosas had his head on a spike in Plaza Victoria, with his two hands cut off and his body strung upside down from a street lamp. Now he's here, reunited with his two hands and his head, a whole man.

And Secilia. The first woman I've eaten. Look at her here in the jungle, fine dress and parasol, hat down over her face and tied round her neck, hair in ringlets and eyes blue like her dress, and with a smile that would still a banshee.

—And what of your crime? Eoin says. —What possible misdeed could have come from one so fair?

Auld wanderin dick, Eoin. Ever a man for the ladies.

Secilia whispered a word against Rosas's daughter in the wrong ear.

—And they hanged you for it?

—They strangled me to death, she says, and round the fire heads shake.

—The man has no shame! Antonio cries. —I've killed a hundred men, but I've never strangled a lady.

—But you raped a few, Eoin says.

Antonio smiles as Teyú rips the other leg from his body with a sharp twist of his scaly neck. —You can have that, Antonio says, —but you'll never take my middle leg.

He grips his crotch and Secilia giggles.

—Who gave this beast license to eat us all anyway? Eoin says. He waves his stump and turns to me, as if I've any say over the deities of this, the other world.

—Teyú is the provider of wisdom, so we give him what he needs in return, I say.

Antonio nods and holds up his bloody stump for all to see. —Take it like a man.

We are six, and soon we'll be more. We will grow and give ourselves to Teyú Yaguá and he will increase our wisdom. And I will grow in wisdom and strength, so I can do what I need to do.

A little gust of air blows outta the trees and the fire flickers, and we all get it at once, a musty goat-like smell – it hangs over the fire choking us. Teyú spits out Antonio's shredded leg, a great tongue flicking outta his mouth. And I know what he's gonna say before he says it, cause I remember that smell.

—Kurupí. Tongue flickering, he turns to nod towards the jungle.

So I get up, the jungle suddenly a few degrees hotter, and they watch me go, Eoin waves at me with his good arm. —Don't get lost out there.

I wink and I turn and wander into the trees into the dark night of caapi, fire behind me and the green sky above, but I don't need light to know where to go, for the caapi knows. It's the great teacher, for through it we know Teyú, and now, Kurupi.

As I wander forth, the stench grows, the goaty semen stench, and soon I'm back at the hut in the woods. As I arrive, he steps outta his door, Kurupi, about half the size of a man. I walk over and he sees me, and what a sight he is: covered in hair, naked, stubbly legs, and with a great length of twine wrapped round his waist. But no – he steps out in front of me and I see clearly, it's not twine around his waist but a great penis, slung thrice about him, tied like a belt round his hairy belly. The stink of goat comes off him heavy, like a rutting beast, and he grips his great willy like a belt and grins at me.

—Kurupi? I say. But I know that it is.

Kurupi stands, squat and buck-legged, hands tucked in his great belt-like prick, grinning. Flicks his head, like, *Come follow me*, and with a single hop he turns round, buck-legged he skips through the forest and I skip after him – *hoo-wee-hee!* – the creatures of the forest scatter at our intrusion, hop-skip we leap along the scattered path, nowhere we go, where we don't know, but Kurupi the foul randy goat leads and I go where he does. We leave the jungle and cross a great plantation under the ale-green sky, wanderwhither here and there, bucking and a-quivering – *hoo-wee-wee!* – Kurupi leads me out of the plantation to the top of a hill where I spot a great walled fortress below, army camp of some sort, prison of men, a place where men go in and don't come out again. But no matter to Kurupi, we go down the hill to the fortress and stop at the wall, and Kurupi takes his great cock, unwraps it from round his waist and tosses it up the wall where it catches at the top, and I know what to do, so I climb that great appendage like an Indian snake rope all the way to the top and Kurupi swings up after me. We're looking down into the courtyard, filled it is with all manner of folk, society and soldier alike, a strange mix I daresay, and I gather someone's getting shot cause right at the front there's a firing squad, rifles in hand. Soon enough the crowd goes hush and two folk are led out, one man one woman. They're stood against the wall. The man sags but stays standing, but the woman, she's pregnant, heavy pregnant and nearing birth too. Tall she is, and heavy. She loses her feet and the man holds her up, but she's not gonna make it and they bring her a chair, two men carry it out, a big hulking wooden thing.

She's put in the chair, her sitting and him standing, the crowd nervous now, don't know where to look, looking at her but trying not to, then the jailer comes out. The Chief Justice, he tells things the way they are, standing on his soapbox pontificating about decency and morals and the status quo, and about how the greatest sin against God has been committed, sins unforgivable, sins that cannot be cleansed or erased. The woman is stoic, defiant, the man doing his best to stay on his feet.

Done with his words, the Chief Justice instructs the soldiers to stand to attention, and, rifles against their shoulders, they fan out, six of them, three per sinner, and at the word they line up their guns, out straight from the shoulder aimed at the heart of the two lovers, the crowd stock still, silent, wordless, for there are no words to describe what's about to happen. Then the jailer speaks, breaking the silence: —*Disparen!* That simple, and as he says it the woman is setting to get outta her seat, she's mid-stand when the bullets cut her down, cut right through her and her man, both of them shot through the heart, the two hearts that brought them to this moment. Dead in an instant. Three lives, not two, gone, the unborn child taken also from this earth.

The crowd is stunned, the jailer silent, for he stands and stares at the woman in the chair, the dead woman in her great wooden throne. Kurupi nudges me with his elbow, points to the back of the crowd, and I follow his finger, seeing her there, right at the back, cowl round her head and shoulders, hidden from view. Hiding maybe. I see the outline of her face and know who it is, it's the gypsy, the woman I dreamed of, the woman from the lake with the wisdom of the salmon, the wisdom of the water and all things dead and dying. She's there, it's her, imbued with the power of life and death.

—The gypsy, Kurupi says.

27

Brother Xavier arrived on the ship from Bremen a day later. I was upstairs to check on Rackham, who was in his usual slumped position on the sofa, still wearing the effects of the night's wine like a shabby gown, face sunken and worn, the stench of alcohol still on him. I heard the cart rattle up outside and stuck my head out to get a look at it, and there he was, Brother Xavier, looking for all the world like the original Jesuit, the very idea of Jesuit, a proper career priest, hat n'all, and he looks up as his driver knocks on the door, and I look down at him and grin.

'Brother Xavier?'

'Yaa,' he says.

'Right you be,' I shout, and downstairs the maid opens the door to the driver.

I close the window and give Rackham a good shake. 'Xavier's here,' I tell him, shaking him by the shoulders.

He stirs. 'Xavier?'

'The German,' I say, and at the word 'German' a terrible roar erupts from Rackham, a strangled cry for help, so I pull him to his feet and put a tea in his hand. 'Get yourself in shape. I'll distract the interloper.'

I head downstairs to divert his attentions. There he is at the bottom of the stairs, and if it's true that half of Ireland is starving then it's also true that in Germany they're living well, cause this fella is robust. I don't know what they're eating over there, but this character grew up on pig and gruel and plenty of it, for he's solid.

'Brother Xavier,' I say, and he holds out his right hand, his left clutching the crucifix at his chest, still wheezing from the effort of getting down off the cart.

'Good day, Brother Oliver,' he says.

'No – you'll meet Brother Oliver shortly. I'm James.'

'Ah – from up country?'

'Yes.'

He takes off his hat and looks around.

'But come in,' I say, and I thank the cabbie as I close the door. 'You'll be needin a cup of tea.'

'Yaa.'

Takes some feeding he does, Brother Xavier, even for a big fella. Three plates in and he's showing no sign of slowing, and that's when Rackham makes an appearance at the table, still nursing his tea, eyes a-blether, face pale. Brother Xavier makes a half-hearted attempt to stand, his fat arse reaching about six inches off the plush cushion before he falls back in the seat. Doesn't want to be getting too far from his food. Rackham holds out his hand.

'Brother Xavier. Welcome to Buenos Aires. How was your trip?' His fine English manner masks the discomfort he's in.

'It was awful,' says Brother Xavier, 'but I won't bore you with the details.'

Rackham clutches his cup. 'I trust you're being looked after?'

'Oh, yaa. I can't tell you how wonderful it is to see warm food.'

—We can tell, ya fat fuck. Gonna eat this one? Eoin whispers. —He'd feed the five thousand.

'We're thrilled that you're here, Brother,' says Rackham. 'We'll give you a day or two to get rested, then we'll get to work.'

'Oh, there's no need. I've been on a boat for a month, Brother Rackham – I'm eager to get started. You'll be surprised at my energy.'

And we are. Brother Xavier eats for three hours, then sleeps for twenty-four. He gets up, bathes, eats for a further two hours, then he's all business. Man wants to get things done. So he's right into the library with the two of us, Rackham now sober but he's got a months-long hangover on him and he's having trouble keeping focus. So I take up the reins best I'm able, pulling out records left, right and centre, accounts for this, that and the other, and soon the table is covered to a depth of six inches in paper. While this is happening, Rackham is getting quizzed on the state of the reductions, and Xavier reads, writes and does a half dozen other things all at once, and we just sit like two spare testicles, me and Rackham, filling in where we can. Well-fed and rested, there's no stopping Xavier. We go through Santa Catalina, Jesus Maria, Candelaria, and soon we get to San Ignacio.

'How would you describe the state of the reduction in your own words, Brother James?' he says.

'Well... I would say we're a happy little family,' I tell him.

'What does that mean, exactly?'

—He means he's fuckin the help. *Thanks Eoin.*

'Ahem... I'd say we've attained a certain societal stability, which means that, for the time we've been there, we've reached the optimum output in crops and livestock to keep the estancia safe and self-reliant.'

—Them's some fucken fancy words outta ya. Who ya tryin to impress?

Brother Xavier closes the book in front of him. 'If only happiness were the goal of the reductions,' he says. 'Which it is, in a way, but not to the detriment of production. Have you heard of Santa Maria de Jesus?'

'I haven't.'

—You're gonna fucken hear about it, though, aren't ya...

'Santa Maria de Jesus was the finest reduction created by the Jesuits. At its height in 1759, its flock numbered close to two thousand and its income was greater than any other Jesuit endeavour on this side of the world or in Europe. There simply wasn't anything that we can compare it to. That is why I've spent the last five years studying the model of the reduction down the finest detail, to see how it might be replicated here in the Argentine Republic. I also have the benefit of a few small but influential businessmen here in Buenos Aires who are going to help us raise our output to a whole new level. So, Brother James, I ask you once again – how would you describe the state of the reduction? In your own words.'

'Middling.'

Brother Xavier nods.

—We know other fat bastards just like this one, Antonio says.

'You know, I've heard a lot of talk about output and production and income since I've been here, but what I'm not hearing about is the welfare of the Guaraní who join us in the reductions. Surely that is the priority here?'

Brother Xavier raises a single eyebrow. 'What you might also be interested to know, Brother James, is the life expectancy of the Indians before they come to join us on the reductions. Do you know the numbers?'

I shake my head.

'An Indian living in the jungle was usually dead before he reached the ages of forty, if he was a man. If she were a woman, she was a little luckier, and might have seen the age of forty-five. On the reductions, an average of ten to fifteen years was added to the life expectancy. What would you call that, if not welfare?'

'I'd call that good business,' I say.

'Call it what you like, but what I'm most interested in are the numbers.'

'You and Brother Rodrigo up in Cordoba are gonna get along just fine.'

—Two fat pigs, Antonio says.

'I hear great things about Brother Rodrigo. I'll meet him soon enough.'

'I'm sure you'll do wonderful things together,' I say.

He doesn't waste any time lining up his business interests. The next day Xavier announces we're all invited to a soirée. Rackham looks horrified, and the novelty of it isn't lost on me, a society event in a city where people are disappearing daily, and where heads decorate the main square like Samhain turnips.

'Sounds like a party,' I say. 'What do priests need with a party?'

Xavier snorts. 'It's not a party. We'll be establishing connections, something which neither of you know anything about, apparently.' He gives me and Rackham a cursory glance, like he's got the measure of us. Perhaps he does. Perhaps the two of us are open books. Rackham's alcoholism seems pretty clear cut, and me, have I convinced of him of my dedication to my life's calling? Who knows. At this point, I'm looking a way out anyway, for me and for Salome and Teodora. The priest's life is losing its sheen. I've had enough of the itchy robes, the early mornings, the forced piety and all the praying. Not that my heart's in it, but how much praying can you really fake? Mornings in church with Brother Theodore saying mass, me at the front, on my knees and hands clasped, or hands raised to the heavens, or head bowed ceremoniously – *In the name of the Father, and the Son...* – and me a father now too, baby on the way growing in Salome's belly, maybe a daughter but maybe a son, and how wonderful would that be, me in a small house in California sitting on the porch – for they have sun there and you can sit outside, not like in Ireland with the whole family crouched round the fire, begging for a little heat – sitting outside in my chair, a chair carved by my own hands, for that's what I'll do when I get to California, I'll build myself a table and some chairs for the kitchen, and a chair for sitting on the porch, and evenings I'll be out there watching the sun go down, young fella on my lap giggling, Salome inside, but I can still smell the sweet aroma of milk and papaya off her, and that's what our house will smell like, milk and papaya, and the bedsheets too, and every morning I'll wake up fine in the knowledge that I don't have to get up and sneak away out like a thief in the night. Yes, every morning her scent in my nose and her hair on my neck, and beyond our young son cries, Seán he's called, and he kicks a stink in the morning he does, young Seán, but that's alright cause Teodora's there and she's a responsible girl, and she gets up and lifts her brother from the crib and whispers loving words in his ear and gets him fed, so me and Salome are there in the bed, and she stirs and looks at me and smiles, and her warmth and her sweet scent get me going, a smell like contentment – no, happiness, that's what she smells of, and her hand squeezes my boyo and he rises like the sun, and with the laughter of our children across the house we make sweet silent love til the sun comes in through the window, then it's time to rise for another day. This is how the days pass for men who've found the thing. And I've found the thing, and it's not in coarse horsehair robes and well-fingered prayer books, it's in the scent of her hair and in the warmth of her belly, and that's where a man needs to be.

'Do you have a layman's attire, Brother?' Xavier says.

Eoin pipes up. —Real mood-killer this one, isn't he?

—I know a good tailor in Buenos Aires, Antonio says.

'I'm a simple man, Brother,' I say. 'I've my plain black suit, and it does me for all occasions.'

'Yes, well, make sure it's clean for tomorrow night.'

—Hear the fat bastard? Clean your suit, ya filthy savage, Eoin says.

'Fuck off.'

Brother Xavier, turning towards the door, spins about. 'What's that?'

'Nothin at all, Brother.'

Priests are not really made for parties, are they? So I play down the Jesuit much as I can: no collars, no crosses, no robes and no Bibles. I even borrow a little talcum powder from Rackham's bathroom cupboard.

Rackham feigns illness so he can skip the party, but I know he relishes the opportunity to stay at home and get drunk alone. There are three of us now in the house not including the housekeeper and the man must be going out of his mind. A man with a guilty private drinking habit needs his own space. So Rackham takes to his room, while downstairs I join Xavier in the drawing room and we wait for the carriage to arrive. Xavier hums like a hoor, pampered and powdered himself he has, in all his fine lotions brought over from Europe. Bit of an old dandy. He's wearing a fine wool suit with an enormous crucifix round his neck, rings on his fingers and a fine pocket watch to boot.

—Look at him, Eoin says.

I'm looking. He's the tartest, plumpest, finest-smelling Jesuit I've ever laid eyes upon.

—If you don't eat this fat little piggy, God may forgive you but we won't, Antonio says.

'Brother James.' Xavier giving me a good look up and down. Checking if I'm fit for the soirée. He sniffs. 'When was the last time you were in decent society?' he says.

'I'm not sure I remember, Brother Xavier. I'd have to say New York almost a year ago. I'm rather used to the rustic life now.'

Xavier is standing by the window, one hand behind his back and the other clutching his crucifix.

'I passed many years in the missions,' he says. 'Six years in North America and three in China. I know the life well. Do you take to it?'

I nod. 'I have to say, Brother Xavier, it has its comforts. I've a found a peace in it I never knew before.'

Eoin whistles. —You found your piece, alright. Nice little black piece, oh yes...

I cough.

'For a man of a certain age, yes,' Brother Xavier says. 'For a man like me, advanced in years, the administrative life suits me much better.'

Then I blurt out the most idiotic question that ever passed my lips. 'Did you always want to be a Jesuit, Brother?'

Xavier turns from the window, looks at me pure puzzled. 'What a peculiar question.' He stares me down. 'Just what about my calling do you think I *chose*, Brother?'

'Well, all I mean is, did you never have your doubts?'

He gives me a last queer look before turning back to the window. 'Never.'

I hear the rattle of a carriage pull up outside, and Xavier turns to me with a twinkle in his eye. 'He's here.'

28

We take a drive round Buenos Aires, night falling and the streets clear, me and Brother Xavier in the back of a fine carriage, him smelling all grand, so I open a window to get a touch of fresh air. Man smells like a hoor's handbag. The streets quiet, the carriage rattles over the cobblestone, and I peer out into those sad, fearful streets and wonder how a place comes to live behind closed doors. The Mazorca are out, the scarlet men, stalling in doorways or out plain as day, they've nothing to hide, but the inclination of them is to the shadows. An occasional carriage or cart passes in a hurry. People rushing off home, and us, two fine Jesuits, off to a party. Strange story.

'You know what's happening in this city, don't ya?' I say.

'I do,' says Xavier.

'What do you think about it?'

Xavier parts the curtain to peer outside. 'After a long absence, we are back in this country by the grace of our Lord. I don't find it expedient to ask questions when our presence here is so precarious. It's enough that we're here. God will take care of the rest.'

—Practical man, Eoin says.

'There's a lotta murder all the same,' I tell him.

'There is always murder,' says Xavier. 'We, the Jesuits, just try to stay right with God.'

'How can we, when we're silent about this?'

'Silent about what? I haven't seen anything,' he says.

'You will,' I tell him.

'Are you trying to sabotage our night, Brother James?'

I sit back. 'So who will be at this fine event?'

'Before I entered the seminary, I studied at the gymnasium with a Tobias Meyer. We studied economics together for three years. We lived together and came to know each other's family intimately, too. We've remained friends ever since. He's here now, in Buenos Aires, with his brother, Finn. The two of them are in import and export. I foresee some very close business ties growing from tonight's affair.'

It hits me then. I'm a sock puppet. Being dragged along to lend some Jesuit credibility to our presence. Me, a fake Jesuit.

'God willin,' I say. *Cause that's what a priest would say.*

We pass the cathedral and pull up on a fine street, this the good part of town, probably the only part of town untouched by the hangmen of Rosas. 'We here?' I say.

'I trust we are here,' Xavier says.

So I hop out but Xavier waits, waits for the cabbie to get down and open the door for him, his perfumed lordship doesn't care to open his own doors, no sir. And outside the carriage a footman opens the entrance to a fine house, columns and all that, glass windows in it, and we approach the door and are ushered inside. Bright lights, portraits, soft violin music, footmen... things men who've scrambled from the clutches of the scabbed earth know nothing of, nor ever heard about or even dreamed of. Big double staircase, one half going this way, the other going that, and meeting above, and hanging down between them a great chandelier like the descendant lights of heaven. Aye, things most men never see. A fine-liveried servant – finer get-up than me – offers us a drink, and why not, cause this is a once in a lifetime for me, I know I'll never be back again. So I take a glass of the sparkling wine, sip at it – doesn't taste like much on its own, but when you throw in the lights and the music and the sparkling chatter of self-satisfied people, it ups the quality some.

'Let's go for a wander,' Xavier says.

We stroll through the fine society of Buenos Aires, women dazzling and men dapper – oh how they live, the other half. And I hear their fine talk too, jolly and exaggerated – '*De verdad? Que sorpresa!*' – people with no concept of what's going on outside these doors, or they know but are perfectly happy to sip at their champagne and blissfully ignore it. And how can I blame them? Heads on spikes and disembowelment, these things don't sit well with fine wines and finger food and talk of curtains and servants, or whatever it is they natter about.

'Es embarazada,' I hear, passing two women in fine gowns, one of whom gives me a right foul eye as I pass... perhaps I don't fulfil the criteria, not cut from the right cloth, as they say, certainly I'm far below the standards of those present. Or perhaps priests aren't just the thing here, maybe the people'd rather not be reminded of their slack morals. Could be. I'm fine with it, no worries – *I have my own problems with the church. Just sayin. But by all means, direct you ire at me.* That's what priests are for. Sure didn't the fella Christ set himself up as a goat so's we could all give him a kick and make ourselves feel better? Sure he did. I'd have probably whipped him myself. They were all at it, save for the Magdalene, hoor with a heart of gold, the one he loved more than all others. And me, I've my own Magdalene, no hoor but a fallen woman all the same, her with child and the father gone. Her up there and me here, strolling among the Pharisees. And right then, I miss her terribly.

'Do you see him, Brother?' I say.

'He's here somewhere. Somewhere here...'

We push on, weaving through the grand salon, past the musicians now, piano and violin and what not, other things I'm not familiar with but enchanted by nonetheless. Music things, heavenly things, even to a man like me. And then a gasp from Xavier and some guttural exclamation in German.

'There he is!'

We approach the party of gentlemen, fine businessmen in fine attire, very German in their way, maybe it's the moustaches or maybe it's the way they hold themselves, but no doubt about it they're German. One strides from the group to grips Xavier's hand, the other hand rising to his shoulder, no embrace just a firm handshake, but the eyes are alight. Old friends reunited.

They shake hands and smile and Xavier is introduced, and then I'm introduced, those stout German fellows are polite and refined and say 'Hello' and 'Good evening' and 'Pleasure to meet you', all fine in their English and in their decorum.

'From Ireland?' one says to me, and I say, 'Aye'.

'We were just discussing your fellow countrywoman,' one says, and I say, 'Who?'

'Who?' he says, and the group look at me, startled.

'Who? The talk is of nothing else. Camila O'Gorman, of course.'

I confess to them that I know no such woman, that I never met her or seen her or heard of her in my puff. More starts of surprise, then Tobias switches to German, directs his chat to Xavier, explaining the extent of my ignorance no doubt, and then they're all babbling in German and me pushed outta the circle, so I slip away, me and my bubbly wine, and I saunter among the crowd trying to be unpriestly which for me is easy. And everywhere I go I hear her name, 'Camila', 'Camila', on the lips of them all, men and women alike, her name whispered in fascination and fear, hushed and quiet like. I try to find a conversation in English so's I can slip in and listen, get the gist of the story, but they're all speaking the Spanish, and me with the Spanish barely good enough to ask where the shitter is.

I wander out into the hall to admire those fine paintings, generals and countesses and viceroys and the like, all fine people with their heads upturned and chins in the air... it's remarkable what a bit of money in your pocket will do for your posture, backs straight heads up, no slouching on these folk. The violin plays all the while and I hold my glass like one of them, and I feel my own back straighten and my own chin rise, my own posture adapting to that of the fine folk.

This gets Eoin goin. —Would ya fucken look at you, gettin all lorded up with it. Check your head, he says.

—A gentleman, Antonio says, and the two of them are laughing at me, proper riotous.

Then they go silent, all animal instinct prey-like, like there's something in the air, and I'm getting it too, coming over all skittish. So I look round me and there she is, standing top of the stairs, one arm on the rail and the other holding a locket round her neck, and she's looking right at me, eyes molten-blue and diamond hard, and I get that old stomach-jitter cause I've seen her before, but only in dreams and hallucinations.

Still looking at me, she comes down the stairs all shouldersung and hipslither, and Eoin and Antonio have the fear, the fear's in them, but me I've something else going on. She descends those stairs all cutswim salmon-like, a jade green dress on her and cut to the thigh, and the thigh like the white shores of Ireland at height of winter, where men crash and die on furious shores, lured by the siren song of cold night whispers. A deep 'V' cuts to her bosom, her still clutching the locket between breasts full and white, and she's coming right for me and I can't tear my eyes away cause I'm caught in her blinding light. She's waylaid at the bottom of the stairs, some well-cut soldier type, and she smiles and touches his arm and breezes on by, and another catches her moving across the floor, she's all smiles and grace as she threads the crowd, they all know her too for they're all after a piece of her. Cuts through them she does, eyes still on me, and there she is in front of me and I freeze, wrecked in the diamond fury of her gaze. Neck like an arched marble naiad, hair black as unholy night, eyes blazing.

'I know you,' I say.

'You do,' she says. 'And I've heard tell of you.' She pauses. 'How many are you?'

Pretence gone, she's straight as an arrow. 'Seven,' I say.

'Come with me.' And she turns and heads up the stairs. I was no man if I didn't follow her, so I followed.

I follow her up the stairs the good folk watching, the poor priest going up the stairs with the jewel, the flawless jewel of the night, but I know her as something else, for there's no mistaking the gypsy.

I follow her up the stairs, me the man behind, watching her all arse and hips, woodsmoke and sex the smell of her, and the sea too and seaweed and dandelion, a rut perfume of the union of earth and ocean. That's what came over me as I climbed the stairs after her, me feeling like a man riding the wave, like a man borne on salty tides, tides that'd carry to him to far shores of blood and wisdom.

The scent of her making me hard.

We climb the stairs, me lost in the marble of her back, the dress split all the way to her arse, and the way the smoky tresses of her hair fall over the aquiline curve of her shoulder, me taken by shoulder and arse and hair and the scent of the sea, some kind of siren song draws me to her shore, and we step into a room and she closes the door, pushes me against it, one hand on my throat and the other on my prick, and slides her tongue in my mouth, and I feel it drip into me, the song of the lust-sleek salmon, all a-prey for the eternal weakness of a man. I feel that tongue in my mouth, testing the limits of my resistance, and the limits are soon found. She releases me and stands back. 'The clothes,' she says, and so I take them off and drop them to the floor, me prickhard and still. She pulls a chair out to the middle of the floor. 'Sit,' she says. So I sit, and she goes into a desk and comes out with a strop razor and hands it to me. I know what she wants and I give it to her. I cut a slice outta the inside of my thigh, blood pouring onto the fine rug, and I hold it up to her and she takes it and devours it. She eats me, then she takes the strop razor from my hand and lifts her leg and places her heeled foot on my leg, and I take a long look up that gypsy-white thigh, and already I feel myself crash with the waves on far shores, carried on torrid swells to perish on rocky bluffs, a place where men die empty but smiling. I reach out and touch her hard calf, run my hand up the length of it, grip it and test the contours for I'm getting ready to climb up there and I need to know the path, feel my way, but before I can climb on up she takes the razor to her own thigh and cuts the flesh, not a wince or a sigh from her, and holds it out for me and I take it, and deep down I hear them, Eoin and Antonio, first a tremble then a shudder, and finally the whimpers of terror, the screams of men who see they are to be consumed. 'Let them die,' she says, and so I swallow her flesh, the flesh of the gypsy that consumes all.

She drops the razor, her bloody and me too, and she takes me by the back of the head and pulls my mouth to the inside of her thigh and I drink the blood of the salmon. I suck on her lifeblood, and when I'm done sucking I start climbing, tongue up the inside of gypsy thighs til I reach the mouth of the river, and there I am, caught between river and ocean, and I lap at the waters, bathed in the river of her cunt, that cunt that marks the shores of the known and unknown. Then she lifts the dress and she takes the haft of me, grips me in her hand, and slides down on me river-like and before I know it I'm setting sail from the mouth towards the ocean, and she takes the essence of me, me screaming, the two of us flailing on the marred surge to spill on far dying shores. Dead men have no thoughts, and so I gaze upward at the brilliant light of the chandelier, lost in the heavenlight, blissfully unaware of the manner of my dying.

I close my eyes and open them, her there in front of me, the lights of heaven gone and only the gypsy in front of me, dazzling as she is, golden, a golden thread of light running from her to me and beyond, out through the walls in all directions, her at the epicentre, and as I crawl up off the shores of the unknown the golden light fades, me cast back into an upstairs room in a fine house in Buenos Aires, spent in a chair and naked and bleeding at the thigh.

'Who are you?' I say, and she doesn't look at me, merely rubs ointment on the wound on her thigh then covers it with gauze, then takes a cloth and cleans her cunt and turns to look in the mirror.

'You know who I am,' she says.

I mark the line of her back and the arch of her shoulder, and the hard curve of thighs that led me out to sea, and the tresses of raven hair that guild the naiad curve of her neck. *Yes, I do, I know who you are.*

She toys with the locket between her breasts. 'Put on your clothes and get out.'

29

'Who's Camila O'Gorman?' I say to Xavier the next day.

'Hmm?' He looks up from his breakfast.

'Who's Camila O'Gorman?'

'The Irish woman? A local of notoriety, from what sparse accounts I heard last night,' he says.

'Do you know of her?' I ask Rackham.

He nods solemnly. 'A poor woman, she eloped some months ago with a priest. Some say he seduced her, some say she was of poor character and was willing. They absconded north, disappearing for six months. But they've just been arrested. They're to be executed.'

'She's pregnant too, they say.'

'And what was their crime?' I say.

An uncomfortable silence falls over the table.

'Their crime?' Xavier says. 'Isn't it obvious?'

'I don't think it is, no. It sounds like they fell in love and ran away to be together.'

Rackham clears his throat, while Xavier wipes his lips with a napkin. 'Brother,' he says, 'you're familiar with the vow of chastity for men of the cloth, yes?'

'Yes, b—'

'And you aren't unfamiliar with the church's views on union outside wedlock?'

'No...'

He doesn't say any more, but picks up his tea and takes a drink, the perfume still on him from the night before.

And in my head is the vision, the vision of the woman in the chair all rage and defiance, hands on her swollen belly, the firing squad stepping out and the rifles lifted – six of them, three per lover – and the cold cry of the lieutenant and the shots ringing out and the blood of her child on her white gown and the dying light in her eyes, behind her the crumpled corpse of her lover.

So I get into a spiel about women and men and unborn children, and the sanctity of life, all life, cause life is golden and belongs to the creator, and *judge not lest ye be judged* and all that shite, I raise my voice and vociferate for the life of Camila O'Gorman, and me not even finished breakfast.

The two men are stunned. And I see in their eyes the first auspices of the unravelling of Brother James Carmichael.

I sit later on the bed, cleaning the wound on the inside of my thigh. The mark of the gypsy. And how will I explain it to Salome, when I take off my clothes and climb into her bed at night, and her hand runs from my manhood up the inside of my thigh and finds the wound cleaved by my own hand at the behest of the gypsy? What story will I conjure for her? The wound is the foul mark of my infidelity.

A dull pain in my belly, there since I ate of the gypsy, grows. My companions have gone silent. Eoin and Antonio, the persistent voices of my appetites, have gone to ground, not a whisper of them to be heard since the previous night's encounter. Of whom have I eaten and at what cost? The silence disturbs me. I need to drink the caapi and venture south to find out what is going on in the vast emptiness of my inner jungle, sit with the souls round the fire, speak with Teyú Yaguá, see Kurupi to avail of his insights and find out what mischief the gypsy has caused within.

So I decide, then and there, to get outta the city, to pack my bag and head north, back to San Ignacio, and once I'm outta the city and back in the country I'll find a spot under the trees and light a fire, and I'll cook up the herb and I'll go below.

I wrap the wound and I get to packing, what little I have, and procure some provisions for the road from the housemaid and put on my robes for the journey to protect me from soldiers and militia and the like, all the while the dull pain in my belly growing.

Packed, I slip out the house, the taint of Jesuit perfume in the air, saying goodbye to no one, and I head to the port to procure a boat up the Rio de la Plata, far from the ocean and Buenos Aires and the gypsy.

For four days, I feel it in me, a pain that grows to an ache, so that by the time I get off the boat at Rosario I'm bent double. I haven't eaten in forty-eight hours, my stomach won't take it, the very smell of food filling me with nausea. Evening, I head to the small hut of Anuncio's friend where my horse is tethered, and with the bare minimum of talk, I take the horse and ride for the jungle. I've broken out in a cold sweat and a great pain stabs my side. An hour outta Rosario on the road to Córdoba, I make camp in the jungle, and I build a fire and lay out my makings on the ground. I'm in excruciating pain now, the silence of my companions going on five days now, Eoin and Antonio and the rest gone to ground, hiding from the gypsy. They're not dead but hunted. She's after them, I can feel it, and though she doesn't speak to me I know what she's out to do. Her dark intent coils round my insides like climbing ivy, swims and slithers through the jungle of my psyche like an asp. I get to cooking the caapi and the fumes of it ease my discomfort, so while it's boiling away I lean in and inhale, suck it in deep, then lie back and wait for it to cook. I doze off and come to and cook some more, and with the night full deep the caapi is ready, so I let it cool and strain the tea. And I pray to Teyú Yaguá and drink, and soon I'm sweating, bent over with the pain, writhing on the floor of the cold jungle, groaning, weeping, til I feel it come up, the bile and the vomit and all the evil that accumulates within a man, the evil that is the poison of the cup of living, and I throw it up, and outta me with the vomit and the bile come snakes, dozens of baby snakes spill outta me onto the jungle floor and slither away into the grass and the undergrowth. I pass out.

I come round with the green sky above me, peering up through the trees at the sky of green fire, and I know I'm back in the realm of the spirit gods and all the souls that accompany the avaporú through the jungle of his psyche, the dark souls that scutter among the shadows of his thoughts, the burning forest of his ego.

But there's a great silence, so I get up off the forest floor and look around for the fire, not a flicker or an ember in sight, and having no other choice I stumble blindly through the dark, tearing my shins on the razor brush and knocking myself against the trees, til I hear a great furious roar from the jungle. I follow that noise and it takes me to the clearing, where I find the fire, the smoking remains of it anyway, for it's not long extinguished, the heat of it fast dying. I see him there, old Teyú Yaguá, a great chain round his neck, him tied to a tree, the god, the great lizard god, a prisoner in his own realm.

—She did this, Teyú? I say.

And old Teyú roars. —The jungle is hers now.

—Where is she? And what of my brother?

Auld Teyú raises his snout, pointing behind me, and I turn round and see them there, Eoin and Antonio and the rest, strung up from the tree by their feet, tied and throats cut and their eyes and tongues cut out.

—She will kill everything, Teyú says, —and there is nothing you can do.

—Where is she, Teyú?

—Find Kurupi and you'll find her.

I untether the chain that binds auld Teyú, for gods are not meant to be chained, and I take a last look at my own brother, dead then alive and now dead again, his soul returned to great lake of sorrows. Antonio too, off on the last journey, so I leave them there, for I've no use for bodies without souls.

—What will you do? I say as I turn, but the lizard's gone, and I alone by a dead fire with a handful of corpses. I wander off through a dark jungle to find Kurupi, only the sorrowful light of a green sky to guide me, pitiful enough light for the night of the dying. But there's no need of light when you have ears, and I hear them in the dark, the consummate couple, moans of them like the ancient beasts of earth under the light of a nonexistent moon, their bodies the cold cries of hunger and satiety. I follow their earthy moans, the only music on this moonless night, and I find them in a clearing, howling like two for whom union is all, praying in their own way to the god of all flesh, their altar a bed of turtle vine and primrose, and I settle in and watch the unholy matrimony, Kurupi's great prick wrapped thrice round the gypsy's waist and up inside her so long it is, and it's reaching places no human prick has ever reached for she's howling murder, like the very insides of her are being torn out, but her cries still have the unmistakable trill of pleasure. Kurupi's tongue flick at her nipples, nipples I had in my own mouth, and I watch the gypsy's own tongue slip into Kurupi's filthy ear. What beast will be born of this union I do not know, but I know one thing, that I'm now hers, the caapi gods, the gods of my own internal dominion, now beholden to her, one enchained and one enslaved to the charms of her cunt, a cunt which subsumed my very own will and sovereignty. I've sold myself down the river and soon I'll drown in the lake of her foul desires. I watch the climax of that impious consummation, knowing wholly and unmistakably that I'll awake the servant of another, a tool of the slyest and wisest creature ever to climb up on a man.

When I awoke the pain was gone. My horse was too. I washed myself in the river and went wandering and found the horse on the edge of the woods near the road. I mounted him and set off, fearing the silence of the gypsy, her buried in the jungle of my psyche, waiting, spying, sitting it out, lording it over my inner gods, sitting over the remains of Eoin and Antonio, and what further hell would she unleash upon me? There was nothing to do but keep riding, so I kept on til night, not hungry and eating nothing.

I arrived at San Ignacio middle of the night three days later.

The place was quiet. I stabled the horse, stirring the animals, them whinnying softly in the dark, so I put them at ease and left them be, and went to my room and climbed outta my robes, and slipped into my nightclothes and tiptoed outta the room, one thing on my mind, round the back to Salome's door, easing it open and slipping in, and me met by a peculiar silent emptiness. The child's bed's empty, her bed empty, and the room empty of all possessions. I climb into her bed and her smell still lingers, sweat and milk and papaya, but the bed is cold and has been cold for some time. So I think, *It's fine, she's moved over to the new huts, them finished now and ready for occupants*, but there's no sneaking over there in the middle of the night and knocking on doors or climbing in windows, me not knowing where she is, so I settle into the bed, push my face into her pillow and drift off to sleep.

30

The next morning I get up, wash myself and sit down to breakfast, and Jacinta and Diego and the kids are at the table and a handful of others too, and I'm chatting and smiling but they're peculiar they are, something wrong with it all, I'm not getting the kinda response you get from friends after a month's absence, so I take leave and head out to the fields, looking for Salome out digging the earth, or Teodora darting among the pear trees, but there's no sign of them, none at all. Brother Theodore appears and I smile but he doesn't, he comes over all solemn, looking afraid and angry and hurt, so I ask him straight.

'Brother Theodore?'

He says nothing.

'Where's Salome?'

'Brother, we had to,' he says.

'What are you talkin about?'

'We sent her away...'

'You did what? What on earth are you talkin about?'

He's blushing. 'The poor woman was—'

'Say it, damnit.'

'She was with child, Brother James.' He pauses. 'And showing. It was clear as day to everyone here that she was carrying... your child.'

My child.

'We sent her away for her good and yours. It had to be done.'

'It had to be done?' Anger builds inside me. 'It had to be done? Her already with one child fatherless and you're gonna go and make it two?'

'Brother James—'

'Two bastards. You're gonna make the woman raise two bastards?'

He's looking at me, uncomprehending. 'You can't be telling me, Brother, that—'

'Two bastards, when they've a perfectly good father right here?'

'B-Brother J-James,' he stutters, 'you... you're a servant of Christ, a Jesuit brother, how—?'

'I'm not a fucken priest,' I shout, out loud so's they all hear me, all of them, digging the earth or picking the trees or watering the plots or just wandering the gardens, they all hear me and stop. 'I'm not a fucken priest.'

I look around, all of them watching, all of them looking in our direction.

'What do you mean, Br—?'

'Where is she?'

'What?'

'Where'd you send her?'

'I'm not sure I should tell you, Brother...'

I lose it. I grip him by his robes and shake him. 'Where is she?'

'Broth—'

'Tell me!' I'm right up in his face.

'We sent her to Santa Fe,' he says.

I let him go and turn and leave. He shouts after me: 'They killed a woman only a week ago...'

I turn around.

'She eloped with a priest. Shot her dead. She was eight months pregnant.'

'What was her name?'

'O'Gorman,' he says. 'An Irishwoman.'

I shake my head and turn and walk away.

'They'll kill you,' he shouts, but I'm no longer listening.

I get the horse and hit the road.

The road is long, I tell myself. *The road is long, but there's happiness at the end of it. There's happiness there to be found, if a man searches. Seek and ye shall find...*

And Christ, I'll find her. I'll find her and Teodora and take them to California, and we'll build our house and have our baby boy, and maybe more, cause there's life for a man there, waiting. This is what I'm thinking as I push east, pushing the horse to its limits, and somewhere in the early morning she gives out and I'm forced to stop and put her to water and go begging for something to feed her. I've stopped eating, me. Don't have the stomach for it, and that's alright cause the next time I eat I wanna be round the table with my family, breaking bread and drinking milk, and manioc and papaya and corn on the table, us fat and comfortable and happy. I'll have it. I'll fucken have it if it kills me, so hitting noon I'm off chasing again, on the horse and roaring, through jungle and over open field, passing through Cordoba like a fiend possessed, like a devil Jesuit on horseback come to reap havoc over the land.

And as I go, strange thoughts creep in, strange gypsy thoughts flash like salmon roe through the dark pool of my psyche, thoughts unaccounted for by my own desperate desires, frightful thoughts of terrible certainty, *Woe the man who makes himself a god*, and *Step not on hallowed ground with chancred feet*, and *Feed poison with poison*, and other things, mad things, these and many others swim through the dark waters of my poisoned kingdom. It's the gypsy and I know it, her vines now stretching out through my being, through the vital passages of my body and up into my mind, and soon the coiled veins of her wisdom will hold me, strangle me. I don't have much time.

I sail on, my horse, too, infected by the gypsy's voracious power. It's her the horse feels when I put my hands on his neck, and lean in close and whisper in his ear, and I wonder if he can't understand the very words that drip into him roelike, for surely the gypsy speaks to animals easy as she pours poison into a man. He's my horse and I go with him, but it's with her wind in our sails as we gallop, for we turn from the direction of Santa Fe and ride north, and I scream and pull at the horse but he won't listen, he just ploughs on, heedless of me. And that's when I hear her for the first time, the gypsy, she rises from her deep jungle abode and speaks into me, a rare echo that invades my being like the dark rumble of thunder in the belly, and that voice is my master, my jailer.

—I have work for you, she says.

And I scream til my lungs bleed, eyes filled with tears, blind to the road and filled with rage. 'I must see her!' I cry, a man alone on a horse screaming at the jungle, the country, the whole continent, the ocean beyond, but she will not be overpowered.

—You will forget her, she instructs.

I keep screaming, but even as I do her sweet poisons are filling my veins, and as I struggle to hold onto her, Salome, her face and her hips and the roughness of her hands on my face, and the weight of her thighs and hardness of her calves, the smokiness of her thick black hair and depths of her eyes, and the moistness between her legs and the scent of milk and papaya, and her cracked lips full in smile, the laughter of Teodora and the smell of my unborn child's head, even as I rage and cling to these things I feel them slipping from me, the gypsy's poisons filling my veins, subverting my purpose, subsuming my being. Soon my face is wet but I know not why, for I'm a man on a horse heading north with a new purpose in his heart, one that eclipses all others, the past a mere lick of a minnow flitting downstream, a strophe in the water, the skirl of the stream – *leuleup!* – and gone.

I wipe the tears from my face and tear on, a man possessed, but possessed of purpose.

And she whispers to me as we go, tells me softly the wherefore of our going, and what we shall do, and how we shall triumph, her words a golden music in my arteries.

On upriver we go, the horse galloping up the western shore, on past Villa Urquiza and Pueblo Brugo, and Helvecia and Santa Elena and La Paz, all the way up past Esquina to Goya where I camped out and waited for dark. I'd near killed my horse, so I set him up with some food and water and said goodbye, for I'd not see him again. And when dark fell I stripped of my robes and bathed myself in the mud of the riverbank, and prowled through the town in the dead of night.

—This is it, the gypsy told me.

I crept round back of the house silent as a killer, me the instrument of the holy gypsy, her the master of man and god alike. I crept through the window and into the house and found him in his bed, crucifix above it, good priest that he was, and I placed my hand over his mouth. He awoke then, terror in his eyes, and surely he tasted the earth and the river from my hands, and surely the whites of my eyes put the fear of God into his soul, for he shat the bed where he lay. I told him to arise and sit down on the chair in the kitchen, and I bound his hands and took a chair and sat in front of him. Then I opened my mouth and he heard her voice, the voice of gypsy from the mouth of a man, words that poured outta me soft and beautiful and poisonous all.

—Tell me what you did, she said.

And he stuttered and spat and wept and pissed himself.

—She is dead because of you. A woman and her unborn child, dead. Now tell me what you did.

Terrible the words, beautiful the voice.

The old priest wept and begged and told the tale, how he recognised the fateful couple and reported them to the Justice of the Peace, family himself of the poor woman, and had them arrested and sent to their deaths.

—What kind of a man, she said then, —what kind of a man are you?

The disgust in her voice palpable.

The old priest begged before God, begged and confessed his sins, sitting in his own piss and shit, and I saw how the man at base was no more than a dumb beast. I got up at her bequest, and took a knife from the drawer and cut out his tongue, 'the viper tongue' she called it, and it was, it was a venomous tongue at that, a tongue that condemned unborn children in their mother's bellies. The old priest gurgled and spluttered and spat, and the life went outta him pretty quick but I cut his throat just to be sure.

—Eat his tongue, she instructed, so I ate it there, raw and bloody. I tasted the venom.

Caked in mud and blood, I left the house. We found the house of Perichon, the Justice of the Peace. Sleeping too he was, so we put him to eternal rest, cutting out his heart and feasting on it raw. Black is the heart that betrays one's own kin, and that's how it tasted.

I washed in the river and was anointed by the gypsy, her the holy compass of my being. I dressed and rose with the morning sun and felt my own godlike power as I stepped in the boat to take me downriver.

We got off the boat at Rosario and sought out Vicente Gonzalez, jailer of the murdered woman, middleman, who had no qualms about his role in her abduction and death. We hung him like a pig from the rafters of his roof, bled him and drank his blood.

Three dead and the gypsy growing stronger, we sailed downriver towards Buenos Aires, and rode on horseback overland til, coming up on a bluff, I saw the prison from Kurupi's vision, Santos Lugares, hard and cold it rose from the green earth, so I rode up to its gates and dismounted and asked to see the Chief of Police. Still in my robes, I was ushered inside to the office of Antonio Reyes. I sat down and looked him in the eye, then I opened my mouth, and the gypsy asked for his confession and he rose in a panic, but she told him to sit and he sat. Hard and unbending he was, and for his blindness we cut out his eyes, filling them with gunpowder and burning them closed, and his screams brought the soldiers. I shot one and killed two with a bayonet, then we left the prison and headed south, the sacred sprawl of Buenos Aires before us.

The last was the lawyer. Maybe the evillest of them all, the one who found justification so that a man could kill a young woman and her unborn child. Sarsfield, his name. Irish n'all, like the priest, the young woman brought to her death by her own countrymen, men of God and men of the law, a shower of bastards the lot. We paid a visit to his house. Rode into the city on horseback dead of night, she knew the way, the streets eerily devoid of even Mazorca, as if she'd connived with the secret police to do her deed.

We found his house, a handsome two-storey place in a fine district, close to the palace too. I tethered the horse in a nearby park and went there on foot, and right in the front I went, the door unlocked, this too the foul will of the gypsy. Up into his bedroom I crept, and sat down in a chair in the dark and watched him sleep, wondering how a man such as himself slept at all. Easy and at peace with himself he was, such was his nature, so I kept my vigil there by his bedside for several hours, marvelling at his silent repose, so untroubled and peaceful and still. One day God will explain how the murderers and rapists and thieves sleep with themselves at all, cause if they're sleeping then they've no soul, and if they've no soul, where does that leave God? Explain that one to me, while I watch over this picture of tranquillity.

After an hour or two he wakes, needs to piss, and he throws his legs over the edge of the bed and puts his feet into waiting slippers, and he stands up and takes a step towards the bedpan, then freezes. Knows that I'm here now, and he looks in my direction, his eyes adjusting to the light.

'Who's that?' he says, voice trembling.

'Sit down,' I tell him.

He sits down on the bed and I see him look towards the drawer, maybe he has a gun in there, so I shake my head all slow. 'It'd be the death of ya,' I say. 'Know why I'm here, do you?'

He shakes his head.

'I need to explain it, do I?'

'I think he needs you to explain,' she says, and I look up and she's there in the doorway, in the flesh, dressed in green head to foot, scarf and all.

'Manuela?' he says.

'Say my name again and I'll cut out your eyes,' she says, and the very words still the room.

'Shall I explain things for him?' I say.

She nods.

So I get up off the seat and walk towards the bed, lay down on it and pull him towards me, cradling him in my arms.

'What's your job?' I ask him, and he tells me. 'And what is it that you do?' I say. And he goes on to explain, telling me about the law and justice and upholding the law, and all the whole schtick he's been repeating his whole life, telling himself and his God and anyone who'll listen, just so's he can go to bed at night and sleep the peace of the dying.

'And how does that sit with killing young women and unborn babies?' I say, and she's there in the doorway watching, I can feel his black heart thumping, him laying against my chest, the body of him trembling, the words coming out all a-stutter, then he breaks down into a kinda whimper.

'I h-had to – he t-told me to,' he says.

'If my father told you to cut your own mother's throat, would you do it?' she says.

The fight's gone outta him. He's a weak man, good only for killing women and unborn babies, so I lean in and kiss him on the forehead, then I lay him down and climb up on top of him, and she watches as I bite into his neck and tear out his throat. Like that, I inflicted death upon an evil man. I held him as he bled out, him pulling at my robes as the light went out in his eyes, and she came and stood behind me and watched it too, and kissed me on the neck and ran her hands through my hair and pulled me into her and embraced me. He fought for a minute and was dead in three. So I let him go and lay down on the bed, and the gypsy lay down next to me, her hand on my chest, my chest sticky with his blood, and she whispered in my ear, words all crystal and cutshimmer, they swam into me like the sunwise salmon in the water, gypsywise her minnow whispers, and I was filled instantly with the wisdom of all things, all things known to men and to women too, and I turned to look at her and she traced a finger over my lips and smiled. And with the peace of the dying I understood that I was to die too.

September, 1848

31

Packing brings me deep joy. I delight in seeing my beautiful things spread out over the bed: books from all corners of the world, the gifts of envoys, or titles I've had delivered from Father's contacts abroad; my jewellery boxes, particularly the one from my mother, silver and lapis and purchased in Paris; my dresses, in all colours but mostly in green, each an exquisite work; my shoes, shawls and parasols – will there be need for parasols in London? They say not, but they'll come with me nevertheless. My soul is irrevocably intertwined with my possessions, and to leave anything here would be to leave behind a part of myself. Call me shallow, but my possessions define me, have come to shape me, who I am and what I shall become. I have become adept at possessing things.

My trunks will be spirited away in the night, silently and swiftly, and in the morning they'll be waiting for me at the port in a berth on the Avila, which will leave at eleven for London. I have told no one. Only Ryan, a fellow whose services Constancia procured for me at the port, knows of our departure. Constancia will come too, of course. She has been at my side since I was fourteen, and I would go nowhere without her. Maximo will join us there. Such a silly boy, but who knows, one day he may make me happy. Not that he knows a single thing about the truth of my nature. And why should he? My life has no call for such complications. Maximo is a simple boy, and it's his simple devotion that attracts me. Men of letters have asked for my hand, doctors and lawyers too, but they are far too full of knowledge for their own good. Note that I say 'knowledge', not 'wisdom' – their learning is limited to word only, for they have no understanding of knowing flesh. How could they? Besides, they don't require a woman but a pet, one in a fine dress to pour niceties and praise upon them at the revelation of their insights and witticisms. I have no need for them. Such men I eat.

Packing is no thing to be taken lightly, so I sip a glass of wine while I fold and roll, store and wrap. I have also banished Constancia from the room. She insisted on helping but I can't have her in the way. Packing is a science and must be practiced alone. It requires will, superb will. And I cannot take everything, of course, some things must simply be abandoned here. The things that'll be left here will be those that cause the greatest offense to my father – those things that remind him of the little girl he thinks I still am, things that speak of a shared childhood long before the horror, trinkets that were gifts from him – no, not gifts, *purchases*, for my father was, *is*, a great believer in buying loyalty. These things of *his*, will stay. Look – I have even arranged some of them on the nightstand for maximum effect. Yes, my father will stay, but my mother's memories will come with me. Her effects will come with me to London, for even dead people live on, and not only in memory. Things, too, contain souls, and the souls of the dead carry on in all kinds of vessels. I know, for I am a carrier of many souls.

I will not sleep tonight. Not out of fear, for I am not afraid. Fear is not a part of me... at least, only inasmuch as it's a part of those I carry within me, but those things are incidental and do not control my motivations. I am in control and so I do not suffer fear. My only anxiety is for six weeks on the ocean with no outlet for my needs. But I have already allowed for this. A woman like me is nothing if not resourceful. So to the extent that I'm able, I have planned and taken precautions, and any eventualities that arise in the interim will simply have to be dealt with felicitously. Besides, the ocean is a vast place with no memory. Things that happen there are forgotten quickly, lost in vague, undulating eternities. I know my anxieties are misplaced, yet I let them in so that they'll swirl in my mind's eddy, before filtering like sediment to the depths.

I don't sleep, but I dream. When you're full with souls, nights are filled with music. The sounds pop like bubbles throughout one's body, a constant harmony of effervescence, a stream of giggles, cries, howls, curses, laughter, whimpers and moans that create a cosmic music of the body. I'll admit, when I first ate a man the sound terrified me, but that was before I came to learn of its beautiful power. Now I hear only the symphony. On this night, I walk the plains of my homeland under a green sky, the unearthly music of souls drifting from the jungle: their fears, their sorrows, their joys – yes, even the dead feel joy, for the soul is eternal and filled with the heart's timeless echo. It is this orchestra that plays to me nights, and on this night, filled with anxiety and the unknown, the symphony is monumental. It fills the country, the continent... all of the land is filled with its song, and I know, fully, definitively, that my soul extends over all of it, like a great mist over the first morning of earth.

The mist settles and the music quiets, and somewhere around daybreak, I fall asleep for the briefest of moments.

Constancia informs me just after eight that the carriage is waiting. Nothing strange about that... it's a Friday, and on Friday I have my weekly meeting with the bishop. Father will be in his study and won't suspect a thing. It will be at seven in the evening, when I don't join him for supper, that alarm bells will ring. And perhaps he'll send a servant to check my quarters, the servant reporting that my drawers are empty, and in a confused rage he'll rush upstairs, and on the dresser he'll see a ribbon of red silk from a childhood trip to Rome, and the collar of our first beagle, beloved by us all, and the master stroke, my first regal tiara of diamond and emerald, given to me on my thirteenth birthday, Father's most coveted gift to me because it was the most expensive. And what will he do when he sees these things? Will he fly into a rage? Perhaps. Smash things? Maybe. But after, he'll start to plot how he can hurt and punish a daughter while appearing to have only her best interests at heart. Yes, he will try to hurt me across the ocean. And he will kill a few people too no doubt. His first response to everything is to demand someone's head. But I am concerned only with my freedom. I can no longer live under the constraints of his household. I must fly, a solitary migration across a dark ocean, but my compass is fixed.

I don't look back as we depart. Little birds don't look back, and we ride in silence, Constancia and I. Buenos Aires, my home, stares back at me gravely as I pass. No sorrow from her, only a chill bitterness in her throat. She is not the same city I remember from childhood; her streets have become fearful and lonely, and dangerous too. My father's atrocities are in evidence on every corner, and I pity the poor people who must stay. I understand why they leave for Montevideo. Even siege and starvation is preferable to this.

My confession: I chose to stay within the satined confines of my father's walled garden. I could've chosen to peek over the wall, to sneak through the scrub at its edges and peer through it to the other side, to see how they lived, how they suffered and bled, the people of Buenos Aires, but I didn't. I was content to live a closeted life, one of gentle resignation, even connivance. I willed myself to believe that the monsters were *out there*, beyond the walls of my garden, lurking on the outskirts of our sheltered, but chaste, lives. Then I discovered the monster within. In our own castle, prowling our own corridors, lurking under our own beds. We built our walls to keep him out, but as it happened he was already within, a symbiotic parasite long cocooned among us. I cannot hate him, the monster. It is him I have to thank for my evolution. For when I evolved, when I was forced to venture outside in order to hunt, that is when my eyes were opened. I saw. And in seeing, I became.

'We are here,' Constancia says.

The carriage has stopped. I see the nervousness in her movements, the fear in her eyes, my little bird. Two little birds on the wing together. *I shall lead, my little hummingbird. Do not be afraid.*

Ryan is waiting for us at the end of the dock. I lower my veil as Juan opens the door and helps us down from the carriage. Juan knows the risk he has taken in bringing us here. I hope my father does not kill him. We have his story prepared.

'Ma'am,' Ryan says. He tips his cap.

'Ryan, is it? Good morning. I trust you've taken care of our luggage?'

'Already on board, ma'am.'

Polite fellow, with an accent like the priest's. Let's hope I don't have to eat him too.

I turn to Juan. In my father's service for six years, he's a good man. I embrace him warmly and kiss him on the cheek. He looks at me grimly and nods. Blessings upon the man. Teyú Yaguá be his saving grace.

'Goodbye, Juan.'

He climbs onto the carriage and departs. Ryan leads us to the gangway and hands over our tickets. He offers me his arm but I decline, and I lead my little bird onto the ship that will carry us away, far over, far from the grasp of lurking monsters. I am not naive – I know that other monsters await us in London. But these will be monsters outside, not within – beasts that we can plan for and defend against. It is the monster within that is the most harmful, and our sailing from this shore is an expulsion, a purification. We will be cleansed. Strong again.

Ryan leads us to our cabin where our trunks are stored.

'The captain asked that I tell him of your arrival, ma'am. I'll inform him forthwith.'

'Thank you, Ryan. Tell him Miss Salome Azul is impressed with her quarters.'

'Yes, ma'am.'

Constancia grins, hearing the name on my lips. I chose it myself. Clever, no? Ryan departs and I close the door and remove my veil, and immediately Constancia starts trembling. I sit her down on the bed and kneel in front of her, and stroke her face and kiss her on the forehead. My aide these fourteen years, I can be her mother this once.

'Don't be afraid. Nobody saw us ride through the city, nobody saw us get on the boat. In one hour, when the boat departs, we are free. Birds on the wing.'

She allows herself a single tear. *My strong little bird.*

Sometime later we hear the ship's horn, a great heraldic blast, and Constancia and I both tremble, sharing nervous laughter. The blast marks a departure in more than one sense – we are leaving many things behind, parts of ourselves too.

I do not go on deck to wave farewell to my country, for it is not my country now and ceased being so some time ago. The country is the mad illustration of a monstrous folly, carved from the imagination of a lunatic. I need no longer share in the picture of it. Instead, I lie down with Constancia, gripping her tightly, and drift off into a golden sleep delighting in the smell of her hair, fuchsia and violet and blueberries, and the beat of her heart close to mine, a heart that has its own dreams, for I can apprehend them very well. We are sisters, after a fashion. We dream together, the warm essence of the both of us melding together in sleep, the golden whispers of distant echoes of buried unknowings.

Some hours later, I get up out of the bed, careful not to trouble Constancia. My little bird has had a stressful few days and needs her rest. I cover her in a blanket and leave her be, and freshen myself up with the small basin of water that has been left by the mate. I rinse my face and peer out of the porthole seeing sea in every direction, feeling the heavy air of the ocean on my face.

When I'm sure Buenos Aires is behind us, out of sight and mind, nothing but a distant dream of the past, I change into something more suited to travel. Something lighter, less refined. I choose green. Green is a fine colour for the ocean, isn't it? Green silk will do fine. Perhaps satin for the evenings. I choose a veil and take my canvas bag, feeling the heaviness of souls within. Books are heavy but souls are heavier, and this bag contains the souls of hundreds. The weight of souls and the weight of centuries, such books no man has heart to lift. Fortunately, I am no man.

Clutching my bag to my chest, I go up onto the deck. Several hours of light remain and I intend to make full use of them. The air is cool and fine. The sea is her usual troubled self. I can't say I've ever felt much of a correspondence with her, but there are those that do. Suffice to say, I appreciate her unfathomable mystery. But I have mysteries of my own that intrigue me more. Such as those I hold in my hand.

Couples and gentlemen stroll the deck, and I search out a quiet corner where I may not be disturbed. One such gentleman appears to follow me there.

'Buenos tardes, señora.'

I recognise him. He's a subject of my father, a lowly government minister. Dispatched to Rio de Janeiro, no doubt, on some trifling business. He stands in front of me, body tilted condescendingly forward, awaiting a response. I don't reply but hiss gently from beneath my veil. This sends him scurrying away in a hurry, a startled look over his shoulder. An unfortunate oversight, his appearance here. Several days here on the boat together, I can't let him live. The man shall have to have himself an unfortunate accident. Let's hope he's alone.

I open the binding on my bag and reach inside, pulling out the two books within. A powerful smell of leather. Recovering the priest's book was easy. It sat on his desk in the corner of his room in that godforsaken estancia in the far-flung corners of the country. It's a pretty but cheaply bound notebook of leather and parchment. I'm not sure what value, if any, it'll have for me. A peculiarity, let's call it. I am already familiar with his soul, since I ate the man, so there can be no revelations inside that'll be news to me. Still, his struggle interests me. An idealistic fool who stumbled into something he could not comprehend. Assuming his mistress's name is my tribute to his heartfelt, if redundant, efforts at greatness. He will be remembered. Somehow. Getting my hands on the other book was a different matter entirely. The old shaman was wily, and powerful. Killing him wasn't easy. He had the weight of ages behind him, but I had something more. So I killed him and hung him above his altar, like the other dead priest impaled there. The priest whose skin now covers this book in my hands, if the stories are to be believed. I run my hands over it now, feeling the weight of its substance beneath my fingers. An entire village bled so I could recover it. This book represents the apotheosis of what I have become.

But it is for another day, for when I am ensconced in my study in London, with all of the materials and requirements at my disposal to make full use of it. So I slide it back into the bag and open the book of Brother James Carmichael, avaporú, a poor one but an eater of men nonetheless. Still, I'll follow your story, padre, of hunger and long journeys and loneliness, and deceit and love lost, and faraway dreams and gods and power, and the power of souls and memory and human flesh. I'll sit back and settle in, and read your pithy tale of suffering. And then, dear fellow, I'm going to reveal to you just what is contained in the vast, devastating soul of woman.

Many thanks to Dave Migman and Adeel Z.

Epigraph from *The Supermale* by Alfred Jarry

Thanks to Bumbayo Font Fabrik for the font.

Latest news at
blacktarnpublishing.com

Available titles:
https://blacktarnpublishing.com/books/

Follow us on Twitter:
https://twitter.com/blacktarnbooks

About the author

Ultan Banan started writing as a way of getting his head straight, discovering in the process that staying busy is the only way to stop oneself going insane. He devotes what time he can to writing, doing his best to avoid gainful employment by increasingly creative means. He lives on the move but dreams of a small cottage on a foul and inhospitable coast somewhere. Currently in Italy.

Printed in Poland
by Amazon Fulfillment
Poland Sp. z o.o., Wrocław

84178401R00146